THE JUSTICE CLUB

By

Patrick M. Shanahan

W & B Publishers
USA

W & B Publishers

For information:
W & B Publishers
Post Office Box 193
Colfax, NC 27235
www.a-argusbooks.com

ISBN: 978-0-6922458-4-2
ISBN: 0-6922458-4-7

Book Cover designed by Dubya
Printed in the United States of America

Acknowledgements

This book is dedicated to the memory of those children whose lives were taken by the worst that live among us.

Prologue

In 1994 the United States Congress passed the Jacob
Wetterling Act requiring states to mandate that sexual offenders register with local law enforcement. The purpose
of the law is to track convicted sexual criminals and to
apprehend potential suspects. The guidelines of the law
vary from state to state with some registering offenders as
far back as 1979, and others not requiring registration for
convicted individuals before 1995.

Although the spirit of the law is good, unfortunately
the letter of the law leaves much to be desired. Teenaged
Romeos are lumped in with rapists, vicious child predators, and repeat offenders, and unless new legislation is
passed they will remain as registered sex offenders for as
long as they live. Currently around 600,000 offenders are
registered, but as many as one third of those are underground and do not have current information on file. Sadly,
many of these are rapists and child offenders, who, instead of being rehabilitated are serial offenders.

Unfortunately, those already convicted and those not
caught don't have large X's tattooed on their forehead,
but instead, live among us and could be anybody. Those
convicted of rape, sexual battery, and solicitation are considered by many to be criminals of passion, but child
predators are a different breed. Their tastes may vary, but
most deal in underground pornography, including pictures

and videos, and nearly all have one thing in common; they hunt victims and seek each other on the internet.

Our legal system, enacted to protect society, sometimes yield unintended consequences and often turn victims into casualties. Raymond Blackburn, a family man in his late twenties, had his life turned upside down when he was pulled into the dark world of child abusers. He decided to fight back and had his own arsenal of tools, including the national sex registry, the internet, and a group of like-minded accomplices. Unlike law enforcement, constricting legal guidelines didn't hamper Ray and The Justice Club, and their conscience was their guideline.

Although our judicial system certainly frowns on any sort of vigilantly activity, and in the past has vigorously prosecuted those who have bypassed the law, in many cases, juries wink, turn a blind eye, and consider the circumstances of the offense. Raymond Blackburn, whose family was destroyed by a child molester, was not the beneficiary of such understanding peers. He got the full treatment, doing hard time. When released he had only one thing to live for, revenge.

Chapter 1

Raymond John Blackburn was sixteen years old the first time he saw her. He was tall and wiry with thick, shaggy dark hair that just touched the collar of his black leather jacket. After dropping the student token into the fare box that morning, he listened in silence as the fare box registered the fare with a sharp metallic ding. The driver automatically handed him a transfer before Ray walked towards the back of the bus. The city bus was nearly empty this early in the day and as he walked to a seat in the rear, he glanced at the beautiful dark-haired girl sitting three rows behind the driver. She never looked up, but as he walked slowly past, he took a mental picture. Her dark hair was pulled back tight into a ponytail and her milky white complexion was flawless. Even though it was only a glance, Raymond noticed the bright red skirt and the dark nylons that disappeared under the pile of books that sat in her lap. When seated at the back of the bus, Ray pulled a filter-tipped cigarette from a crumpled pack, lit it, and cracked open the window next to him. When smoke drifted to the front of the bus the driver gave a long glance into the rear view mirror, but said nothing. He didn't need the seats of his bus slashed just because he hassled a kid. Several adults turned in their seats to also register their displeasure, but the girl never looked up and continued reading from the notebook she held in her hand. Ray got off the 87th street bus at Halstead, but before he did, he stared at the girl, but as before, she was oblivious of him.

The year was 1977 and the city was Chicago, Illinois. Ray was a junior at Dirksen Vocational School on the city's West side, where students—after two years of required subjects—learned a trade. This was not a college preparatory school and did not adhere to certain district boundaries, and any male student in the city was eligible to enroll, but mostly those with poor grades and troubled backgrounds attended. Profanity in class, although not encouraged, didn't raise any eyebrows and did not bring reprisals or any other punishment. Fights were common, although seldom in the classroom; that did bring quick and harsh punishment. The best way to avoid trouble was to mind your own business and that's the code Ray lived by. He kept to himself for the most part, and after several fights, was left alone as being somebody not to mess with.

Thoughts of the beautiful girl accompanied Ray all that day. Who was she, where did she come from, where did she go to school, and why hadn't he seen her before? He tried to dismiss such thoughts, but found himself looking forward to the following morning when maybe, he could by chance, see her again. Normally, Ray wouldn't take such an early bus, but he had a project that needed finishing, and although he had a car, the school forbade students from parking them either at the school or in the surrounding neighborhood.

The next morning as he waited by the Holland Road bus stop, located between two viaducts, his heart raced as he saw the green and white city bus come into view. After boarding, he neglected to put his token into the fare box, as his eyes scoured the nearly empty bus looking for his dream girl. She wasn't there. The driver's voice brought him back to reality. "This isn't free, son. You gotta pay or you can't ride."

"What? Uh, I forgot my money. Let me off."

Ray walked back the half block to the bus stop and hoped she'd be on the next one. She was. This time he walked slowly past her and as she raised her head he smiled. She pretended not to notice and simply looked out of the window. He "forgot" his money three times during the next week and every day managed to see her, although she completely ignored him. He wanted to know this girl, but she wasn't making it easy, so he decided to stay on the bus and see where she went. He noticed that she glanced up when he didn't get off at his usual stop, but quickly went back to the book she was reading. When the bus stopped at Ashland, a noisy group of kids wearing Luther South sweaters and jackets got on, and a tall good-looking boy wearing a sweater with a varsity football letter sat next to her. Ray watched as she gave him a quick smile and moved over slightly to allow his big frame into the seat. The jock did most of the talking and from watching, it was clear the guy wasn't her cousin. At that instant Ray hated him. A boy he didn't know anything about, but a rival just the same. He berated himself. What right did he have being jealous of that kid for trying to make time with a cute chick. He decided to get off the bus and walked to the rear door and pulled the cord, ringing the bell. He was completely dejected until, at the last second, before he disappeared from the bus, he noticed she glanced over her shoulder and was watching. What did it mean? Maybe nothing, but just maybe she had shown a spark of interest.

***

RAYMOND JOHN BLACKBURN lost his mother when he was five and soon after, his father disappeared into a whiskey bottle. His thirty-year-old married brother, Ralph—an auto specialist—put a roof over Ray's head, but never assumed the role of a parent. There was little discipline in Ray's life as long as he didn't bring trouble home. Ralph did side jobs, using the home's two-car detached garage as a workshop. At times Ray assisted, earning spending money, but spent most of his spare time working on his 1968 Plymouth Road Runner. The car had a solid body, painted in charcoal primer, but had obviously seen better days. With his older brother's help, Ray had rebuilt the hi-performance 440 cubic inch Commander V8, re-worked the torque-flite transmission and did a total brake and suspension re-build. Mechanically the car was like new, and although the interior was worn, he kept it clean.

Ray was not interested in school and his grades showed it, but he did manage to acquire enough credits to keep up and planned on graduating the following school year. He didn't have any close friends and when he felt like a night out, he just went to the local schoolyard and hung out. On weekends some of the guys would get beer, smoke grass, and try to entice neighborhood girls to join them. The few dates Ray had were with girls the guys passed around, and in his mind if this was what women were like, he decided he would never marry.

***

AFTER A WEEK the bus drivers were on to Ray, although the dark-haired beauty seemed clueless. If she wasn't on the bus, they simply waved and drove on. During the second week he walked slowly past her, slow enough so that the mystery girl would look up. Her quick glance each morning always found the same greeting, a warm smile as he passed. Ray hadn't smoked a cigarette on the bus since the first day and secretly hoped she had forgotten about that. He wasn't trying to look like a hard guy, at least not to her. Finally, he decided to test the waters; he would greet her as he passed. His heart beat hard with excitement as he turned from the fare box and grabbed the handrails behind each seat as he started down the narrow isle. He paused slightly as he neared her and when she glanced up he muttered a nearly incoherent, "Good morning." As he passed he heard her soft reply, "What?" Oh god I blew it he thought as he realized too late what had happened. That entire day he beat himself up as being stupid, and decided that he would try again the next day, when hopefully things would go better. He practiced over and over in his mind until he again approached her seat. This time he stopped. "Good morning." She looked up and smiled as he just stood there.

"Is there something you want?"

"Uh, no." *Damn,* he thought, *I blew it again. She must think I'm some kind of dork.* He felt so bad he missed his stop and again watched as the football letter sat next to her after the Ashland stop. He was so dejected that he rode the bus all the way to Luther South and watched as "his girl," with the letterman at her side, walked toward the school. By this time the driver figured out what was going on and after turning the bus around called over his shoulder, "C'mere, kid."

Ray walked to the front of the bus while reaching for another token. "Yeah, I know, another fare."

"Put your money away, son," The driver said as he handed Ray a cigarette and pulled out a silver lighter.

"I've watched you for a couple of weeks now and, man, am I seeing a rookie. Your hair will be as gray as mine before she notices you if you don't do something. Something that takes balls, you understand?

"No."

"Next time you see her, plop your ass down and say something. And don't try to be cute, just be natural. What can she do, reject you? You already got that. That big turkey that hangs on her... he's the right tackle on the football team that hasn't won a game in two years. I know him. He went to middle school with my kid and he's dumb as a post. But he's got a little moxie. Are you listening, boy?"

"Yeah, I'm listening."

The driver opened the door and both he and Ray tossed their butts out.

"You live on Swede Hill, people up there have to scrap for everything they have. How bad do you wanna know her?"

"I get it, mister. Thanks."

An old lady, with a large shopping bag, struggled up into the bus as the driver called over his shoulder to Ray as he walked toward the back, "Her name is Elizabeth, I saw it on her student I.D." As the driver watched in the mirror, Ray turned and smiled his thanks.

***

IT WAS SEVERAL DAYS before Ray got his chance with Elizabeth. He decided that practicing in his mind would be useless so he winged it instead. This time when Elizabeth glanced up, Ray saw that she had books lying on the seat next to her so he sat across the isle. "Hi! My name's Raymond, what's yours?"

"What? I mean…. what for?"

He shrugged his shoulders. "I just thought that since we see each other nearly every day it would be nice to know your name."

"Elizabeth."

"Do you go by Lizz or Lizzy?"

"My Name is Elizabeth," she said icily as she lifted her book high enough to block Ray's face. The gesture made it plain that she had no interest in what he said, or of knowing him either.

Ray got up and moved to the back of the bus, cracked a window, and lit a cigarette. Normally, he would be grumbling profanity under his breath and silently calling her every name he could lay his tongue on for rebuking him, but somehow with this girl, this woman, it was different. There would be another day. He promised himself that. When he got off the bus at his stop, instead of being dejected, he felt elated that he had the courage to at least approach her. Several days later Ray again rode with his driver buddy and was advised to be patient and to not push anything. The encounter with Elizabeth happened in early November and since Ray started taking the later busses, he didn't see Elizabeth all that winter, but he hardly forgot her.

Chapter 2

It was a chilly Friday night in early March when Ray, along with two friends, Worm and Bug, sat in the basement of Bug's apartment building, drinking from stolen pints of whiskey. Worm was extremely tall and skinny, and Bug was short and fat with bulging eyes, thus earning them the nicknames. Both wore black leather jackets identical to Ray's and had similar, long hairstyles. Ray never took his car out when he did alcohol or grass and later that night the boys piled into Worm's '62 Ford Fairlane. They rode around 'bird-dogging chicks', but didn't have any luck, so after burning a hand-rolled, they decided to get a sandwich at Melody Lane..

The restaurant was crowded with kids coming from the area high school basketball games and a line formed nearly to the outside door. The trio waited patiently for a table, but when their turn came the host seated a group of six that were in line behind them. Ray just wanted to leave, but his friends were having none of that. Worm grabbed the host by the arm when he came back. "Hey, what gives? That should have been our table." The middle-aged restaurant manager shook off Worm's hand and replied, "When I get a table for three I'll seat you, and that may be awhile." The implication was clear; they were not welcome. "You boys have been drinking and I don't have to serve you." Bug pushed past the man and grabbed a service cart filled with coffee pots and water pitchers, then dumped it over. The man grabbed a telephone and called the police. In a matter of minutes the three boys were in handcuffs and on their way to jail. Ray got the last word just before the police officer took him by the arm and led him to the squad. He whispered to the manager, "Unless you want real trouble you better not press charges, 'cause if you do, you'll be applying for unemployment benefits when you get out of the hospital." On the way out, as Ray was led through the crowded waiting area, he briefly locked eyes with Elizabeth, his dream girl. No charges were ever filed and other than an hour at the station, no damage was done, except to Ray, as he could only imagine what Elizabeth thought of him.

***

SEVERAL WEEKS LATER, on a rainy Thursday afternoon, Ray was bugging out the Road Runner after resetting the ignition timing. It rained hard all that day and he had to be careful since the streets were wet, and with over 450 horsepower it would be easy to lose control on slick pavement. As he whizzed past, Ray noticed Worm's Fairlane pulled off on an adjacent side street. The passenger door was open and as he got closer he saw Bug with his hand on a girl's arm. He smiled to himself as he thought it was a girl from the neighborhood, but when he pulled in behind the Fairlane he could feel the bile rise in his throat as he realized that it was Elizabeth. He couldn't imagine what this was all about, but knew something was definitely wrong. When he climbed out of the Road Runner he ignored the boys. "Elizabeth, you're lost. Thank god these guys found you. This can be a bad neighborhood. Get in my car and I'll take you home." Elizabeth never hesitated as she broke free and got into the Road

Runner, locking the door behind her. Now Ray had to deal with Worm and Bug. Worm started it. "What gives, man? You know that chick?" Ray knew he had to be careful. Running with these guys was like running with a wolf pack, stumble and the pack turns on you. "She's my lady."

"Since when?" Bug asked. "You ain't never said nothing about having an old lady."

Ray reached into his jacket pocket and slipped his hand into a set of brass knuckles. When he held his hand up the ½ inch long spikes sent shivers through both Worm and Bug. Worm grinned. "Damn, bro, that is nasty. Where did you get that?"

Ray ignored the question as he back-pedaled to the car. "Catch you dudes later." As Ray guided the Road Runner slowly through the nearly flooded streets, he questioned Elizabeth. "What's going on? Why are you on foot around here, girl?" She sat still for a very long time and didn't speak, instead dabbing her eyes with a hankie. Finally Ray pulled over to the side of the street, shut the engine off, and looked at her. "Well!"

"Okay, the viaduct where you catch the bus is flooded and the driver said he had to turn around and go back. I got out and thought I could walk over the viaduct and catch a bus on the other side, but the railroad police warned me not to go up on the tracks or I'd be arrested. So, I decided to walk back to that little grocery store that's about two blocks from the flooded street and call my mother. That's when those two guys tried to pick me up. If you'll just take me back to a safe place, I can call home."

"You're safe now." Their eyes met. "You really are." She reached over and patted his arm. "Thank you, Raymond." Ray was amazed that she remembered his name, but was pleasantly surprised. "If it's okay, I'll take you to my house and you can make your call. And when the water recedes, I'll take you home."

"Thank you, I'd appreciate that."

Ray couldn't help but hear the conservation Elizabeth had with her mother. "I'm fine, Mother. Raymond is going to take me home as soon as the viaduct is passable....No he doesn't go to Luther...I don't know, but I know him from the bus....He lives with his sister." She looked at Ray. "She wants to talk to your sister." Ray called his sister in law to the phone. "Elizabeth's mother wants to talk to you." After explaining the circumstances again, Mary Blackburn handed the phone back to Elizabeth. "I'll be home as soon as I can, mother." With that the inquisition was over, and as she hung up the phone she smiled at Ray. "Mothers! She wanted to know why can't I go around the flooded street and why it's taking so long." She shook her head. "Why can't there be peace on earth? Some things we just don't know the answers to."

After a meal of hamburgers and fries, Ray and Elizabeth drove down to the flooded viaduct. "It's gone down," Ray said, "but it'll be a couple of more hours before they open the road."

They sat in the car in front of Ray's house for a long time while they got to know each other. "I go to Dirksen Vocational and I'm a junior. Now you know all about me." He looked over at her in the fading daylight. "Your turn."

She turned toward him in a friendly gesture. "We just moved here last summer. My father works for US Steel and was reassigned. I grew up in Dayton and that's where all of my friends are. It's really hard to move when you're fifteen."

"So you're fifteen?"

"No. Actually I'm sixteen now. My birthday was in October."

"Reassigned? Is your dad some kind of big wheel at the mill? I mean they don't transfer the hardhats."

"I guess so. He's a boss over the accounting department or something, but he had no choice in being transferred. It's not a promotion. At least I don't think it is. Really, my father doesn't discuss his career with me."

"Sorry. I don't mean to be noisy about your family. So, are you going steady or dating anybody?"

"I wasn't allowed to date until I turned sixteen, and I've only dated a few times." Now it was time to pop the big question and Ray could feel his heart rate jump.

"What about the guy that sits next to you on the bus, the one who acts like he owns you?"

"Nobody owns me," she shot back. "Joseph is just a guy at school."

"From what I see, he looks like your boyfriend."

"I don't have a boyfriend. I haven't since I was in seventh grade."

That was great news to Ray. He had a chance, even though she was a bit agitated by his line of questioning. They made small talk for the next hour and finally Elizabeth looked at her watch. "It's after ten; the road should be open by now."

The Road Runner easily navigated the ten inches of water still covering the roadway, although officially the road remained closed and was blocked by the Illinois state animal, yellow saw horses with hanging red lanterns.

Ray pulled the car into the long driveway set off to the side of the white, freshly painted, three-story Colonial style house that was known as 8636 Yates Avenue. The house and grounds were lit up like 1600 Pennsylvania, Avenue; the White House in Washington D.C. Ray stopped the car and looked the building up and down. "Which apartment do you live in?"

"It's not an apartment building, silly. It's our house."

That information prompted a single word response. "Whoa."

The Commander engine, with the racing camshaft, idled so hard it actually shook the ground and vibrated the windows in the old house, and that brought mother out onto the porch in seconds. Elizabeth turned to Ray and offered her out-stretched hand. "Elizabeth Barrett, and I'm pleased to meet you. I'm also sorry for the snub on the bus."

"Apology accepted and I'm Ray Blackburn," he said as he gripped her hand. It was a bit redundant, but they both got a chuckle out of it. By this time her mother was halfway down the stairs and met Elizabeth on the side-walk. They both watched silently as Ray backed out of the driveway and disappeared into the night. Elizabeth smiled to herself with memories of the boy she just met. Her mother turned for the house without a word, she had a mission. Write down the license number she just read from the car's plate.

When mother and daughter were behind closed doors, the interrogation began anew. "Who is that boy and how did you wind up at his house? Where does he live and where does he go to school? What about his family? Who are they?"

Elizabeth ignored her mother's questions and started up the stairs to her second floor room. "I'm tired, mother, and I'm going to bed. I have to get up early to do the homework I couldn't do tonight."

Rosemary Barrett stood at the foot of the stairs with her mouth agape, not believing the insubordination of her oldest child. Knowing that her husband was so involved with his work that it was her responsibility to monitor the children, she promised herself that this matter wasn't over, not by a long shot.

***

IN THE PAST, Ray, like his friends, chased short skirts and long-haired girls. Girls he would never want a long-term relationship with, but with Elizabeth it was different. She was wholesome and good, and he wanted to know her.

He started taking the early bus again and Elizabeth sat in the first seat across from the driver so Ray could see her from the street. They sat together and each looked forward to the ten minutes a day they spent together. After several long phone conversations, Rosemary Barrett decided to monitor the calls and always seemed to intercept them, telling Ray that Elizabeth wasn't home or couldn't come to the phone; and they always went unreturned. For the time being the meetings on the bus had to be enough, and although Ray asked her out, because of her mother, she always had an excuse not to accept.

Several weeks later Rosemary confronted her daughter. "Elizabeth, you're not to see that boy anymore. He's not the kind of person you should be interested in. He goes to a school for delinquents and will never amount to anything. He comes from a place surrounded by railroad tracks called Swede Hill, a neighborhood that's filled with old, run-down houses. And that brother he lives with will never amount to anything either, he's just a grease monkey and works at a gas station."

Elizabeth was nearly speechless, but soon recovered. "Mother, maybe Swede Hill isn't Knob Hill, but for the most part the people there are hard-working and honest, and how dare you judge Raymond. And what did you do, hire a private detective to check him out? You had no right to do that."

"Your father is a powerful executive and his company has people that do background checks. He just called in a favor. Besides that's not what this is about. That boy will only bring you trouble. Listen to your mother."

"I am and it's making me sick."

"Sick or not, you stay away from him. And I don't want him calling here anymore."

Elizabeth was embarrassed to tell Ray what her mother said, but she felt he was entitled to the truth. "I don't care what your mother and father think. I care what you think. And if you want to see me, then we will."

Although her mother wanted Elizabeth to attend only school and church functions involving Lutherans, she gave in and took turns driving Elizabeth and her friend Martha to various teen dances. At first Ray met her at these hops and spent the evening talking and dancing with Elizabeth. After two months of seeing each other this way, every Friday and Saturday night, the young couple would meet at the dance and leave for the evening in Ray's Road Runner. They did things Elizabeth was sure her mother would never approve of, no matter who the date was; roller-skating, the show, bowling, and the other usual things young people do on dates. After two months the jig was up. Already suspicious, Rosemary went into the Holiday Club Teen Mixer at ten o'clock instead of the usual eleven thirty, and when she couldn't find her daughter called the police, who arrested Ray when they returned. Rosemary signed a complaint accusing him of contributing to the delinquency of a minor. Ray posted bond and was released into the custody of his brother. The case was thrown out of court the following Tuesday, but by that time Ray wanted his say with Rosemary and drove over to the big house on Yates Avenue. He didn't have to blow the horn as the thunder from the loud exhaust brought Rosemary from the house. He backed his car up over the sidewalk onto city property and motioned for her to follow. When she stood several feet from him he started in. "Mrs. Barrett, I don't care what you think of me personally, but I do care what Elizabeth thinks and that's why I'm trying my best to be civil and courteous to you; and that's only because you're her mother. Now you need to understand some things. I've fallen deeply in love with your daughter, and no amount of your interference will discourage me. The only reason I'll get out of her life is if she tells me too, and not because you coerced her into it. And only if that's honestly what she wants. I think she loves me and I want to give our relationship the chance to see if our feelings are real." He paused for a moment before continuing, "I love her like I've never loved anything or anybody in my whole life and I hope to marry her someday. And with or without you blessing I intend to see Elizabeth as much as I can."

Rosemary Barrett walked up to Ray, and with her face just inches from his began. "Okay, I let you have your say, now I'll have mine. And excuse me if I'm a bit blunt. You, sir, are not good enough for my daughter and you never will be. And it's not a case of money. It's a case of class and values. You are what you come from, it may not be your fault, but that's how it is. And where you live is who you are. Am I making myself clear?"

"Perfectly. You're a snob."

"I knew you wouldn't understand. Look, Raymond, Elizabeth enjoys a privileged life style that I'm sure you could never offer her. If you really care you'll leave her alone. She'll get over you and I want it to happen before she has four kids and a miserable life. Am I getting through to you?" Ray didn't reply. "Elizabeth is a God-fearing young woman brought up with Christian princi-pals. This whole family, including Elizabeth, believes in strong religious values. Do you go to a church, or even believe in God?

He shook his head no. "Of course I believe in God. And no, I don't go to church, but I was baptized Catho-lic."

"Figures. My mother warned me about Catholic boys and you fit the bill, mister. Now you listen to me, and lis-ten carefully. Until she's eighteen she lives under my su-pervision, and I'm telling you to stay away from her." With that Rosemary stomped off up the driveway.

That night she decided to lay it on the line with Eliz-abeth and cornered her in her bedroom while she was studying. "That friend of yours came by today and I ran him off. I explained that he wasn't good enough for you and that since you're not eighteen, you will abide by my rules."

"You did what? You told Raymond that he wasn't good enough for me? How could you? I love him, and someday I want to marry him. He's a good person and he loves me too."

"Love? What a laugh! What's love? Living in a cold-water flat in the inner city? Is that what you want? Is love going to put you in a nice house and buy a decent car or put money in your checking account? You have a lot to learn about life, girl."

"No, Mother. YOU haven't learned about life. Let me tell you about you. You have a great house, a nice car, and money in the bank. You also have a marriage that sucks. I see how you and father look at each other and how you never even say good morning or good night to each other. And you never even kiss him when he comes home or leaves the house. What kind of marriage is that?"

Now Rosemary was angry. "The kind that will never leave me or my children out in the street no matter what happens…. that's the kind of marriage I have. And if it's a little short on the romance part, so what."

Elizabeth stood up and stood nose to nose with her mother. "I'll spend as much time with Raymond as I can, just so you know. And I don't give a crap about all your security, Mother. They can carve that on your tombstone.

Chapter 3

Rosemary Barrett made it extremely difficult for the young couple to see each other and decided to drive Elizabeth to and from school. The only activities allowed were student sock hops and functions sponsored by the school or her church, and Rosemary always drove her daughter to and from these affairs. She also warned school officials about Raymond Blackburn, the boy who was stalking her daughter. Most mornings, as Ray waited for the bus, he watched Elizabeth's sad face as she whizzed bye in her mother's Audi on their way to Luther South. Their stolen moments were few, and other than the phone calls Elizabeth managed to sneak, contact was practically non-existent.

Several months later Ray was surprised to see Martha, Elizabeth's friend from school, on the bus. She slid over as Ray took the seat next to her. "I normally take a much later bus," she explained, "but Elizabeth asked me to give you this." She handed him a plain white envelope. He stared at it and thought the worst. Martha smiled. "It's not a Dear John letter; we just thought that you two could communicate through me... if you want to."

"Of course I want to."

"Good. I'll take this early bus once a week and you two love birds can pass letters back and forth." She scribbled on a piece of paper and handed it to him. "This is my phone number in case you ever need to get a message to her."

Once a week, Martha exchanged the long letters that the couple wrote, but instead of filling a need, they only created a stronger desire to see each other. This worked well during the school year, but during the summer, other than an occasional telephone call from Elizabeth, the couple had no contact. Late that summer, on hot August day, as Ray and several friends swam at Lake Michigan's Calumet Beach, he saw Elizabeth sunbathing on a large beach towel while her mother sat nearby in a lawn chair reading a book. Eventually, Elizabeth looked up at her mother, said something, then rose to her feet and walked to the concession stand. This was the chance Ray was waiting for and soon followed. When she saw him she casually walked behind the stand and greeted him with warm kisses and tight hugs. They only had minutes and didn't waste them on talk. Finally, Ray, holding both of her arms lightly, stepped back and drank in the loveliness of her body. At nearly seventeen she was all woman and although her yellow, two piece bathing suit was a long way from a French Bikini, it didn't hide much either. He again embraced her and murmured, "You're beautiful. I love you." And then she was gone.

In late September Martha came up with an idea. Her boyfriend, James, would pick up Elizabeth for a date to the Homecoming Dance and then pick up Ray and Martha at Martha's house. Although the school was supposed to be on the lookout for Raymond Blackburn and required identification from everyone entering the school, they never connected the dots. After several hours and the usual portraits, Elizabeth's picture taken with Martha's boyfriend, the couple enjoyed a late night dinner at a posh

downtown restaurant. On the way home, as they whispered to each other in the back seat, the lovers were hungry for each other's touch, each other's kisses, and each
other's hugs.

***

IN MID OCTOBER ELIZABETH'S parents were
treated to a ten-day all expenses paid trip to Montego
Bay, Jamaica. It was called a business seminar on paper,
but the inner circle of US Steel executives who attended
knew different. Although Rosemary Barrett didn't trust
her daughter, she had no plans to miss this trip. Her husband neither cared nor worried about what Elizabeth did,
after all, she was just his stepdaughter, a fact never shared
with Elizabeth. Rosemary was married at sixteen and divorced at seventeen, with a brand new baby girl. Remarried at nineteen with no living family, it was decided
that the secret would always be that, a secret.

A nanny, hired to stay with the children since her
brother was only four years old, was given instructions
about what Elizabeth was allowed to do and not do. But
each morning her mother was on vacation, Elizabeth
walked to the bus stop and was picked up by Ray in the
Road Runner. He drove her to school several times, but
other days, they just skipped school and enjoyed each
other's company. It didn't take long for Elizabeth to realize that the nanny could have cared less about what she
did and the couple took full advantage of it. Ray took her
out every night and even spent an evening in the big home
on Yates Avenue. Rosemary Barrett called every day before dinner, at nine sharp, insisting to speak to her daughter. Her logic was that with the call at that time, it was too

late for Elizabeth to sneak out. She was wrong; it was only six in Chicago.

When Elizabeth turned seventeen, during her parent's
vacation, she enjoyed a very special day with Ray. They
drove to the Indiana Dunes State Park and walked bare-
footed, holding hands for miles along Lake Michigan's
sandy lakeshore. Later, as the surf crashed onto the shore
the couple lay on a blanket while smothering each other
with kisses. Before returning home they dined at
Westfalls, an upscale steak house in nearby Chesterton.

It was past eleven when the couple returned to the
house on Yates Avenue. Neither of them wanted the evening to end and as they sat in the car Ray finally pulled her
close and whispered, "Good night, darling." She clung to
him, and pulled even tighter when he tried to break away.
Ray could feel her warm tears on his neck. They embraced for a very long time and when Elizabeth pulled
away slightly it was only to kiss him. She gently pushed
him down onto the seat and kissed him passionately as
she lay on top. Ray responded, and in a matter of moments their hands were everywhere exploring each other's
body, places formally off limits. Ray tried to reason with
her as she smothered him with kisses. "Elizabeth, we gotta stop. If we don't..." She reached down and unzipped his
trousers, saying nothing. Minutes later it was done. They
went all the way. All their plans about waiting to be sure
of their feelings, the waiting until they were older, were
gone. This time when they embraced it was Ray who softly wept. "I'm sorry, Elizabeth. I didn't mean for this to
happen."

"Shh. You didn't do anything wrong. I wanted to. I
love you, Raymond."

***

MOTHER AND FATHER RETURNED home three days later and from what the nanny told them things went well while they were gone. Elizabeth counted the days until she had her period and breathed a sigh of relief when it happened. Neither Ray nor Elizabeth liked the way they had to sneak around, but learned to live with it until a call from the vice-principal of Luther South changed that. "Mrs. Barrett, Raymond Blackburn was turned away from admission to several of our school events. You asked to be notified if he stalked your child again, and so I'm warning you, that he is attempting to have contact with Elizabeth."

When Elizabeth returned home from school that day they had it out. Rosemary started it. "I know you've been trying to see that boy again and I'm tired of being a cop. Either you stop it or I'm sending you away to school. I don't care if you only have six months until graduation, don't push me, girl. Even if you don't know what's best for you, I do."

"Mother, I've had about all of your bullshit I'm going to take."

"Listen to the way you talk to your mother. Did he teach you that?"

"No, you listen. I'm going to tell you how it is and if you don't like it, I'm going to court to have myself declared emancipated. Do you know what that means, Mother?" Rosemary remained silent. "It means you're not responsible for me anymore and that I'm legally able to make my own decisions."

"You wouldn't dare."

"You don't think so? Now you listen to me for a change. I'm going on eighteen, not eight, and I have a right to make decisions concerning my life and who I want to see. I'm not going to sneak around to see Raymond anymore. Either he is allowed to come over here, to my home, either to spend time with me or to pick me up for a date, or I'm out of here."

"Where do you think you'll go, and what about school?"

"That, Mother, will not be your problem."

Rosemary dabbed her eyes with a tissue and whispered, "I was there once, Elizabeth, where you are now. I got pregnant when I was sixteen, had you at seventeen, and divorced at eighteen."

"WHAT. You mean Norman Barrett is not my father, and you were married before?"

As she continued to dab her eyes, Rosemary went on, "Of course he's your father. He adopted you when you were two and always treated you as his own." Rosemary grabbed Elizabeth by the arm. "Don't you see, I thought I knew everything too, but look at what happened to me. I just don't want to see you make that same mistake. Can't you see, that boy can't take care of you like he should, and you have no guarantees that he'll even make a good husband. How is he going to provide for you with the kind of education he has. He'll wind up digging ditches for a living"

Elizabeth pulled away from her mother. "I don't care if he sweeps the floor at McDonalds, as long as we're together."

Rosemary gave in. "Okay, we'll try it your way for a while, but remember, I warned you."

Although she gave in, Rosemary had an ace in the hole, Elizabeth would go out of state next year to attend college and she doubted that Raymond would be able to follow. Yes, the small, tight knit Christian College in Alabama would be just right, and plans had already been made for Elizabeth to attend.

***

FROM THAT POINT ON things were better. If not bubbling with love, at least Rosemary was civil and polite to Ray, and of course he reciprocated. After graduation, that summer was spent with lazy days at the beach and long drives into the country. Although they tried, they were unable to avoid the temptation of sex, but always used protection. Although it was never the centerpiece of any outing, the couple often shared a cheap bottle of wine or a six-pack of beer. At times they would double-date with Martha and James, going to amusement parks and rock concerts, but mostly just enjoyed spending time together. As the summer waned they started to worry about their future. "I leave for school in two weeks, Ray. Are you still going to do mechanical jobs with your brother?"

As they swung gently on the porch swing at her house, he paused for a moment before answering, "I joined the Army." She put her foot down and stopped the swing abruptly. "You didn't." He pressed his lips together.

"Yeah, I did. I'm not college material and I need to learn a marketable skill, one that will give us a decent living. I'll be out when you finish school and when I have liberty, I'll come to you." Elizabeth put her head on his shoulder and cried softly.

"I'm going to miss you."

"I'll miss you too, but we'll see each other every couple of months and I could even get assigned to an Army post close to you."

They sat there for long time swinging gently, both with their own thoughts. Finally, Ray lifted her chin with his index finger until they gazed into each other's eyes.

"I want to marry you the day I get discharged. Will you have me?"

She threw her arms around his neck. "Of course, darling. I can't wait." She hesitated briefly and pulled away slightly. "There is one thing though; promise me you won't use illegal drugs anymore. I don't want any of my babies having life long health issues because either of us used."

"I've never use hard stuff, only grass, but I promise."

She again embraced him. "Thank you."

Chapter Four

Although he was sworn in during early September, Ray didn't have to report for induction until the first week in November. After Elizabeth left for school his brother Ralph came to him with an interesting proposition. Ray and his Road Runner were well known in the area and an older guy with a hi-performance Corvette challenged him to a race. The guy had deep pockets and offered to put up 10k against the title to the Road Runner. In the past Ray street-raced for a case of beer or twenty dollars, but never for such high stakes.

"Think about it," Ralph said. "If we work on the car a bit, I think you can take him. But this guy won't race on the street. If it happens, we race at US 30 drag strip under NHRA rules, and the track officials will hold his money and your title. It'll be "run what ya brung" heads up, one pass only. Interested?"

"I don't know?. What'd you know about his car?"

"It's a '67 with the L88 engine, 435 horsepower, tweaked transmission, and a stock gear."

"Do you know how he runs?"

"My buddy from work, Jerry Hammond, is a racer and Ham says the guy runs at the track all the time, and runs high tens."

Ray caught his brother's gaze. "Since I never took my car to the track, I have no idea what it'll do. And I don't want to lose my car by being stupid and drawing on the wrong guy. He's sitting on at least twenty more horse than me, even with the hi-lift cam shaft, steel crank, and the forged pistons we put in."

"Brother, we upped that engine a lot from the factory 390 horse power. Let me take the car to work and I'll put it on the dyno and we can tell."

"I don't know. I don't wanna lose my car."

"You won't."

"What's in it for me?"

"Five thousand and you know that Plymouth is only worth about $1500. The other guy knows that too, but he's so sure he'll win he doesn't care. Since nobody ever said anything, we'll install a nitrous kit and change the differential gears to .456. That'll give your Road Runner some legs."

"We'll need new tires, and that'll cost."

"Ray, we put two grand into the car, you get five, I get two, and Ham gets the other one."

"What's Ham got to do with anything?"

"He's gonna drive. If you wanna win, you gotta drive it like you stole it; and I know you won't do that."

Ray paused for a moment, and then gave in. "Okay. I'm gone for four years anyway. Let's do it."

Arrangements were made and the big race would take place in four weeks, on the last weekend the drag strip was open. Three weeks later the car was ready, but the only place it was towed was to the shop where Ralph worked. After power timing the engine on the dynometer, Ralph looked at his younger brother. "It's a bear. It'll do mid 9's. I've dyno'd enough racecars to know. The only thing we have to worry about is a catastrophic failure. We'll blow the doors off that Vette."

***

RAY KEPT HIS WORD to Elizabeth and didn't smoke pot, but with his friends, he drank enough to make up for it. On a Friday night, Ray, along with Worm and Bug cruised the city in Worm's Fairlane when Bug decided he needed cigarettes. Worm accompanied him into Jonny O's Food and Liquor while Ray parked the car around the corner. He suspected his pals might try to heist a bottle and he didn't want anyone seeing them get into the Fairlane. Minutes later, Worm and Bug charged around the corner and jumped into the car. Both were screaming, "Go, go, go."

A block away Ray looked at his friends and laughed. "Did you grab a jug?"

Silently, Bug, who sat in the middle, held up a deep blue, snub-nosed revolver and offered an explanation. "When the guy saw Worm put a bottle under his coat he freaked and grabbed this. I jumped him and when me and Worm tried to get the gun, it went off and hit the guy."

"You shot the guy? Jesus Christ what were you two dopes thinking?"

Worm leaned forward and turned toward Ray. "Nobody saw us, man. We're in the clear."

"In the clear, my ass," Ray yelled. "I'm going home and I better not hear from the cops, 'cause if I do, I'll hunt both of you idiots down if it takes forever. I don't know nothing about this, and if either of you get caught, my name better not come up. This shit could ruin my life. Am I making myself clear? And get rid of the gun."

That night as Ray lay in bed he had nightmares about the police kicking in the front door and dragging him off to jail. The story was all over the news and the talk of the neighborhood. The clerk suffered a gunshot wound to the leg, but was expected to recover, and with his eyewitness description, police were expected to make quick arrests. Ray knew it was only a matter of time before his pals went away, and he could only hope they'd keep their mouths shut about him. Two days later both Worm and Bug were arrested, the gun recovered and as ludicrous as it sounds, the hapless clerk was charged with possession of an unregistered firearm. Eventually both pled guilty to aggravated battery and attempted robbery, and Bug, as a minor, got fifteen months in a juvenile facility and probation until he turned twenty one. Worm was eighteen and got the full treatment, especially since he had a long file with the police. He wouldn't see freedom for eight years since his sentence stipulated no parole or early release. Ray was never implicated and soon put the incident in the back of his mind.

***

WHEN THEY GOT TO US 30 Drag-strip Ray, Ralph and Ham watched as the sunshine-yellow Corvette made several passes through the ¼ mile. "Shouldn't we make a pass or two before we race?" Ray asked.

"That's up to Ham," said Ralph.

"No," was the reply. "We know what the car will do and if we break before the race, we lose. I can come off the line without practice, don't worry."

The yellow Corvette was putting on quite a show and the spectators loved it as each pass brought a gasp when the clock at the finish line displayed his elapsed time. When Ray looked at the sign, his heart sank, 9:21. He looked at Ralph. "I don't think we can beat him. He did something to the car." Ralph sniffed the air and shook his head. "He's burning alcohol. We're in trouble, brother."

When the time to race finally arrived, the crowd roared as Ham did a burn out, a process by which the tires are made sticky and thus attain better traction. As Ham slowly backed up into the blue haze of tire smoke the Corvette lunged forward in the opposite lane disappearing into the cloud he created. The noise was deafening and the track officials, standing nearby, covered their ears. After a brief time the smoke drifted away, revealing broken drive shaft parts behind the Vette. The other driver appeared, and after removing his helmet, slammed it down on the pavement. All Ham had to do was run down the quarter mile and the Road Runner would be declared the winner. When he got the green light he didn't overtax the car, never spraying the nitrous, and ran a 10:6. The Corvette owner was a good sport and said that maybe they could try again in the future. Ray knew it would never happen and was grateful for the five thousand he now had. Money that he hoped someday would be the down payment on a house, after he married Elizabeth.

Chapter 5

Elizabeth wasn't exactly on her own at Faith Christian College, her best friend Martha was also enrolled and shared a dorm room, with plans of securing off campus housing for the following semester. Both were Liberal Arts Majors and came to Faith Christian with excellent high school grades. They were serious and there to get a good education like most of the other Faith students, and not looking for parties and freedom from parental control that many college kids seek. Martha and James had an understanding that each could date while they attended separate universities, but Elizabeth, wearing the inexpensive engagement ring, remained true to Raymond.

When boot camp started, the twice-weekly phone calls stopped and although she carried a heavy load of eighteen credit hours, Elizabeth wrote every day, even though she knew that while in boot camp at Fort Leonard Wood, Missouri, Ray received no mail. Still, when writing, she felt close as she shared her college experiences with him. He promised that when boot was over he'd come to her and Elizabeth lived for that day.

***

RAYMOND BLACKBURN may have grown up with very little discipline, but he easily made the adjustment and understood the reasons recruits were subjected to ridicule and embarrassment. If they were going to crack, the Army wanted to know before they endangered any mission. Raymond had a tattoo on his left bicep of an angry cartoon character with a scroll proclaiming ROAD RUNNER in its mouth. The instructor saw this and because of his name started calling him "Blackbird." The other recruits laughed while Ray pretended irritation, all to the delight of the Sergeant. The recruiter had promised Ray a job in the motor pool, but on the first day all recruits were informed that they could forget about any promises made to get their enlistment. Ray expected this and also knew that during basic training he would be given a series of tests which would decide where he would be placed. He earned the recognition of expert on the rifle range and although he considered himself a proficient street fighter, the hand-to- hand training dramatically improved that skill. Basic is always tough, but during peacetime, when the need for trained personal is at a minimum, the training is always much tougher.

After thirteen weeks the recruits were ready to graduate, but would have to wait another week until the General had time to attend. The boys were getting their first liberty, a 48-hour pass and their instructor was worried.

"Gentleman, don't let the little head do the thinking for the big head." He knew it was useless to tell them to stay celibate. "Use protection if you find a girl, and don't drink so much that you can't protect yourself. And men, don't get arrested or get into any fights. You won't graduate if you wind up in the brig." The sergeant always made the same speech and always had the same results; two or three out of this group would come back with the MP's, spend thirty days in the brig, and do basic training over.

The soldiers knew that Ft. Leonard Wood was not a party town and most decided to take the two-hour bus ride to St. Louis, a town with plenty of action. Instead, Ray rode along with a buddy to Springfield, Missouri, only an hour away. The soldier lived there and had his girlfriend pick him up, and along with Ray, took two others to Springfield. The three were let out downtown and told that since they had to be back by six Sunday evening, he would pick them up at four sharp Sunday afternoon, on the same corner.

The soldiers got a room and found the nearest bar. Ray was wise to what happens to soldiers in strange towns and brought a change of clothes, but his pals didn't and those uniforms brought trouble. First, it was two local girls who just loved soldiers in uniform, and of course that brought the locals who didn't like the idea of those pretty boys hitting on their woman. Ray tried to stay out of it and hardly spoke to the girls, but one, a redhead, wouldn't leave him alone and insisted that he dance with her. He tried to keep a proper distance, but she snuggled up and was cheek to cheek before he knew it. "Are you a soldier too?"

"Yeah."

"Are you a General or something?" she whispered into his ear. "How come you aren't wearing your uniform?" Ray never had the chance to answer, and as they turned to the music he spotted a beer bottle being swung at his head. He instinctively ducked as the girl was hit across the forehead, producing a large gash that bled profusely. Now the battle was on and the odds were not in the soldiers' favor. Five locals jumped on the soldiers swinging bottles and throwing glasses. Ray back-pedaled until he reached the wall behind the pool table where he grabbed a cue stick and quickly broke it across the face of the guy that charged him. When another attacker dove for him he picked up a cue ball and bounced it off his skull. Now it was even and the other locals, seeing what was happening, decided to take an early hiatus. It was over in less than a minute, but that was long enough for the barkeep to call the police. Ray and one of his fellow soldiers half dragged the other soldier out of the door and quickly disappeared down the busy street. There was no telling how bad the civilians were injured and Ray was sure that the bartender would back up any story that the attackers came up with. The soldiers knew that the police would be looking for them, and wearing Army uniforms they wouldn't be hard to spot. After they were safely back in their room it was decided that Ray, since he wore civies, would go to Wal-Mart and get the two other boys a change of clothes.

Later, after changing into the new clothes the boys listened to the local news, but heard nothing of their escapade, so they again hit the street. This time they took a cab and wound up at a dance club frequented by the Springfield jet set. Ray just watched his friends as they became drunk and spent a king's ransom buying drinks for every pretty woman who would sit with them. Finally, around midnight, they wanted Ray to party with three girls at their apartment. As much as he felt the need, Ray begged off as thoughts of Elizabeth filled his head.

The next morning he smiled as his friends recounted the evening with their "dates." Both were broke, but would have a wild tale to tell when they returned to the base. Ray only thought about the fifteen-day leave after graduation, when he again would hold Elizabeth in his arms. The wait would be worth it.

***

FEBRUARY 14TH THE DAY after graduation, Rau finally got his leave. Ghat was the time between boot camp and AIT, Advanced Infantry Training. He took a bus to St. Louis and caught a flight to Montgomery, Alabama where Elizabeth and Martha met him and brought him to their rented two-bedroom house. When they saw Raymond they hardly recognized him with his military haircut, high, tight, and short on top. The fresh flowers he bought at the airport were in water when he unzipped his travel bag and presented Elizabeth with a large red Valentine heart, wrapped in a matching red bow. "Sweets for the sweet," he said as he presented her the box.

She set the candy down and threw her arms out and hugged him for a very long time. "I missed you," she said.

"I missed you too," Ray replied.

They aborted all pretenses as Ray put his things in Elizabeth's bedroom. They both agreed that those two weeks were the best they ever had. Martha, respecting the couple's privacy, stayed away most of the time while Elizabeth cut numerous classes.

***

TWO MONTHS LATER RAY finished AIT and with his high-test scores was placed as an aircraft mechanic. The bad part was that he was stationed in Seattle, close to the Canadian border, and would not be able to see Elizabeth on any regular basis, although they talked at least twice a week on the phone.

In mid October he got a call from Martha. "You need to come as soon as you can. Elizabeth needs you."

"What's wrong?"

"She's pregnant and due any time."

"What! Why didn't she tell me? God, I have a right to know."

"Look, Ray, she doesn't even know I called you. Said it's not your problem."

"Okay, I'll talk to the CO, or the Chaplain, or somebody, but I'm on my way. Tell her that, will you? I'll call you when I know my flight."

The CO wasn't very agreeable to an emergency leave, but with the Chaplain's help Ray was on a plane the next morning. When Martha picked him up they drove straight to the hospital. "She's been in labor for fourteen hours, poor thing. I guess I should tell you what's going on. When her parents found out about the baby they refused to pay her tuition and threw her out of the house. She didn't go to summer school like she told you; instead she went to work at a family restaurant as a waitress and stayed in the house we rented."

"Why didn't she tell me? I wanna take care of her. Doesn't she know that?"

"Raymond, she's scared and confused and doesn't know you're coming. The rest is up to you."

When Ray explained that he was the father he was given a hospital gown and allowed in Elizabeth's room. When she saw him her eyes filled with tears as she tried to smile. "I guess I really did it this time."

He leaned down and kissed her softly on the lips. "You're so handsome in your uniform," she said. "I just want to eat you up."

He took her hand and smiled. "I'm here now and I won't leave until I'm sure you and the baby are alright."

Elizabeth's eyes filled with tears. "Raymond, I signed papers. I gave the baby away for adoption. I thought that would be best for the baby and you."

Ray felt frustration, but he understood her reasoning and just squeezed her hand.

A heavy-set woman in a nurse's uniform, carrying a clipboard, ignored Ray and spoke directly to Elizabeth, "Ms. Barrett, you need to sign this form, too." Ray took the paper off the board and read it.

"What the hell is this, lady?"

"Who are you, sir?"

"I'm the father."

"Well, Mister..."

"Blackburn, my name is Blackburn, the same one our baby will have."

"Mr. Blackburn, Ms. Barrett signed papers allowing the baby to be put up for adoption, but we do have a slight problem."

"Yeah, we sure do. She changed her mind. We're taking our baby home with us."

"I'm afraid, sir, that is impossible. Ms. Barrett already signed away her parental rights and listed the father as unknown. You're too late. Now for the problem. Ms. Barrett had no prenatal care and we didn't know until a few minutes ago that she's carrying twins. The ultrasound confirmed that. Now we need her to sign this form for the other baby."

Ray took the nurse by the arm and practically dragged her from the room. Once out in the hall he kept his voice low, but his message was loud and clear. "Lady, pigs will fly out of my ass before Elizabeth signs any more of your papers, and we want our other baby too."

"Look, Mr. Blackburn, I don't think you understand. The papers that Ms. Barrett signed gave up the baby in consideration for paying all of her related expenses. So, as you can see our hands are tied."

"I'm taking her out of here."

The nurse stood her ground. "Go ahead. You'll kill both babies and probably the mother to boot. She's fully dilated. Do you know what that means? ... I didn't think so. Now understand, she hasn't given up the other baby and you can still take that one home. Please, don't do anything stupid. You'll only hurt yourself and your girl-friend."

And that's how it went down. The first baby, a boy, went unnamed by his natural parents, but John Raymond, born second was named reversing his father's names. Two days later Elizabeth returned to the rented house with her baby and Ray went back to Seattle to fulfill his Army commitment. Two weeks later, using most of his savings and with a lot of help from Martha, Elizabeth and little Johnny Ray flew cross-country and moved into a small house on the Army base. That same day the base Chaplain married Ray and Elizabeth.

Chapter 6

The next eleven years passed quickly and found Ray and Elizabeth still deeply in love and residing in St. Charles, Missouri, a St. Louis suburb. At thirty one, Ray, a certified aviation mechanic, was the mechanical supervisor for Haggrity Aviation, a company that leased corporate jets and helicopters to deep-pocketed clients. Elizabeth was a stay-at-home mom for Johnny Ray and his six year-old brother Cory, an energetic kid who adored his older brother and wanted to be just like him. Johnny was a gifted athlete and the star of his little league team. Cory faithfully followed his older brother to every practice and game, riding his 18" bicycle behind his older brother with his baseball glove hanging from the handlebars, just like Johnny Ray did, and always hung around the field until his brother was ready to go home. Johnny didn't always want his little brother around, especially when he wanted to walk a girl home from the game, but Cory followed him like a shadow. Johnny Ray tried to explain it to his mother. "Mom, he just follows me everywhere I go. Can't you make him stay home or something? Can't he just come to the games when you and dad go? Why doesn't he hang out with his own friends? I mean... my friends are getting tired of my little brother following us everywhere we go."

"He looks up to you, and he loves you. You know, when you grow up those friends might not be your friends anymore, but Cory will always be your brother. Think about that. If it makes you feel better, I'll talk to him and maybe he can do a little more without you."

***

THINGS DID CHANGE, Cory only went to the games, not the practices, but in return Johnny Ray made a point to spend time with his younger brother. He played catch in the back yard and even helped Cory build a tree-fort with his friends. Several weeks later severe storms swelled every body of water in the area with widespread flooding. Cory took Johnny Ray two blocks from home where floodwater emptied into a huge culvert that went into an underground storm sewer. He had pieces of cardboard, thin sticks, and several sheets of notebook paper. Johnny knew his brother loved to play in water and often crafted small sailboats out of similar materials. "We can have races, Johnny." As Johnny Ray looked at the rapidly flowing water, he warned his brother. "Okay, but don't get too close to the culvert."

"I won't."

They played for nearly an hour, and after releasing the boats the brothers would run ahead to a spot where the flow narrowed and catch them. Johnny Ray tired of this and decided to let his boat "get away" and sail into the flooded sewer. When Cory saw that Johnny Ray missed his boat he ran ahead and waded into the water and was immediately sucked into the current. He screamed for help, but Johnny knew that if he went into the water both boys would drown. Instead he ran ahead and waded into the water at the culvert gripping an iron screen that was partially closed. The Bureau of Public Works long ago abandoned the screen, installed for the purpose of catching large debris. As he was swept bye, Johnny grabbed

Cory's shirt and swung him around grabbing the opposite side of the screen. The force of the water was so strong that Johnny couldn't pull his brother back around to rescue him. "Johnny, I'm scared."

"I know," shouted Johnny over the roar of the water. "Just hang on."

"I can't. The water's too strong."

"Yes, you can. Listen to me. I need to get help."

"No, don't leave me. Johnny, I can't swim."

Johnny raised his voice hoping to reassure Cory that he knew what to do. "I'm going to put my belt through the fence. Hold on tight with one hand and put it under your arms, then give me the other end. Now listen, you can't let go. Do you understand?"

Cory tried not to cry, but it was hard as his voice trembled. "Yeah."

He couldn't get the belt under his arms and instead put it under his right arm and over his shoulder before handing the end to Johnny. After buckling the belt to the screen Johnny yelled to his brother. "I'm getting help. Just hold on. I'll be right back... and don't cry, only babies cry."

Cory sniffled, "I won't."

Ten minutes later Johnny was back with a homeowner who dove into the water and wrapped his arms around Cory while he waited for the rescue squad to arrive. By that time, Elizabeth stood anxiously by, clutching a hankie. When he finally reached dry ground, he ran into his mother's arms and was swept up in her embrace. Cory, Johnny, and the Good Samaritan were all taken to the hospital where their worst injuries were cuts and scrapes. Johnny Ray expected to be punished for the episode, but instead was praised for his quick thinking by his parents.

After the close call, there was no way Cory was ever going to leave his brothers side. Where he idolized Johnny before, he now worshipped him. Johnny Ray didn't care, he loved his little brother and didn't care who knew it.

***

THE PRACTICES AND GAMES were held in a large park that always attracted the usual summertime crowds. Mothers pushing strollers with small children hanging on to the sides, kids on bicycles surrounding preteen girls sitting on park benches, small crowds cheering at the softball games, and the ever present people walking their dogs.

A big man with thinning brown hair became a familiar fixture around the park that summer. He always walked with two energetic, mongrel puppies. The cute black and white dogs always attracted a crowd of eager children wanting to pet the friendly canines. As the dog's tails beat the air while being petted, the man was often questioned about them. Nobody knew his name or where he came from and since he had only a partial index finger on his right hand, the older children referred to him as "two thumbs" while the younger kids knew him as "Uncle Bob." Cory Blackburn started spending a lot of time with the stranger and developed a strong attachment to the dogs.

The man seemed to favor Cory over the other children and even let him help name the dogs, Barney and Clyde. Johnny Ray often saw Cory, along with other children, petting the dogs, but thought nothing of it as he concentrated on his baseball. Unknown in the community, the man was a child predator and lived quietly for over a year in the area. Like all stalkers he waited for his opportunity, the chance to get Cory alone. He hated the big brother, the one who was always around, but he knew that someday he would get his chance, and finally that day arrived.

It was nearly dark after the game ended, when a cute thirteen-year-old whispered into Johnny's ear, "Wanna come over to my house for a little while, my parents aren't home." Johnny was flattered that a woman, two years older that he, would actually make that offer. He looked at the slender blonde, visualizing his first make out session. "Uh, yeah, I can do that." The girl hopped on her pink bicycle and sped off into the twilight, closely followed by Johnny Ray.

When Cory saw this he tried to follow, peddling as hard as he could, but could only watch as this brother disappeared. Johnny only glanced back once, seeing his little brother wiping tears from his face with a fist. He could barely see Cory's open mouth as he called out for his big brother to wait, but Johnny never heard. The last thing he did was shout back, "Go home, Cory."

The friendly man with the puppies saw the whole incident and in a matter of seconds was at Cory's side. "That was mean. Is that your brother?" Cory bobbed his head yes between sobs.

"Hey, I got an idea. Barney and Clyde need a bath, would you help me? I only live on the next block."

"I'm supposed to be home by the time the street lights come on and it's almost dark now."

"Okay, but you'd really be a big help. You know how hyper these guys are, and besides, you can call your mother from my house." For the clincher the man added. "We can have cookies and ice cream when we finish."

Nobody seemed to pay any attention to the little boy walking his bike beside the man and the playful puppies, since it looked like a family outing and not a child abduction.

***

BY THE TIME JOHNNY RAY got home it was well after ten. He knew he was in trouble, but it was worth it he thought. Elizabeth was angry with Johnny and raised her voice into that mother's threatening tone, "You're in big trouble young man. Where's Cory?"

"Isn't he home? I told him to go home."

"No, he's not home. Where were you?'

"I walked a girl home. I'm sorry. I shouldn't have left Cory alone. I'll go look for him."

"Stay here. Your father is out looking for the both of you, and when he gets back I wouldn't want to be you."

An hour later Ray came home and when he found that Cory was still missing, the police were called.

Ten minutes later two police detectives sat in the Blackburn's living room filling out a report. "How long has the boy been missing?" Ray did the talking as Elizabeth and Johnny Ray sat quietly by. Ray looked at the clock on the wall. "About three hours, I guess." The officer making the report folded his notebook closed. "Mr. Blackburn, in the case of a juvenile we can't file a report for twenty-four hours and in the case of an adult we wait seventy-two. The boy could be at a friend's house or maybe he just ran away. We can alert our local department to watch for him, but we can't file a missing report until the twenty-four hours are up."

Elizabeth burst into tears. "He's only six years old. Where on earth do you think he's going to run to?"

"I'm sorry, ma'am, but we have procedures to follow."

***

THE POLICE FINALLY got serious three days later when no trace of Cory was found and the story received statewide coverage. Accounts of the friendly stranger with the puppies created plenty of police concern, but at the time, he was only considered a person of interest. When the police finally found him he stood up under questioning and was dropped to the bottom of the suspect list. Meanwhile, community volunteers searched every nook and cranny of the St. Charles area, including all vacant fields, bodies of water, and wooded areas, but no trace of Cory was found.

Ray didn't go to work; instead he and Johnny Ray joined the searchers while Elizabeth stayed close to the telephone in case any news was forthcoming. After a week the doorbell rang one afternoon and a small boy looked up into Elizabeth's face. "Are you Corey's mom?"

"Yes. What can I do for you?"

"Well, I just want to tell you...you know, Uncle Bob, the man with the puppies? I saw Cory's bike over by his house the day before the cops were looking for him, but when I went back later it was gone."

"How do you know it was Cory's?"

"'Cuz, Cory has his baseball glove on the handlebars. Everybody knows his bike."

After thanking the boy Elizabeth walked the two blocks to the man's house to confront him. His address was no secret since newsreels of the small cottage were shown on television when he was a suspect. The barking puppies tied to leashes on either side of the porch wagged their tails at the sight of Elizabeth. When Uncle Bob answered the door, he swung it wide and stepped back allowing Elizabeth to enter. Before closing the door he surveyed the area looking for reporters and nosey busybodies. Seeing none, he felt safe as he closed and dead-bolted the lock with a key.

***

THE FOLLOWING DAY Ray was nearly out of his mind with worry as he confronted investigating detectives. "What the hell are you doing? Now my wife is missing. It's that Uncle Bob guy. Haven't you been listening to the kids at the park? He could be holding my family prisoner and all you two do is interviews, asking the public to do your job."

"Look, Mr. Blackburn, we can't go around harassing citizens without proof. That's against the law. What if you're wrong?"

"Kidnapping is against the law. And what if I'm right?"

"We know how you feel, sir. Let us do our job. We know what we're doing. Don't do anything you'll regret later."

"No, you don't know how I feel," Ray shouted. "And you never will unless you're in my position." With that outburst Ray stomped out of the police station, got into his car, and drove straight to Robert Morgan's house. When he banged on the front door and got no response he rammed his shoulder into the wooden door. After it flew open Ray stepped through the splintered door frame into the living room where "Uncle Bob" stood in front of him with a crow bar.

"Where's my family, you bastard."

"I don't know what you're talking about, mister. You better leave. I've already called the police."

Instead Ray charged past the large man and started a room-by-room search. Robert Morgan walked outside and stood in the yard while he waited for the police. Several minutes later uniformed officers, with drawn guns, entered the house. When they found Ray he was holding his son's baseball glove and rubbing it gently against his face. He was pushed to the floor, handcuffed behind his back, and finally led to the front yard just as the detectives working the case appeared.

"We warned you," said one of the detectives. "Now you're in big trouble."

"Ask him how Cory's baseball glove got into his house."

Robert Morgan screamed at the officers as they started to put Ray into the back of the marked squad, "Get him out of here, I'm pressing charges." But the lead detective stopped that. "Wait a minute. What glove, Mr. Blackburn?"

"Cory's glove is on the bed in one of the bedrooms."

The detective, realizing that a search warrant wasn't needed in this case because he already had probable cause, followed Ray into the house while the uniformed policeman held Uncle Bob's arm. When they came out of the house one of the detectives held the baseball glove and ordered the policeman, "Take the cuffs off of Mr. Blackburn and watch this guy." Ray was told to stay outside while the detectives went through the house looking for either the missing mother and son, or evidence that they were there at some point. This type of search, a walk through, was allowed by law under the circumstances. But without a signed warrant, legally, they were restricted from going through drawers, cabinets, or anything else concealed from the naked eye. Ignoring this rule, the detectives, anxious to break the case, did not dump anything out, but they did open drawers and cabinets. Who'd ever know, they reasoned, and besides, if they found anything, they'd simply get a judge to sign a search warrant and come back while Robert Morgan was held for questioning. They didn't find anything upstairs, but when they walked down to the basement and flipped on the light they entered a different world. The area had no partitions and was filled with tables of small animals in various stages of taxidermy, and two large workbenches that were filled with related tools. Over the benches were several shelves holding numerous bottles of chemicals. They looked at each other and started to go through several cardboard boxes they found under the benches. Realizing that the boxes contained clothing for a small boy and garments worn by an adult female, they looked at each other shaking their heads. One detective spoke, "Let's bring this jerk in, get our warrant, and really go through this place." His partner didn't hear that, he was busy inspecting a large upright freezer wrapped with a heavy chain that was against the far wall.

The lock, a cheap hardware store type, was easily broken. The lead detective opened the door and let out a loud groan and mumbled, "My god." The other detective turned and gently pushed his partner aside while he opened the freezer door. He quickly closed it and sank to the floor, resting his back against the door. They remained like this for a long moment before one spoke, "That bastard."

They called the coroner and the Chief of Detectives on their radio explaining that they were needed at this address as soon as possible. Ray heard this and immediately grabbed one of the large decorative stones lining the driveway and smashed it into Robert Morgan's head several times before officers were able to restrain him.

Uncle Bob went to the hospital where he would remain under police guard for three weeks, and Ray went to jail. He was charged with home invasion, attempted murder, felony assault, and disobeying a police officer. He posted the required ten percent of the one hundred thousand dollar bond and was released. When he returned home the next day, Elizabeth's best friend Martha, and her husband James, met him in the driveway.

Martha hugged Ray for a very long time, neither one saying anything. At this point Ray only knew that his loved ones were dead, he didn't know the circumstances, but the newspaper Martha handed him pulled no punches.

"MISSING MOTHER AND SON FOUND DEAD"

St. Charles police made a grisly discovery late yesterday afternoon at the residence of Robert Morgan. The decapitated heads of 30-year-old Elizabeth Blackburn and her 6-year-old son, Cory, were discovered in a basement freezer by detectives investigating their disappearance. Robert Morgan was placed under arrest and charged with two counts of 1st degree murder and one count of kidnapping.

Raymond John Blackburn, the father and husband, is also under arrest on various charges unrelated to the deaths. Blackburn attacked Morgan as he was being arrested and the resulting injuries have put Morgan in the intensive care unit of Good Sheppard Hospital.

The story went on and gave detailed information concerning the case, and the effort made to solve the mystery. Ray sat on the concrete stairs leading to the porch and cried. He couldn't believe what had happened, in just a few days his life was destroyed and it wasn't his fault.

Martha's voice brought him back to reality. "Johnny Ray is under the care of Child Services. I've checked with them and he doesn't know what happened. He thinks both Elizabeth and Cory died in some kind of accident. I guess you know I'm a licensed child physiologist and a school counselor. Anyway, Child Services has agreed to let me take Johnny Ray until you get through this legal mess."

He hadn't thought about that. "You mean take him back to Illinois? What about school?"

"Martha spoke softly, "We still have schools back there. I really think this would be best for your son."

Ray thought for a minute. "Okay, but don't tell him what happened. He thinks this mess is his fault."

Martha cried softly. "I had to identify them for the coroner, Ray. It was horrible." She fell into his arms, as both wept unashamed.

Chapter 7

The recovered remains of Elizabeth and Cory were kept in a police freezer in the hope that someday the rest of their remains would be found. When the State's Attorney prepared the case against Robert Morgan, he asked the opinion of the presiding district judge about admitting the evidence obtained at the suspect's residence. Judge Carolyn Retter decided that since the officers had no probable cause, and no warrant to conduct an in-depth search of the premises, they illegally opened the freezer, and therefore the evidence was inadmissible. As for the baseball glove, that was discovered by a suspected home invader during a home invasion and also not admissible in a court of law. The public outcry was deafening, but under the legal system, the state didn't even have a weak circumstantial case against Robert Morgan. The best piece of evidence was the eyewitness account of the playmate seeing Cory's bicycle near the suspect's house, and the state refused to try the case on the testimony of a five-year-old. The State's Attorney had little choice but to drop the charges in hopes that someday new evidence would surface to support a solid case. If the case was tried with flimsy evidence and the suspect found not guilty, under the double jeopardy clause, the suspect could never be tried again and would be free as a bird.

When he recovered from his injuries Morgan was released from custody and promptly moved out of his rented house to a place far from St. Charles, Missouri, but that was hardly the end of the matter. He promptly hired a trial lawyer and sued Raymond Blackburn for ten million dollars for injuries he caused during the illegal search.

Ray had other legal troubles. His criminal case was coming to court and his public defender advised him to plead out. He refused, since pleading guilty to home invasion would bring a mandatory sentence of at least seven years. Ray took his chances and lost. He was found guilty of felony assault, attempted murder, and home invasion. The only charge he was not found guilty of was disobeying a police officer, and only because all the police involved refused to testify against him. If it would have been a jury trial the outcome may have been a lot different, but since it was impossible to seat twelve jurors and two alternates who hadn't heard about the case, the judge decided on a bench trial where she alone decided guilt or innocence. At sentencing, the judge explained her reasoning before imposing sentence.

"Mr. Blackburn, this court sympathizes with you, but you need to understand that there is no place in our society for a vigilante. You have been judged on your actions according to the law and found guilty. As much as it pains me to impose sentence, my oath to the people of this state requires me to do so. You are to serve not less than eight or more than fifteen years in the state of Missouri penal system. Because you have been found guilty of a class X felony, you will not be eligible for any kind of early release according to laws enacted by the Missouri state legislature." When the judge banged the gavel it was over. There would be no appeal, that cost money, and with the civil suit looming, Raymond Blackburn's assets were frozen by the court.

The civil suit was fast tracked, and again with a pro-bono defense, Ray lost. The judgment, for actual damages, including hospital bills and physical therapy, was set at $115,000. Punitive damages, including permanent disability were awarded at two million dollars. In essence, all of Ray's worldly property, including his house, bank accounts, savings plan at work, and even his beautifully restored Road Runner were seized and ordered sold at auction to satisfy the judgment. Ray didn't care; as far as he was concerned his life was over anyway. As long as Martha looked after Johnny Ray, nothing else mattered.

***

WHEN HE GOT OFF the bus at Fulton State prison, Ray stopped for a moment and squinted against the midday sun while looking up at the tall limestone tower. He felt himself being pushed as a guard shouted in his face, "Come on, you. This ain't no field trip... get moving"

After a delousing shower, the group of new inmates, wearing prison issue, stood in a line as the assistant warden gave his welcoming speech. Ray never heard a word as his head filled with his own private thoughts. Finally, each man was issued a blanket, a washcloth, two towels, and bed sheets, then told to put all of their civilian clothes and any other personal effects in a plastic bag that the guard put a seal around. When they were marched through the cellblock they were greeted by loud shouts and wolf whistles. This ritual intimidated even the hardest first-timers and everyone was glad when they were assigned to a cell.

When Ray's cell was opened he briefly stood in the doorway until the guard pushed him inside. When he heard the door clang shut he came back to reality. A big, shirtless man sat at a small table against one of the inside walls. Nearly every inch of his exposed body, except his neck and face, were covered in tattoos. Along the back wall was a small washbowl with the toilet next to it. Ray looked at the two cots littered with clothes, books, and other personal items. "Which one is yours," Ray said. The man only glanced at Ray. "They're both mine." When Ray set his blankets down on the cot furthest from the man and started to shovel everything over to the other bunk, the guy jumped to his feet. "I guess you don't hear so well, sonny. I said they're both mine." The inmate was bigger and younger, but Ray knew he had to stand up for himself or be branded a wuss, and in prison that was disastrous. He knew what harsh penalties were attached to fighting, but he also knew he had little choice.

"I heard you, chum. Now you have to ask yourself if it's worth getting your ass beat trying to show me how tough you are, because if I'm going to solitaire for kicking your ass, I'm gonna put you in the hospital. Do we understand each other?"

The man chuckled. "Just seeing what I drew for a bunkmate, pal. No harm intended." With that he held his hand out, which Ray ignored. "Jimmy Sullivan, and I'm doing fifteen to life for murder." Ray realized that somehow this kind of a sentence must be a status symbol.

"Tell you what, Sully, I don't give a fuck if you whacked the Pope; that's your business. Just don't jack with me and we'll get along fine."

Sullivan grumbled as he turned away. "By the way, I know all about you, man. Between the grapevine and the newspapers you're a very famous guy around here."

***

THE FIRST TIME RAY was out in the prison yard a familiar face came up to him. It was his old buddy Worm, a lot heavier, but with the same face. "What the hell are you doing in this place, Worm? Last I heard you were doing time in Illinois."

"History. I met some guys in that place and moved to Kansas City when I got out. I got railroaded and here I am."

"Life's a bitch, ain't it?"

"Yeah. By the way, sorry about what happened."

Ray could feel the lump in his throat as pictures of Elizabeth and Cory filled his mind. "Yeah, thanks, man."

Worm changed the subject. "Don't call me Worm. It's Fast Eddie now. Everybody knows me as Fast Eddie around here."

"Okay, Eddie it is. So what's up? What happened to Bug?"

"He's a union painter, got married and has a couple of kids. Still lives around Chicago."

"Who in the world would ever marry him?" Ray laughed.

"Remember Helen Kren? She lived in the neighborhood."

"Yeah, Hot Helen. Good for the Bug."

"Look, man, there's some shit you need to know about this place. You gotta get hooked up or you ain't gonna survive. There's four gangs in here, Whites, Niggers, Beaners, and Gooks. Join the Whites and we'll cover your back. Stick with us, Ray, and you'll be safe. You'll be a turd at first, until you do something important for the gang. You gotta take orders and do what you're told without question. Everybody starts out that way. Those are our people and we need to stick together. Don't join and you'll be considered a traitor to you own kind and become a target of theirs. Believe me, Ray, without protection you're just lunch for everybody."

"Look, Worm,... I don't give a shit no more. Can I make it plainer?"

"Really, man. When you got a bunch of horny bastard packing your ass, you'll damn sure give a shit. And I promise you, that'll happen."

"I'll think about it."

"Don't think too long. By the way, watch your celli. Jimmy Sullivan is a whack job. He got mad and killed his wife because she didn't buy his beer. Since he's been here he's killed two Mexicans and smashed a Custody Guard's face into a brick wall; and he's marked, so stay away from him outside of your cell. And don't take nothing from nobody. If a guy gives you a cigarette today, he'll want three back tomorrow."

Ray extended his hand. "Thanks, buddy."

***

RAY DIDN'T JOIN THE Whites right away and nearly paid the price. He was assigned a job in the dining room with several other inmates preparing and cleaning up after meals. A week after his talk with Worm it happened, five black convicts jumped him in a utility room behind the kitchen where paper plates, paper cups, and plastic dinnerware was stored. He was grabbed from behind and immediately knew what he was in for. He screamed for several seconds until a large hand smothered his face. Then the door was closed muffling out any outside sounds, but while Ray was held and his pants half down, the door burst open and a group of Whites, led by the Worm, rushed in and fought the attackers off.

Minutes later, as Ray sat in the dining room; Worm brought him a glass of water and joined him at the round, picnic style table. "You okay, man?"

"Yeah, I'm alright, but now I know what you mean. I worked with those assholes for almost a week and they were so nice to me... and then this."

"Tomorrow, when were out in the yard, look for me. I'll introduce you to Retread. He's a biker, a lifer, and also our leader. Talk to him, unless you want this to happen again."

The next day when Ray met Retread, a big, barrel-chested man with a clean shaven head and a short goatee, he was filled in on what prison life is. "Eight years? You won't make eight weeks without help. This isn't Great America. It's a class three prison; everybody here is considered violent. Now, my people watch all the new guys, white ones that is. We saved you last night, but it won't happen again unless you join us."

"Okay, if I join up what's that mean. And what do I have to do?"

Retread looked over both shoulders and lowered his voice. "You do what we say, when we say it. Mostly you'll be a mailman, deliver messages, take orders and deliver product."

"What product?"

"Are you that naive? We supply merchandise to our customers and we'll expect your visitors to help us get some of it in here."

"What if I don't have any visitors?"

"Get some, or we'll get you some. Look, I'm not here to negotiate. I'm telling you what you'll do. We're like Walgreens, we get the order and we fill it. If we haven't got it, we'll get it. A few of the CO's are in on it and when they work visitors, we bring in our shipments."

Ray looked at the biker tattoos up and down Retread's arm and spotted a skull and cross bones, meaning he'd killed for his gang.

"Is that it?"

"For starters. Later we might ask you to get close to somebody, and then when the guy trusts you, shank him. If we tell you to shank your own brother, you do it. Or you get what we sent you to do. Do you understand me? As long as you're in here you belong to the Whites."

"I get it."

"Good. Tomorrow go to the barbershop and ask for Roy, he'll cut your head bald. That's kind of an initiation."

Retread turned his neck and turned down his collar exposing a small Nazi Swastika. "After that, Jimmy Sullivan will ink you, and everybody will know you're one of us." When Retread offered his knuckles Ray reciprocated with a fist bump, sealing the deal.

The rest of that day Ray struggled with himself trying to figure out what to do. Back in his cell Jimmy Sullivan never mentioned Ray becoming a White. They weren't friends and never would be, but outside of their cell they would die for each other. That was the code.

"Ray lay awake late into the night. Soft tears rolled down his face as he reminiscenced about his life and how much he missed Elizabeth. White gangs, black gangs, Mexican gangs, that was his life now. He was not religious growing up, but the last few years he accompanied Elizabeth and the children to church every week. Silently he cursed God. If God was so great, why did he allow this to happen? As quietly as he could he twisted the bed sheet into a rope and after he heard the CO make his hourly round, got the small chair, stood on it and tied the end of his makeshift rope to the bars on the door and made a noose. Before he slipped the rope over his head he thought about how much he wanted to be with Elizabeth and Cory, but then he thought that there was only one thing he wanted more, revenge. He quietly got back into bed and decided he needed to survive. There was a score to settle.

The biggest problem he had now was the swastika. He wasn't a raciest and he hated what Hitler stood for, but remembered what Retread said about negotiating and decided no matter what, he'd get through this.

Prison time is hard, but Ray found a friend in an unsuspecting place. Warden Pells turned out to be a car buff and was restoring a 1970 Dodge Super Bee, a first cousin to the Plymouth Road Runner. Remembering newsreels of Ray's confiscated classic car, he gladly assigned Ray to the prison motor pool where he was allowed to lead the restoration of the Super Bee, although his friendship with the warden was at arm's length, since he didn't need the reputation of a "snitch."

Eventually the public outcry over Ray's conviction subsided and after several months the crusaders, always looking for a pot to stir, moved on. Even though the prison population knew of the raw deal Ray got, all inmates are viewed the same by other inmates, unless of course, the prisoner is convicted of a crime against a child, then he becomes a target.

***

RAY MANAGED TO KEEP his record clean and was released on a warm spring day. He was not the same guy who entered the system eight years earlier. Even if his record was clean, his conscience wasn't. He'd done things to survive that he never would have believed he was capable of. He did dirty work for the Whites, things that if caught would mean he'd never breathe free air again. A lot changed in the eight years he spent in that sewer. Jimmy Sullivan was shanked during a movie one night and Retread somehow turned rat and was doing his time in segregation, a custody that allows no contact with other prisoners. Ray got lucky, his new celli, an old timer, just wanted to do his time with no hassles and the change at the top of the Whites didn't mean anything to him.

Martha sent Ray several letters at first, but stopped after his one letter to her.

> Martha
>
> I consider my life over and don't want to have any contact with anyone. I hate everybody and everything. I don't want to hear about how you or anyone else knows how I feel or must feel. You could never know.
>
> Under the circumstances, I could never be a proper father or a good influence to Johnny Ray. I have no idea what has to be done, but if you'll take care of it, I'll sign papers giving up any parental rights. Please, tell him I died in prison; I want his nightmare to be over.

It took almost two years, but finally Ray's request was granted when he signed the custody papers in the warden's office. Martha and Jim Burns were granted temporary custody and since they asked for no financial help from the state of Missouri, officials looked the other way and had no plans to place Johnny Ray within its system.

Chapter 8

Upon his release Ray wore the same clothes as the day he was incarcerated and like that first day, he again looked up at the tall flagstone tower, vowing that no matter what, he'd never spend another night in this place or any other like it. Physically he was in the best shape of his life. Like many prisoners he had spent hours each day building up his body, but emotionally he was drained. He did have one great stroke of luck. After befriending his celli, he found that the convict once taught classes in personal protection and Ray spent countless hours with him learning Karate, the Oriental art of self-defense.

Standing in front of the prison, Ray read from the back of the warden's business card. **Jeffery Rusk, University Hospital, Columbia Missouri.** This he realized was payday for restoring the Super Bee. Two other released inmates waiting for a bus tried to persuade him to join them in St. Louis. "C'mon, man, we'll get laid, get drunk and get laid again." Ray declined, saying that he was going the other direction to meet up with his brother in Kansas City.

It was just after noon when he stepped off the bus in Columbia, Missouri, only twenty miles from the prison. He walked out of the bus station carrying the navy, blue duffel bag that contained everything he owned. Counting the $50 the prison gave him, he had $68 in his pocket. He toyed with the idea of going straight to the University

Hospital, but decided to have a cold beer instead. After all, it had been eight years.

A half block later he walked into "The Tiger Tap" a play on the name Missouri Tigers, nickname of the University Of Missouri. Columbia was home to the University and with a large student body the city was a college town. He stood just inside the door for several moments to adjust his eyes to the dark as the familiar bar smells reached his nostrils. He quickly scanned the bar. It was long and narrow with tables along the opposite wall. There were two groups of mixed college students laughing and chugging beers at the tables, and two guys and one girl that sat alone at the bar. One of the guys was reading from a textbook while the other talked with the barkeeper. The girl just stared ahead as Ray took a stool several seats away from her. The bartender glanced at Ray as he continued his conversation.

After several minutes Ray looked over and yelled, "Hey, You!" The bartender looked up, obviously irritated, and walked toward Ray. The man, wearing a white bar apron, was about fifty, a bit overweight, with thick salt and pepper hair. "You in a hurry or something?"

All conversation stopped as the patrons waited for the next act. Obviously this guy thought he was tough and wasn't going to take any guff from a kid. Ray knew how to hold his temper; he controlled it for eight years because he had to. But he didn't have to take it now. "Look, Gramps, just get me a large draught beer, okay?" The bartender reached under the bar and grabbed a police baton.

"I know how to handle smart guys, buster. Get the hell out of here before I...." He raised the club in a menacing manner, but in a split second Ray was over the bar and ripped the baton from his hands and hit him two quick shots to the head. The bartender went down like dirty water in a sink and lay motionless. Ray again jumped over the bar, grabbed his duffel bag and started for the door where two of the students blocked his exit. He stopped and softly announced, "Boys, step aside or you'll spend the rest of the day in the hospital." They looked at each other and stepped aside. When he got through the door he stopped briefly, trying to decide which way to go when a female voice filled his ear, "Follow me." When he turned he realized it was the girl who sat alone at the bar.

"C'mon, the police are coming. Do you wanna go to jail?" She didn't run, but instead walked at a brisk pace to the corner where she broke into a dead run as she ran down the side street. Ray followed, he didn't have a choice. After a block, she ran to the driver's side of a beat-up Honda Civic and yelled to him, "Get in."

Minutes later, as they left the business district, she looked over. "Where to, champ?" Ray immediately knew that this was a streetwise girl. "I just got off the bus. I'm new in town." She didn't reply, but instead nodded her understanding.

As she drove in silence Ray turned in his seat and studied her; mid twenties, long blonde hair with a good body and that street-smart look. She wore dark-blue slacks with a modest white blouse and had a silver necklace around her neck. After a ten-minute ride she pulled into a gravel driveway next to a small house. After shutting the engine off she looked over at Ray. "Not exactly the Taj Mahal, but I call it home." Ray followed her into the house and left his bag by the door. He looked at her. "Okay, what's this all about? Why are you helping me?"

She grinned. "Looking a gift horse in the mouth, huh?" She stuck her hand out. "Sugar O'Day!"

Ray automatically took her hand and hesitated briefly. "Ray Black, and thanks. I don't need to spend the night in jail."

"I know where you came from, those shoes are prison issue and if you get busted you'd be in a world of hurt." Ray nodded his agreement.

"Geno, the guy you clocked, is a bully and is always pushing people around. You finally gave him what he deserved."

"If he's such an asshole, what were you doing in there?"

"I was waiting for the owner. I collect his tax every week for my boss."

"Who's your boss and where do you work?"

Sugar didn't answer him. Instead she went into the kitchen and returned a minute later with two cold cans of Bud Light.

Ray held the can up. "Good luck." And then drank half in one swig. "First beer in eight years, thanks."

"I'm a dancer at "The Hallo Club" and I think my boss would like to meet you."

"Why?"

"He's always looking for tough guys, and from what I've seen, you fill the bill."

Sugar looked directly into his eyes. "You can crash here for awhile, but don't get any ideas; I'm a dancer, not a hooker."

That night Ray was introduced to Mr. Big, John Mullio, owner and manager of The Hallo Strip Club. "Sugar tells me you can take care of business, Mr. Black."

"Ray, Mr. Mullio, and I can handle myself."

"Call me John. She says you just got out of Fulton. What were you in for, and how long?"

Ray decided to tell the truth, but not more than necessary. "Yeah, I put some time in. Eight years for home invasion and felony assault."

"What happened? Were you drunk or high?"

"The man hurt my family."

"Okay, I can understand that, but I don't need any loose cannons around here. Here's the deal. I need a floor manager for Friday and Saturday night. You start at 9 pm and work until we close. Usually, you're out of here by three. No drinking on duty, and if I find out you're using drugs, you're gone. I pay $300 a night. Interested?"

Ray chuckled. "A bouncer.... hmm. Will I be alone or what?"

"No, you'll work with two other guys. Now, you need to understand that I don't want you busting people up. Most of our cliental are college kids and I don't need any angry parent suing me. We only use necessary muscle, and we try not to mark anybody up. You'll get a Z-Force Extra Stun Gun; that's 300,000 volts." It's not the most powerful stun-gun, but we're trying to stop trouble, not give somebody a heart attack. Some clubs use Mace, but that could cause a stampede. Anyway, if you need to use the stun-gun, you never let the customers see it."

"Sounds good, Mr. Mullio. Can I start tomorrow night?"

"Yeah." As they shook hands John Mullio added one thing. "Geno, that guy you popped in the grill, is in the hospital. You fractured his skull. Don't worry about that though. The police report will be lost." He ended the conversation with a wink.

***

THE FIRST WEEKEND went well. Most of the patrons were regulars and after Ray collared several troublemakers his creditability was established. The following Monday morning Sugar drove him to the University Hospital where he met with Jeffery Rusk, a small man close to retirement. He wore University issued coveralls with a nametag proclaiming him "Rusk." His comb over and potbelly nearly brought a smile to Ray's face, but he managed to control himself.

"Warden Pells gave you a very high recommendation young man. Says you can work on anything mechanical. Any idiot can work on anything. I need to know what you can fix."

"Mr. Rusk, I can't fix everything, but I am a pretty good wrench. I've worked on all kind of vehicles and equipment, gasoline, diesel, and even some electric. But I don't know anything about air-conditioning, boilers, or heating systems, if that's what you're looking for."

"You can learn, can't you?"

"Yes, sir. I can learn."

"Okay, the job pays $3200 a month, if you want it."

"When do I start?"

"You already have. Now let's get a couple of things straight. First off, call me Rusk, everybody around here does. And Warden Pells told me your story, about your family and all. I'm truly sorry for that. As far as I'm concerned, you didn't deserve the time you did and as long as I work here it will never be an issue."

"Thanks. One thinb, Rusk. I wanna use the name Black. Is that alright?"

"Not a problem."

Ray knew this funny looking little man was a straight shooter and immediately liked him.

After several months Ray fell into a routine. He worked the "Hallo" on the weekends and liked the action, although he had to be careful not to let his pent-up anger push him past what he needed to do. His job with the University proved a challenge. Keeping the fleet of cars and vans running was easy, but when Rusk saw how talented he was, he started teaching him how to repair delicate hospital equipment, which required him to read and understand wiring schematics, diagrams, and blueprints. After a year Ray was transferred and worked out of the shop in the basement of the hospital. When he asked for more money the University Hospital didn't hesitate and raised his monthly salary to five thousand dollars per month, much more than he expected.

With money coming in Ray knew it was time to move off of Sugar's couch and within a month, he made the short trip to Sugar's bed. He knew she developed strong feelings for him, but to him she was just a pretty girl that he was living with. He definitely liked the arrangement, but he'd never love her or any woman ever again. He just grinned when Sugar did her routine and flirted with the customers while sneaking glances at him, all in the vain hope of making him jealous.

After several weekends of "bouncing" at the "Hallo" John Mullio wanted Ray to work for him fulltime. After thinking about it, he declined. He knew that eventually this world would be a ticket back to prison, and although sidetracked, he vowed to find the bastard that wrecked his life. That's what he lived for that.

There was never a day that the face of Robert Morgan didn't haunt him, and the faces of Elizabeth and Cory filled his mind reminding him of his mission. He believed his loved ones could never be at peace until that monster was stopped. He thought often about where that "two-thumbed bastard" was, what he was doing, and how many more children he harmed. Even in prison he tried to keep track of Robert Morgan, but soon discovered that the name was nearly as common as Smith or Jones and that thousands of Robert Morgan's dotted the United States. And besides, there was no guarantee that Robert Morgan was even his right name. But one thing was for sure, he had a stump for a right index finger, and that couldn't be hidden forever.

Chapter 9

It was around seven one night when Ray rode the elevator to the third floor hospital cafeteria. He was hungry and often grabbed a sandwich when working late. He was glad the day was over since his back ached from leaning over a temperamental MRI machine most of the day. As he sat alone at a corner table in the nearly deserted cafeteria a familiar voice interrupted his thoughts, "Mind if I join you?" He looked up into the smiling face of Mary, the hospital social worker. She was in her fifties, heavy set, with short black hair, and wore small, silver-rimmed glasses. She had a quiet confidence about herself and the ability to cheer up even the most despondent patient.

"Of course not, glad to have company."

"I'm going to be very frank with you, Raymond. I know about your past since I have access to all personal records and I like to know about the people who work here. Call me nosey, but I've noticed on many nights you work way past four and I just wondered why. You don't seem to have a life away from here." She paused for a moment waiting for a reply. When there was none she continued, "Ray, I don't mean to intrude, but I really care about you. I chair The Grief Help Group, and I'd like you to come to a meeting."

Wanting this conversation to end Ray stood up. "I'll think about it"

She looked up into his face. "The weekly meeting starts in about ten minutes in 1A Conference Room.

Please come. Even if it's just once, I think we can help you get on with your life."

As he walked away he automatically repeated, "I'll think about it." He liked Mary, but what right did she have to pry into his life? On the other hand, he knew she was sincere and really wanted to help. He finally decided that he could spend an hour listening to other people's trouble; at the very least it would get Mary off his back.

When he walked into 1A Conference Room there were twelve chairs arranged into a half circle, with ten of them occupied. Nobody seemed to pay him any special attention, other than the little smile Mary flashed when she saw him. Everyone wore a nametag, and before sitting, Mary handed him a hand-written temporary tag that read "Raymond." She sat at the head of the circle and at exactly eight, walked over and closed the door. She again took her seat and sat with a large blue notebook on her lap.

"Okay, folks, lets get started. Tonight we have some new faces so I'd like to go over some of our basic rules. The first rule is that like Las Vegas, what happens here stays here." That brought a chuckle from the group.

"Next, we're here to help each other, not to criticize anyone. Remember, everyone here is dealing with a personal tragedy, so try to be compassionate. And lastly we only use first names. Alright, anybody want to start?"

The group remained quiet like it always did at this point. Later, Mary knew, she wouldn't be able to get a word in. "Okay," she said as she opened the blue notebook, "Last time we were discussing about how Ellen's family didn't seem to have the sympathy she expected when husband James passed away. Has anything changed, Ellen?"

"No. When I asked my granddaughter how she felt about losing Grandpa she told me, 'He was old, and old people die'." With that said Ellen dabbed her eyes with a tissue. "We were married fifty-three years, James and I."

Mary looked at the group. "Anyone have anything for Ellen?"

An elderly man spoke, "You should have swatted the little bitch."

Ray nearly bit his tongue in half trying not to laugh, but Mary calmly went on.

"Now, Howard, I think you need to apologize to Ellen."

Ellen stood up and walked over to the sitting man and leaned over him. "Listen, you old son of a bitch; I ought to swat you."

Mary set her notebook on the chair and quickly restrained Ellen and led her back to her seat.

Ray and most of the other people were laughing hysterically. This was the first time he laughed in eight years.

Mary calmly addressed the group, "That'll be enough of that. Now, Ellen, you need to understand that many people don't realize the pain you feel. They seem to think that just because you had all those years together, somehow death doesn't hurt as much as it would if you lost him when you were younger. But you also need to understand that not everyone feels that way; this group feels your pain."

Ray sat in silence, but couldn't help but subscribe to the former mindset. If he could have had Elizabeth and Cory for fifty-plus years, and lost them to old age, he would get down on his knees and thank God. *This woman is a whinny old bag who didn't know real pain and just felt sorry for herself.* At this point he almost left, but the group moved on to another story, one that peaked his interest.

"Helen, do you have anything for the group?" Everyone turned to a young woman of around thirty-five.

"I'm trying to adjust, but now I need to find a job. The insurance money is about gone and that man fled the country. Last I heard he jumped bail and went back to Mexico."

Mary then explained that Helen lost her husband and two children in an accident caused by a drunk driver, an illegal with no insurance; and that she had three other children to care for. That was pain Ray could feel. Several people offered advice and one even promised to help her find a job.

After an hour of the two-hour meeting most of the people present had participated in one way or another. Only Ray and a sad-looking young woman had remained silent. Mary looked at Ray. "Would you care to tell the group your story, Raymond?"

"Uh, not tonight, Mary."

"Okay. How about you, Jill? You've been here three times, but haven't told us anything about yourself. Would you like to share tonight?"

In a loud, defensive voice Jill answered, "My twelve-year-old daughter was raped and murdered, and my husband divorced me because he says it's my fault." She started crying and whispered, "Maybe it is my fault." With that she stood and rushed from the room.

If anyone at that meeting felt her pain, Ray did, and he automatically followed her into the hall where he caught her as she walked briskly toward the large, glass, double doors that exited to the parking lot.

"Wait! Jill, we need to talk. Please." The woman acted like he wasn't there as she continued walking.

Ray tried one more time. "Jill, my wife and little boy were murdered, and the bastard got off. I know how you feel. God in heaven, if anybody knows how you feel, I do."

Jill stopped dead in her tracks and turned to Ray. "You poor man. I'm so sorry. I know that pain, Raymond."

Ray whispered, "I know you do. Can I buy you a cup of coffee or something? The cafeteria's still open."

She smiled. "Sure, I'd like that."

***

JILL BLEW ON THE steaming, black coffee while Ray watched. In a very soft and comforting voice he urged her, "Tell me what happened." It took a moment while her mind retraced the events that changed her life. Finally, in a weak trembling voice she started. "Amy was my only child and I loved being her mom. I was a room mother for her class, recording secretary for the PTA, and I taught Amy's Sunday-School class. We always had a house full of her friends and I was constantly driving them someplace. You know; to soccer, school events, the usual places kids go." She looked away as she continued, "It was a Saturday morning and Cliff was golfing when Amy and her friend Arlene asked me if I would drive them to the mall to see a movie. At first I said no. I didn't want girls that young to be alone in the mall, but Arlene asked that if her older sister went, could Amy go then. Her sister was sixteen and since the movie was rated G, I gave in. Anyway, they got the sister to go and I drove them, but when I went into the mall after the movie I found the sister, but I couldn't find the girls. After looking for an hour I went to the mall manager's office and they alerted security, but it was too late, Amy and Arlene were gone. The big sister said that she met some friends and cruised the mall while the girls went to the movie. We aren't even sure if they went into the theater, nobody re-membered seeing them." She looked into Ray's unsmiling face as tears streamed down her cheeks. "The police brought in a canine unit and scented the dog with Amy's sweater, but the trail ended in the parking lot. I should have taken the girls myself, not trusted a dopey teenager to do my job."

Ray reached over and patted her hand.

After a moment Jill regained her composure and went on. "Three days later a fisherman found both Amy and Arlene's bodies in tall weeds close to a lake. Both girls had been strangled and were naked from the waist down. The medical examiner determined that all kinds of horrible things were done to those children while they were still alive." She faked a smile. "And now Cliff blames me for what happened."

Ray looked deep into her eyes. "It's not your fault. Cliff can't handle it and blaming you is how he deals with it. But God knows it's not your fault."

She stared at her coffee. "Cliff was the police chief's main suspect and they put him through the wringer, since he's not Amy's biological father. I was sixteen when another boy got me pregnant and abandoned me. Cliff married me anyway and always treated Amy as his own. The detectives started asking both of us all kinds of questions like, 'Is she authorized to go with anyone besides you and do you have a code word you use?' We didn't. Then they zeroed in on Cliff. They gave him a polygraph test and because he was so nervous it came up inconclusive. Next, they searched our entire house and Cliff's truck looking for evidence. They kept telling him they knew he did it, or knew who did. Three weeks later, DNA evidence cleared him, but he never got any kind of apology from the police. They acted like they were sorry he wasn't guilty."

Both sat silent for several minutes before Ray spoke, "I never thought anyone else could hurt as much as me." Now it was his turn as he relived his nightmare. Five minutes later Jill knew his story. Everything that needed to be said was said. Finally, they rose and embraced. Jill looked up into Ray's face. "Will you come next week?"

"To the meeting?"

"Yes. I think we should both give it another chance. Will you go, please?"

"I guess so."

***

THE NEXT MORNING MARY found her way down to Ray's workshop. "I'm sorry about last night, Raymond. We've never had such a disorderly meeting. I hope you'll give it another chance."

He set the micrometer down on the workbench and looked at Mary. "Sure."

"I have to ask you something; did you leave because Jill upset you?"

"No. I followed her, because we both live in the same hole. We went to the cafeteria and talked for a long time."

Mary hesitated momentarily. "I don't usually ask about another group member, but did she say if she's coming back next week?"

"Yeah, she said she was."

Ray couldn't get Jill out of his mind and thought about her constantly. It wasn't any kind of romantic thoughts; it was the same kind of concern that two people in a leaky rowboat would have. For the first time since it happened he felt someone else's pain, and more importantly, for the first time he cared about someone else.

Even Sugar noticed the difference. "Why are you so quiet, Ray? If things at the college are getting to you, you know Mr. Mullio will hire you full time whenever you want."

"I know. I'm good, Sugar. Thanks."

***

THAT SATURDAY NIGHT Ray got himself into trouble. While working the floor at the "Hallo" a middle-aged man accompanied by a gangly boy, who was obviously under age, sat at a table drinking beer. Ray talked to Horse, the guy working the door.

"Did you let that pair in?" The other bouncer glanced over at the table.

"Yeah, he's a regular. That's Father Dollar."

"Father Dollar? Is that a joke?"

"No. The guy's really a priest and he's a big wallet. Mr. Mullio said to give him the VIP treatment."

"You sure he's a priest?"

"He wears a Roman collar under that turtle neck and says he's a priest." Horse grinned. "Anyway he sure spends a lot of money on those altar boys."

Ray watched Father Dollar most of the night. He watched as Father Dollar gave the kid dollar bills to stuff into the dancers g-strings. He hated it, but controlled himself until he saw Father Dollar slide close to the boy and reach down his pants. Without a thought he rushed to the table and grabbed the priest by both collars and started dragging him to the door. The teenaged boy followed, dumbfounded. The club was crowded and few saw what was taking place. Three steps outside of the club Ray pushed the priest into the parking lot with a warning. "And stay out of here, you sick bastard, or next time you'll need an ambulance to leave."

The priest pulled down the turtleneck exposing his religious collar. "You just attacked a Roman Catholic priest, mister. You're in big trouble my friend. I know a lot of important people."

Ray had enough, priest or no priest. "Well, I hope you know a good doctor, Father, because if you open that pedophile mouth of yours again, you'll need one."

Ray turned his head just in time to see the boy swing the tire iron that grazed his neck. When he fell back both the priest and the boy attacked him. One karate blow to the throat sent the kid to the ground and a rapid series of punches to the face left Father Dollar in a bloody doubled–up heap. Father and his young friend went to the hospital, and Ray went to jail charged with aggravated battery. Using the name Ray Black his past never came up and bond was set at $500 cash.

John Mullio was angry, but he posted bond anyway. Later, Ray and his boss sat in the club office long after closing. "Ray, do you have any idea what you did tonight?" He answered his own question. "You know that this place is a front for the organization and that we launder a lot of money through here, right?"

Ray looked at the floor and whispered, "Yeah."

"Okay, tonight you put the heat on us. What the hell were you thinking? That guy might be a scum sucking child abuser, but that's not our business. Now I gotta burn up some favors to make this go away, because if it doesn't, and they run your prints, you're going away. The only good thing we got going for us is that the church doesn't want any publicity. They got enough lawsuits to deal with and don't need any more angry parents dragging them into court. By the way, you did a good job on that prick. He has a broken nose, a broken jaw, and three teeth knocked out. What the hell did you hit him with?"

Ray just shook his head no and didn't speak.

"You gotta use your head, tough guy."

Ray's voice was barely audible, "A child abuser murdered my wife and son."

John Mullio's mouth flew open. "OHH…. Alright, let's just see how this thing shakes out.

Even though Father Dollar wanted to sue Ray and the club, the church squashed the whole thing and all charges were quietly dropped. When healed, Father was simply transferred to greener pastures where he wasn't known. Sadly, this practice was all too common with troublesome priests.

***

JOHN MULLIO DECIDED TO put Ray 'on other things'. He had a nice side business going. He called it "problem solving" and it was all his, and as long as he kicked 20% upstairs nobody ever tried to muscle in on it. The concept was simple, go to a club or profitable business after hours, always after the owner left, and bust up the place. Beat on the help and tell them the boss was lucky he wasn't there because they were there to kill him. The next day the owner would get a visitor claiming that he was offered $50,000 to put the guy's lights out, but if he gave him the fifty, he'd see that the problem went away. Nobody ever turned that offer down. The scam was foolproof and only the ransom changed, with some "clients" paying as much as $100,000.

Ray, along with two well-armed goons visited "A Bit of Paradise" late one Saturday night. They tore the club to shreds and scared the life out of the three women left to set the club up for the following night.

The following Tuesday John Mullio handed Ray a wad of cash. "Your piece of the pie from that little deal the other night." Ray knew he had to make a decision. If he stayed working at the club he'd eventually wind up in big trouble since John wanted to keep him on 'other things' and take him away from the day to day routine of bouncing. "You got more talent than to keep the customers away from the girls and throwing out drunks. You can make some real dough if you want to."

"Mr. Mullio, I can't take a chance on going back to prison. I'm going to find the piece of crap that killed my family and I can't do it from a jail cell. It's time I moved on. I appreciate the opportunity you are offering me, but I must respectfully decline."

Mullio paused while rubbing his chin. "Okay, I understand. You know I have connections. If I can ever help you with anything, just ask."

Ray shook his hand. "Thanks, Mr. Mullio. Thanks for everything."

A week after Ray left "The Hallo" Sugar confronted him. " I quit. I got a great offer from a club in Dallas." She watched for Ray's reaction. When there was none, she went on. "You're welcome to come with me, but I know you won't." She paused for a moment. "I've tried to love you, but I know it's useless. Whatever you're looking for, I hope you find it, because under all that anger there's a really sweet guy."

"Sorry, honey, you deserve a lot better than I've been giving you. Good luck."

She walked into the bedroom and returned with two large suitcases that she set by the front door. She turned to Ray. "If you want to stay here the landlord's address is on the kitchen table. Mail the rent to him, and just pay the utilities." Ray nodded his agreement. She threw her arms around his neck and hugged him tightly for a brief moment. As the smell of her expensive perfume filled his nostrils he wondered why such a good person chose the life she led. In another moment he stood at the door and waved to her as she drove away and out of his life.

***

RAY AVOIDED THE grief meetings and one afternoon, three weeks later, Mary confronted him in the hallway. "Raymond, please don't give up on our little group. I still think we can help you."

He wanted to get rid of her and started to walk away. "Okay. I'll think about it."

Mary knew she was being brushed off. "You know Jill has come every week and she looks for you. If you won't go for yourself, go for her. That girl is hurting. I know I shouldn't tell you this... but she's really depressed, maybe even suicidal. Please, if not for yourself, come for her."

He did go to the next meeting and although neither Ray nor Jill participated, they did make eye contact. A lot was said without ever uttering a word and when the meeting ended they met in the hall. Jill spoke first as she smiled, "Buy you a cup of coffee, mister?

Ray laughed. "Sure."

Again they sat at a table in a far corner of the cafeteria.

"I thought I said something wrong," she said.

"What'd you mean? You didn't do anything wrong."

"You didn't come for the last three weeks. Why? I thought you said you would."

"I'm sorry. I had some major issues to deal to with."

"Is everything alright now?"

"Yeah, everything's fine."

Chapter 10

Johnny Ray was stripped of his childhood the day Cory disappeared. Even though Martha took him out of state, the story became national news and followed them back to the Chicago area. Her hope to shield him from the tragedy became futile as newspaper and television people camped outside of the upscale North Shore Colonial Jim and Martha Burns called home. When Johnny Ray yelled and cursed the reporters, it only added fuel to the story and helped it live a longer life. Commentary pointed to Johnny Ray as an example of the temper his father had and that created, in some minds, an underlying opinion, branding Ray as an out of control bully.

When Martha read Ray's only letter, she debated whether to follow his wishes or not. Finally, she decided that it was not her decision and as gently as she could, told Johnny Ray that his father had passed away. "I don't know the details, honey. The prison officials didn't elaborate. Just that he died of illness last Tuesday."

Johnny Ray fought back the tears as he pressed his lips together. Martha tried to hug him, but he pulled away. She spoke softly, "It's okay to cry."

He turned to her. "I'm not gonna cry. I'm not a baby anymore. I'm a man and men don't cry." Martha dabbed her eyes with a tissue as he continued. "Aunt Martha, why did this have to happen? If I hadn't ditched Cory...."

"It's not you fault, John. That monster would have just done it another time."

He kept his word and didn't cry, but his eyes filled with tears as he finished. "Aunt Martha, I'm going to find "Two Thumbs" someday and he's gonna pay for what he did to my family." She took him and held him tightly to her bosom as he cried softly.

**

JOHNNY RAY WAS an angry young man and was involved in numerous fights while growing up. He didn't care about being in trouble, but he knew it hurt Aunt Martha, so when possible he tried to avoid it. During high school he found the outlets he needed. Football because of the contact, where he became an all-state line backer, and wrestling in the 180# division. When his reputation as an extremely aggressive defensive back circulated throughout the league, several teams marked him and tried their best to injure him. That proved to be their mistake, as he sent many opposing players limping to the sidelines. His coach loved his aggressive nature, but had to warn him of injuring his teammates during practice.

Coach Johnson knew of his past and tried his best to mentor him. "John, there's a recruiter from the Naval Academy that's been asking about you. This might be your best opportunity. You could have a bright future in the Navy. Even though you're only a junior, it's not too early to start planning your future."

The night after the last game of the season, Johnny Ray piled into his teammate Allen's old sedan, and like many high school kids, got a twelve pack of beer and cruised the town. At a stoplight the passenger of the car next to them jumped from his car and pulled Allen from the driver's seat and started punching him in the face. John leaped from the car, pulled the man off, and gave him a good pounding. At this time the driver jumped on Ray, but got an elbow to the face for his trouble. Next, a woman came at him swinging a tire iron. She was obviously pregnant and Johnny simply gave her a good push. She fell back dropping the iron and retreated to the car. From the shouting and profanity it was clear that the other driver felt he was cut off. The attackers, in their thirties, started yelling for someone to call the police. Johnny Ray knew it was time to exit as he helped his friend into the passenger seat and then climbed behind the wheel, burning rubber as they fled the scene.

That was hardly the end of the matter. Through license plate information, Allen was arrested at his home and implicated Johnny Ray. Jim Burns took the late night call and drove Johnny Ray to the police station where he was arrested and charged. Jim was not the loving step uncle that Martha wanted him to be; instead he merely tolerated Johnny Ray. On the ride to the police station he had his say. "Martha and I have tried to give you a good home and this is how you repay us. You're just like your father, always in a scrape."

Johnny looked at him in the dark car. "I loved my father and want to be just like him."

"Well, you are."

From the time Johnny Ray was arrested, it was clear that Jim wanted no part of it. Allen was from a single parent family and his mother called Coach Johnson, who was already at the station house when John and Jim arrived. Jim, after identifying himself as Johnny Ray's guardian, stepped off to the side. Coach Johnson, on the other hand, tried to reason with the arresting officers. He knew what happened to suspects who were unruly and didn't want either boy beat up or attacked by other prisoners and he made that plain. His reputation as solid community figure cemented the deal. The boys were not put in the bullpen, a crowded and dangerous one size fits all detention cell, but instead spent the night in a holding cell by themselves. The watch commander insisted that they stay the night, since they were underage and had obviously been drinking.

They were both charged with assault, battery, and underage drinking. As the boys slept it off, the guys Johnny Ray wailed on confronted the coach as he made arrangements for bail. "Mister, my wife is pregnant and I'm worried your boy hurt my baby." Coach Johnson never said he wasn't either boy's father. "Take her to the hospital and send me the bill." He reached into his wallet and handed the man his business card. "And I think he loosened some of my teeth." The coach glanced into the man's mouth as he talked and took note of the crooked and yellow stained teeth.

"Get the fuck out of my face before I loosen the rest of the 'em."

As he turned to walk away, the man finished the conversation. "We're suing your ass, mister."

Neither boy knew the fix was in. Coach Johnson was a Democratic precinct captain and simply called the Alderman who put a bug in the judge's ear. Martha agreed with the coach that this could be a good learning experience for Johnny Ray and neither of them told him that the charges would be dropped. When the case was called, the bailiff read the complaint as the two boys stood before the judge. When he finished, the judge asked, "How do you plead, guilty or not guilty?

Johnny Ray didn't know how to plead, nobody told him what to do. Coach Johnson, Martha, and the judge all held their collective breath. If he pleaded guilty, the judge was helpless and everyone, except Johnny Ray, seemed to know that. After a long moment Allen broke the silence. "Not guilty, Your Honor." Johnny Ray followed suit, and after a good tongue lashing the judge dismissed the charges.

After they exited the courtroom Coach Johnson put his arms around each boy's shoulders. "Boys, I hope you learned a lesson from this."

Just then the guy with the pregnant wife and the bad teeth walked up to the trio and stuck out his hand to the coach. "I'm glad the boys got off." The coach snapped back. "Get out of my face before I knock you on your ass, you jerk." The man spun around and made a hasty exit.

The next day Johnny Ray sat in the coach's office. "Okay, John, this is how it is. You got a pass this time, but if the judge sees you again, you can kiss any scholarship money goodbye. No matter how good you play, no coach is going to want a loose cannon representing his school, either on or off the field. Do you understand me, son?"

"Yes, sir."

"John, I told you the Naval Academy is interested and that could be your ticket to a great future. Make football your steppingstone, not your life. One injury could end it all and you'll have nothing, but a good education will follow you wherever you go. You need to stay out of trouble to get the chance. Don't make me look bad by recommending you."

"I won't, Mr. Johnson."

Chapter 11

Ray and Jill became regulars at the Grief Management meetings and always had coffee afterwards in the hospital cafeteria. Several months later they invited a small group to join them. A group that shared one thing in common, each one grieved over the loss of a child. A middle-aged black couple, Luther and Dee, lost their daughter to a hit and run driver. May, a middle-aged librarian, lost her son to a cult. Brooke, a younger woman and a clerk for the city police, was still waiting word of her six-year-old brother who disappeared while walking to school several years earlier.

Ray looked at the Group. "You know we can sit around and feel sorry for ourselves until the sun sets in the east, or we can fight back. You know my story. Someday I hope to find the monster that destroyed my family." He lowered his voice to a whisper, "It's not just talk. I can't even the score, but I can stop that bastard from hurting anyone else if I can find him. And even if I never do, I can stop people like him from hurting any more kids. You're here because I think you're hurting enough to want to do something about it too."

Dee looked at Luther. "Tell them the rest."

Luther's shoulders sagged as he spoke, "It wasn't just a hit and run. The guy tried to pick up a little boy and when spotted, ran down our baby while speeding away." His voice broke as he continued, "She was only five."

Ray looked into each person's eyes before speaking. "All of us are here because somebody intentionally harmed our child. I want to do more than go to meetings and console each other. I'm gonna fight back."

"How?" Brooke asked.

"Find out who they are and stop them. You do know that convicted sex offenders have to register with the police; it's the law and that information is public knowledge. We just Google "sex offender" put in a zip code, and wham, it tells us who they are, what they were convicted of, and where they live and work."

Luther wanted to know. "How we gonna stop them when we find 'em?"

"I'm gonna put their fucken' lights out, that's how I'm gonna stop 'em. If anybody doesn't want to help, leave now. But before you do, think about what these people do and how they ruined our families."

Dee asked, "Who do we target, everybody in our zip code?"

"No," Ray replied. "We'll find those still active."

May took the floor. "We got a guy that comes in the library and uses the computers to view child porn. By law, I can't monitor what he views, but just walking past I see the most disgusting things you can imagine. I know the sites he visits. I just recall history and there they are, all kiddy porn and MY SPACE blog pages. I don't know why he just doesn't do it at home, but he doesn't. He's only allowed one hour a day, but he has several library cards and just goes to another library. All of the librarians know him and don't like it, but under the law he's protected by the First Amendment."

Luther asked, "You mean he can just walk into any library and view smut? How is that possible?"

"He logs on, brings up the site, enters his credit card number and he's in."

Ray interrupted, "Forget about the law. That's why the whole thing is such a mess. I'll bet the reason that this guy is at the library is because he's already been convicted of a crime and isn't allowed to own or use a computer. And I'd bet money that he's using an alias. May, get everything you can on this guy and I'll try to check him out."

Brooke smiled. "I can do that. I'll run a criminal check on him. Remember, I work for the Columbia Police Department."

Ray looked at Jill. "We'll be working without a net. Are you with us?"

"I'm with you, all the way," she whispered.

***

THE NEXT EVENING Brooke called Ray. "There's nothing on Louis Avery. He's using an alias."

"Figures. I'll do a little detective work and see if I can find out who this slime ball is and what's his thing."

"Ray, let me talk to May. I do fingerprints at work and if she can get me the mouse he used on one of the library computers, I can run his prints through The Automated Fingerprint Identification System.

"I've heard of AFIS. What are the chances he's in the system?"

"If he's been arrested and charged with a crime in the last ten years he's in the system."

***

A WEEK LATER MAY called Brooke. "I switched the mouse and put the one this Avery guy used in a baggie."

Late that afternoon Brooke brought a fingerprint kit to the library and simply sprinkled a dark gray powder on the mouse clicker, which revealed a perfect right index print. Next, she used a special tape and simply lifted the fingerprint from the clicker and transferred it to a police formatted index card. She smiled at May. "I'll run this tomorrow."

The following evening the small group met at a McDonalds close to the hospital. It was decided that meeting in the hospital cafeteria was not a good idea since Mary was in and out at all hours and they didn't need her wondering why none of them were attending her meetings anymore. They had their own meetings with a much more aggressive agenda and referred to themselves as "The Justice Club." The restaurant was nearly deserted that late in the evening as they crowded around a large table in the rear of store.

Ray looked into Brooke's smiling face. "You have good news?"

"Yes. We got a hit on the fingerprint. The guy's name is Joseph James Como and he's been a very busy guy for a long time. His juvy sheet is sealed, but he's been really active since he turned eighteen." She opened a large manila envelope and pulled a color picture of James Como from it and held it up. "Is this your guy, May?"

May bobbed her head up and down. "His hair's longer, but that's him."

Ray stared at the picture for a long moment. The guy didn't look dangerous. On the contrary, he looked like a typical thirty-year-old man. His hair was short and his smile appeared genuine. "Tell us about this guy, Brooke."

She again reached into the envelope and produced several sheets of paper and began the journey of Joseph

James Como's life. "Since eighteen he's had the usual kid convictions; under-age drinking, drug charges, retail burglary, and then he went big time, breaking and entering, felony assault, grand theft auto, receiving stolen property, and possession of drugs with intent to distribute."

Ray grew impatient. "Brooke, I don't care if he hijacked a shipment of DVD's headed for Best Buy; what about child porn?"

"I'm getting to that. After all the other was said and done, he spent six years behind bars. Now, he's a registered sex offender and you were right, Ray, he's not allowed to own or use a computer until his parole is up in two more years. It doesn't say why he did the time, but he's had numerous sex convictions. In '96 he was convicted of statuary sodomy 2nd degree, and of aggravated sexual abuse with bodily harm. In '98 he was arrested for indecent solicitation of a child and pleaded no contest. And in '99 he was convicted of criminal sexual assault. He must have been incarcerated by then because that's when the trail ends." She looked up into Ray's unsmiling face.

"Or when he started being more careful," Ray said and added. "So he's a tough guy and likes to beat on his victims. Hmm, very interesting."

For the first time Jill spoke, "That's a power thing. He was probably a victim himself when he was a child."

Luther ended the discussion on physiology. "Now what?"

The Group discussed what action should be taken and all agreed that before anything was done they needed to be sure Joseph James Como was still a threat to children. It was decided that May would watch him carefully and, if possible, see if he communicated with anyone.

May waited in vain for weeks before he finally showed, being careful not to ask any other librarians if he visited their libraries. The group decided that the less attention that Joseph Como was given the better. That afternoon she told him that the computer system was having trouble and that he'd have to wait a bit before he could log on. She brought him to a room where free coffee was available and poured him a cup. "Cream and sugar?" she asked.

"What?"

"Do you drink your coffee with cream or sugar?"

It was obvious that he had little interest in coffee, but mumbled that black was fine and accepted the cup. May hoped he'd drink several cups and would need to use the washroom before his hour was up, which would give her time to see if he was talking to anybody on line. After a short wait and one cup of coffee, he logged on. Thirty minutes later he turned off the screen and headed for the washroom, which was downstairs and several minutes away. May quickly turned on the monitor and saw he was visiting My SPACE and having a conversation via Instant Messenger with a computer friend named "youngstuff." More importantly she found his screen name, "mrTed." Her investigation only took seconds since she didn't read any of the correspondence, but she got what she wanted.

That night the Group again met at McDonalds and with May's information, Dee took center stage. I'm kind of shy, but on the internet I feel comfortable, so I spend a lot of time surfing and talking to people." Luther bobbed his head in agreement as Dee continued, "A lot of young children aren't properly monitored and do things they shouldn't on line. Unknown to their parents some kids have built blogs that anybody can visit. The personal information they share with strangers is unbelievable and most of them try to act grown up and actually want to talk to adults. I suspect that's what this 'youngstuff' is doing. I presume she's a girl, but who knows, it could be anybody. On the internet you can be who or whatever you want and nobody will ever know the difference."

Ray questioned her. "Okay, Dee, what can we do to smoke this guy out? Do you have any ideas?"

"Yes. I'll go to MY SPACE and start a blog and see if mrTed takes the bait. I'll call myself "hot2trot." I'm sure that'll get a lot of attention."

Brooke looked concerned. "Be careful, Dee, that could be dangerous. Some of these perverts are really computer savvy and could find you. Remember, every computer has a serial number and can be traced. Sometimes we do it at the station and if we can do it, so can a lot of other people."

May solved that problem. "Come into the library when I'm there and you can spend as much time as you need on the computers and nobody will follow you home."

***

DEE WAS RIGHT, perverts came out of the woodwork like picnic ants and showered hot2trot with all kinds of attention, but mrTed wasn't one of them. Brooke had an idea—talk to the parents of youngstuff and get her off line. If that opportunity were gone, mrTed would be on the prowl again. Using her police tools Brooke found that youngstuff was a twelve-year-old girl living with her grandmother several hundred miles away in rural Kansas. After grandma got the "heads up," youngstuff's career as a computer tease was over and mrTed was again trolling for a new playmate. He was extremely frustrated that the time he spent with youngstuff was lost, but rationalized that those things happen.

Joseph Como liked to sit at a certain bank of computers and knowing this, May always seated Dee across the large room at the other bank. Finally it happened, on a Thursday night when the library was extremely busy and he sat at his computer terminal, he took the bait. Dee sat across the room brushing off potential suitors when she got the "hit" she was waiting for. It was mrTed.

mrTed: hru (how are you)

hot2trot: fine

mrTed: what are you doing tonight?

hot2trot: just finished my homework ewww. I hate homework

mrTed: I hate it 2

hot2trot: r u still in school?

mrTed: no I graduated

hot2trot: lucky u

mrTed: do you have any hobbies?

hot2trot: I collect posters

mrTed: r u kidding I'm an events co-ordinater. I get all kinds of posters.

hot2trot: awesome

mrTed: maybe I'll send you some. Where do you live?

hot2trot: I live in a pooie old town in Missouri

mrTed: where?

hot2trot: Outside of Jefferson City. Where r u

mrTed: Chicago

hot2trot: my god that is so cool. I am sooo jealous

mrTed: Have u ever been to Chicago?

hot2trot: my mom is bugging me I gotta go

Dee sat at the terminal for several minutes before strolling up to May's desk. "He took it, all of it and he wanted more, but I logged off. Don't worry, he'll be back tomorrow."

Dee was right, Joseph James Como was back and he came back every day looking for hot2trot, but Dee only played the game twice a week. After three weeks, Joseph Como found out that hot2trot was almost thirteen, smoked cigarettes, and even drank beer once. Her parents were a drag and didn't know anything, and that she couldn't wait until she was sixteen when she could quit school and be on her own, all music to his ears. Como passed himself off as a twenty-two year-old free spirit who understood completely where she was coming from. When she told him her name was Carol and that she was very mature for her age he knew he was home free. He needed to meet with her. Then he'd show her what life was all about, whether she wanted to or not.

mrTed: I've missed u where have u been?

hot2trot: my mother caught me smoking and grounded me for a week. The bitch.

The time was right. He was careful not to scare Carol, but now she was ready.

mrTed:. I know I shouldn't, but I hate your mother. My parents were mean too. Can I come to u? I know it sounds stupid but I think I'm in love with u.

hot2trot: I don't know, I'd like to meet you but...

mrTed: Wherever you say. I'll come. We'll do what you want to do. You're a grown woman, Carol, and I'll treat you like one.

hot2trot: Let me think about it. I gotta go. Bye.

He hoped he hadn't scared her off. He put a lot of time and effort into that little bitch and deserved a reward.

That night, as he lay in bed, he fantasized what he would do with her, whether she was willing or not. He planned out the whole scenario. Three days in the deserted summer cottage at Osage Beach would be just about right; either way she would never see her next birthday. Six years in prison taught him well, dead people don't testify and they can't turn on you either.

At the next meeting Dee grinned. "People, we got him. All we have to do is tell him when and where." Ray looked at Luther. "Now it's you and me, bro. Are you up to it?"

"I'm up to it, but I think we should wait a bit. Have you thought about what we're going to do with him when it's done?"

"No. I guess I haven't."

"Try this on. The guy who buried my baby had his daughter raped about a year ago, and the guy got away with it because she took a shower and destroyed the evidence. The slug that did it is a tinhorn from the neighborhood and brags about it to whomever will listen. If we do this guy, the funeral director is our friend forever."

"So, what does that mean.? We clip this guy and Digger O'Dell gives 'em a nice funeral? Look, Luther, we can't take on everybody's cause."

"Ray, this dirt-bag is a sexual predator. too, but listen to the good part. Mr. Brown has a crematorium on his property and if we do him this favor, I'll bet he'll turn our jobs into ashes. Anybody we eliminate will just be a missing person."

"Are you sure? I mean once we start there's no turning back. Can we trust this guy and are you angry enough?"

Luther looked at Dee. "Yeah, and I'm angry enough."

Chapter Twelve

Ray walked into the Hallo Lounge late in the afternoon and headed straight back to John Mullio's office. The boss was glad to see him. "Good to see you, Ray. How've you been?"

Ray broke into a smile. "Good, Mr. Mullio. Better than I deserve."

"What brings you here?"

"John, you said if I ever needed a favor, to come see you. Well, I need a favor."

"Okay. What can I do?"

"I need a dependable handgun and two Z Force high volt stun guns."

John Mullio never asked why, that wasn't his business. His only concern was helping his friend. "Okay, I can fix you up with a Glock. I have a .40 caliber, compact semi- automatic, with the big magazine. But I can't get the stun guns for a couple of days. Will that work?"

"Yeah, that's great."

"I'll call you."

Ray gave him his cell phone number and was surprised when John called the next afternoon and told him to meet him at the club that night.

Late that evening, Ray knocked lightly on the door marked 'Manager' and opened it when he heard John Mullio's voice inviting him in. The music and din from the club disappeared as he softly closed the door. Mullio stood, hand outstretched to greet Ray.

"Alright, I got what you wanted." He reached into one of the bottom desk draws and pulled out a small cloth bag. He set it on the desk and removed a model 27 Glock and an extra clip. "This came off the street, but out of state, so you should be alright if you get stopped. You do know that in Missouri you can carry concealed in your vehicle?"

"John, I'm an ex-con and not supposed to handle a firearm anywhere. That law makes it bad for me. Now the cops are always looking for weapons when they make a traffic stop."

"That reminds me. I got a present for you." He opened the top drawer and handed Ray several cards. A Missouri drivers license, a concealed carry permit, and a voters card, all current and all in the name Raymond Black.

As Ray thumbed through the cards he mumbled, "God, Mr. Mullio, how much do I owe you?"

"I told you, this is a present. I got these ID's when I thought you were going to work steady for me. What am I gonna do with 'em?" He walked to a coat closet and brought out the Ultra Z Force stun guns and set them on the desk alongside the Glock. "This isn't your father's stun gun, Ray. These could give somebody a heart attack." He looked at the weapons piled on the desk. "Altogether, this hardware is a grand and change. But let's just say you owe me a favor. Okay?"

Ray walked around the desk and embraced the man as he spoke, "Just call me, Mr. Mullio. I'll come running."

"Good hunting, son."

***

TWO NIGHTS LATER it was just after midnight when Kenneth Jones slid behind the wheel of his Cadillac Escalade, parked a half block from Giddy's Lounge. After starting the engine he felt the hair on the back of his head tingle an instant before the high voltage hit and paralyzed him. His body arched and then sagged as he was rendered helpless. Ray climbed between the split seats and frisked Jones, relieving him of a small .32 caliber Berretta, and a large knife that he wore in a leather sheaf strapped above his left ankle. Ray then rolled and pushed him to the passenger seat and secured his hands with several plastic ties.

Moments later, wearing thin police issue gloves, Ray drove the Escalade and followed Luther to Brown's Funeral Parlor and Chapel. On the way Kenneth Jones tried to talk his way out of a bad situation. "Hey, man, give a brother a break. You want my ride? Take it. You want money? You got it."

Ray looked over at the trembling man. "I already took your ride, chump. Next, I'm gonna take your money, and them I'm going to deliver you to Mr. Brown. You remember him don't you? You know, the father of the girl you raped."

"Hey, man, I didn't rape nobody. You got some bad information."

"You know, I don't care if you did or you didn't, but Mr. Brown sure cares."

"C'mon, man, you know how it is with chicks. They say no, but they really mean yes."

"Well, chum, I guess you never learned the difference, did you?"

When they got to the funeral parlor Able Brown was waiting. Luther pulled a diamond-studded money clip from Kenneth Jones' pocket and counted out $800, which he quickly pocketed. When Jones saw Luther throw his money clip into the crematorium he realized his fate and started kicking and screaming at the top of his lungs. Another jolt from the Z Force quieted him enough so that the trio was able to stuff him into the furnace. When Able Brown slammed and latched the door, Ray and Luther left. They drove the Cadillac to an all night restaurant and left it there. The gun and knife were thrown into a forest preserve lake. Kenneth Jones would become just another statistic and another missing person. With his reputation the police wouldn't be very aggressive in its investigation and the whole matter would just die a quiet death.

***

A WEEK LATER THE Group was ready to deal with mrTed. It was after hours at the library and the computer room was closed to the public, but not to a certain group that crowded around the screen. mrTed wasn't using the library computers anymore, apparently he found another source to prowl the Internet. Dee sat at the terminal and fended off the "hits" until mrTed appeared. As usual he instructed her to a private chat room where he planned to finalize his plan to meet hot2trot in person.

hot2trot: my computer crashed and I just got my mother board back today. I missed you.

Those were words that Joseph Como lived to hear. He knew he had her.

mrTed: I REALLY missed u 2. I was on a business trip arranging a concert in Denver.

hot2trot: Who and when?

mtTed: Bon Jovi. It's still in the planning stage. Probably next summer.

hot2trot: omg (oh my god) are u serious? I love him.

mrTed: It's not a done thing, but it looks good. I can get tickets if u want to go.

hot2trot: My parents would never let me go. Besides I wouldn't have the money.

mrTed: Tell them you're staying overnight with a friend. I can send my corporate jet to pick u and a friend up and bring u back home the next morning.

hot2trot: You have your own airplane? Awesome!

mrTed: It's not exactly mine. We lease it, my partners and me. If u could stay away for an extra day, we could ride horses at my ranch.

hot2trot: A ranch. U are unbelievable. I love horses. That would be so cool.

mrTed: I'd like to meet u face to face. Maybe u won't like me.

hot2trot: That is soo not possible.

Nobody said anything as Dee lured Joseph Como into the trap.

mrTed: U don't want to meet me?

hot2trot: YES YES I want to meet u. And I already like u.

mrTed: Before we meet I need to know a few things. What do u drink and do u do grass? I never do hard drugs, that stuff is bad for u.

hot2trot: Bud Lite. I never smoked marijuana, but I'd like to try it.

mrTed: Okay. Another thing. I'd like to bring u a present, some sexy lingerie. What's your size and favorite color?

hot2trot: omg are u serious?

mrTed: Of course I'm serious. You are a woman aren't u?

hot2trot: I'm a size two and I like red. Do you need my bra size?

mrTed: Just your cup.

Hot2trot: C cup.

For the first time Ray spoke, "You better arrange a meeting pretty soon, Dee. Before this guy's pecker gets so big he knocks over his friend's computer."

mrTed: I'm going to be in St. Louis tomorrow morning. I could meet you in Columbia in the afternoon. Could you work something out at home so we could be together tomorrow night? I'd like to take you to a nice restaurant and then maybe we can find a dance club.

hot2trot: brb (be right back)

Luther laughed as he looked at Dee. "He's probably waxing his weasel while he's waiting."

Even though the mission was serious, and the comments vulgar, everyone enjoyed a good laugh. Then five minutes later hot2trot came back.

hot2trot: I called my friend Nora; she'll cover for me. I told my mother and she said that I'd have to talk to my father, but he's easy. Can you meet me after school around four at McDonalds on Blyth St? I'll wear a red hooded sweatshirt and I'll sit in a booth by the window. Is that ok?

mrTed: Sounds great, Carol, I'll be wearing a western style hat and boots. I'll see you there. And call me Ted.

hot2trot: Okay, Ted. I gotta finish my homework. xoxoxo.

After Dee logged out, the six conspirators high-fived each other and went into one of the library offices. Over a pot of coffee they planned the downfall of mrTed.

Ray looked at Jill. "You'll be the bait. Can you do this?"

She looked at Ray. "I'd climb Mt. Everest to get retribution for what was done to Amy and Arlene."

"Okay, just sit by the window and when the dirt bag shows, me and Luther will take care of the rest." He looked over the group slowly before speaking again. "Everyone here understands what we're doing, right? If you're not up to it, now is the time to leave. Just keep all this to yourself. But if you want some payback..."He stood up and made a fist and put it out over the table. One by one each person stood and put their fist on each others. "We're with you, Ray," Brooke said. "To me, this is the guy that took my little brother." Everyone nodded agreement.

***

THE FOLLOWING AFTERNOON at McDonalds, Jill sat at a window table facing the parking lot. She pulled the red hood over her hair leaving only a small portion of her face exposed in case Joseph Como slipped past Ray and Luther. Maybe she didn't look twelve, but even at thirty she could easily past for eighteen. Meanwhile, sitting in Luther's white Ford Explorer, straight across from the window, Ray and Luther had a perfect view. The trap was set an hour early just in case mrTed decided to case the scene before making contact.

Ray glanced over at Luther. "Nervous?"

"Yeah, a little bit."

"Alright, let's go over this one more time. When we approach him we both show our badges, tell him he's under arrest, read him his rights and cuff him. Got it?"

"I got it."

"Those detective badges Brooke got us should fool him and I don't think he'll resist."

Luther grinned. "Bluff and cuff, right?" Ray nodded his agreement.

Ten minutes later a maroon Dodge Intrepid, with a man wearing a black western style hat, slowly circled the restaurant several times, and as he drove in front of Ray and Luther, rubber necked while looking back at the red hooded figure in the window. Ray dialed his cell phone. "He's here, Jill." Both men put on law enforcement rubber gloves before Luther pulled out behind the Intrepid and followed it until it pulled into a parking space. When Joseph Como stepped from the car Luther pulled in front, blocking it in. Ray and Luther both jumped from the Explorer and in seconds each had one of Joseph Como's arms. They flashed the police badges as Ray shouted, "Joseph Como, you're under arrest for solicitation of a minor. You have the right to an attorney…

"I know my rights. What the hell is this all about?" After cuffing his hands behind his back with a plastic tie Como was searched and pushed into the back seat of the Explorer. Ray retrieved a large dark gray travel bag from the Intrepid before jumping into the Explorer and shouting, "Go." He looked over the seat as Luther drove. "Looks like you'll be keeping that thing in your holster, cowboy."

"Is that what this is all about? She told me she was eighteen."

Ray pulled the Z Force from his pocket and gave mrTed a ½ second burst. mrTed screamed out in pain. "That's just a taste, JC. Next time you lie to us you get the full treatment. Now, hot2trot is a decoy and you just got caught."

Joseph Como didn't say anymore and just stared out the window for the short ride to Brown's Funeral Parlor. When Luther pulled the Explorer down a ramp to the basement, mrTed spoke, "Hey, what's this. This ain't no police station. Are you guys real cops?" Silence was his reply.

Luther unlocked the door while Ray pulled mrTed out of the SUV and pushed him towards the door. Luther retrieved the travel bag and in moments they sat around a small rectangular table while Ray pulled items from the bag. "Duck tape...rope...some rags...chloroform." He looked at Joseph Como for a long moment before continuing, "Condoms, KY...Flex cuffs...two bottles of Peach brandy and ...what's this, a present?" He tossed a brightly colored box on the table and ripped the bow and tissue paper off. He held up a skimpy red nightie. Next, as he looked in the bottom of the bag he was grateful for the hand protection and was almost sick when he viewed the array of sex toys mrTed planned to use on hot2trot. Luther looked at Ray and wondered what was going through his mind. He thought about youngstuff and how this could have been her fate if they didn't step in.

Ray grabbed mrTed by the lapels and pulled his face within inches of his. "Quite a party you had planned."

He pushed him back into his chair.

"Look, man, let's talk about this, huh? I was just looking for a good time; I wasn't gonna hurt her. I ain't never did nothing like this before. Just let me go. It won't happen again. I promise." Luther pulled his Z Force out and gave him a shot so long Ray had to restrain him. "Stop, you'll kill him." As he lay on the floor groaning Luther pulled mrTed to his feet and again sat him in the chair.

"Okay," Ray began, "now that you know what happens when you lie, I'm going to ask you some questions. How you answer depends what we're gonna do with you. First, you're right. We're not cops. You're not that lucky."

Joseph Como knew he was in the worst jam of his life and tried hard to talk his way out of it. "Look, man, I got a record and I'm on probation. If I get convicted again I go away for a very long time."

Ray replied, "Tell us the truth and I promise you won't go back to prison."

"What'd you wanna know?"

It was agreed beforehand that many of these perverts knew each other and anyone they catch would be questioned about cases pertaining to the Group. Ray doubted that he'd have information about his case, but since the others were local, he needed to try for them. He fished for information concerning Brooke's little brother and Jill's girls with no luck.

"Look guys if I knew anything, believe me, I'd help you. I wanna get out of this." Luther tried. "A six-year-old girl was run down walking home from school about two years ago. The guy that did it tied to pick up a kid and was running away. He drove a gold van. Know anything about that?"

mrTed thought for a moment. "I heard about it. I don't know the guy's name, but he drove a gold Ford Club Wagon. It was either a 98 or 99. I know because my mother had a blue 99."

"That's it?" Luther asked.

"That's all I know. Now can I go?

Ray picked up the roll of duc tape and the rope. "Just out for a good time, huh? I don't think this girl was supposed to come home. And how do we know you didn't do some other kid before? You know; like a serial thing?"

"Please, I'm telling you the truth."

"Okay. Luther, put a bag over his head. I don't want him to find his way back here."

Luther, as planned, put two large, green garbage bags over mrTed's head. Ray pulled out his Glock .40 and before Joseph Como could utter his final farewell, put two rounds into the back of his skull. The bags weren't out of compassion. That was a trick assassins use to keep from making a bloody mess. In the next minute mrTed and all of his possessions were loaded into the crematorium, then Luther called Able Brown into the room.

"Everything is ready, Mr. Brown. And remember, we don't keep anything, no matter how valuable."

It was done. The Justice Club, by law, were all considered murderers, but nobody had any remorse, although nobody celebrated either. Their work had just begun.

Chapter 13

Several days later the Group met and discussed the information obtained from mrTed. As usual Ray led the meeting. "Brooke, can we do anything with that vehicle information we got?"

"I'm sure the perp doesn't own it anymore. Criminals always dispose of cars that can link them to a crime. I can get into Motor Vehicles and run the information we have, but since the titles don't show color, we're looking at a lot of vans. It'll take a while though, we're talking about records from two years ago and I'll have to search archives for that information. Another thing, these guys usually come from outside an area to do their dirty business, but this is a good place to start."

Dee reached for Luther's hand. "Maybe we could actually catch the person who killed our little girl."

"Maybe, baby," he replied. "But it's a long shot."

Ray spoke, "Maybe it's not as much a long shot as you think. If Brooke can run all the 98 and 99 Club Wagons within, say 100 miles, and we get some names, we can compare them to the registered sex offender list. And folks, just maybe, we can get a hit. Luther, what do we know about the guy besides the van? Anything you forget to tell us?"

"I don't think so. He's black, probably in his forties, with short hair and a mustache. That's all we know, besides the van."

"Any witnesses?"

"Look, Ray, in that neighborhood people don't see nothing. If they do, they never see anything twice. You know what I mean?"

Ray banged his fist on the table. "I don't give a shit about the code in the hood. Some pervert killed your child and if somebody saw the bastard, I'm going to find him. Are you with me, Luther?"

Luther lifted his head and everyone could see the tears as they rolled down his face. His voice was a whisper and chocked with emotion, "I'm with you, Ray."

***

BROOKE PULLED UP the registry of vans from Boone and nearby counties while working to compile a useable list. The vans that changed ownership during that period were eliminated and that shortened the list considerably. She targeted vans that weren't reregistered in the immediate area since most perverts stay away from their own homes. Meanwhile, Ray and Luther worked the neighborhood looking for any possible witnesses. Ray's white face didn't exactly bring a firestorm of cooperation and after several trips to the area both he and Luther were confronted by an angry group of young adults. An especially enraged man, wearing a blue bandana as a do-rag, stepped in front of the group, blocking the sidewalk in front of Ray and Luther.

"Hey, niggar, what the hell are you and this cracker doing in our hood? Luther stepped in front of Ray and started to speak when the man pushed him aside and grabbed for Ray. With his training in Martial Arts and his bouncer experience, he put his assailant down in an instant. When the others rushed forward grabbing Luther, pulling him to the ground, Ray quickly reached into his jacket and pulled his Glock semi-automatic from his Bianchi shoulder holster. After he fired a warning shot into the air the struggle stopped. When the group started to back off, Ray called to them. "C'mere, guys." When he put the Glock back into its holster they slowly came forward. Up to that point Ray and Luther hadn't told anybody the circumstances of why they were interested in a hit and run from years earlier.

Ray turned to Luther. "This man is your neighbor. He lives close by and his little girl went to that school." He pointed down the street. "Two years ago some slug tried to abduct a child from this street. It could have been your daughter or your little sister. Anyway, some of the mothers stopped it and when the guy ran, he drove over this man's five year-old baby. We're trying to find out who. And no, we're not cops. We're just two guys hell bent on a little street justice. What's my interest in all of this? My wife and son were murdered by a pervert that the legal system let walk."

The leader wiped his mouth, looked at the blood on his hand and wiped it on his pants. He walked up to Luther, gave him a half hug and mumbled, "Sorry, bro." Next, he did the same thing with Ray. "Tell us what you need to know."

Ray explained that they knew about the gold van, but not who owed or drove it. "What we need to know is if anybody in the neighborhood owned a van like that, maybe a grandmother or something. Our boy could have borrowed it, or maybe he was on vacation here. We don't know. He's probably from out of town, but we need to check it out."

After the confrontation Luther questioned Ray, "I had no idea you were carrying a piece. That saved us, man."

Ray smiled. " I've got a concealed carry permit from my bouncing days."

After that run-in they had the key to the neighborhood and several eyewitnesses came forward, but all they could do was give the same general description and verify the license plate was Missouri. At that point, although they had some of the pieces, they weren't even close to having enough to find out whom.

***

AT THE NEXT MEETING Brooke gave the results of her investigation. "I found three possible, guys in the system for a sex crime that owned a Ford van like the one we're looking for. I checked the VIN #'s with the car manufactures and none of those Club Wagons were gold, at least not from the factory. Anyway, all of perps are white. Now I'm working St. Louis County. Instead of looking for a gold van I'm just getting a list of owners and running them through our system. So far I'm up to the G's and I've got two possible." She reached into a large office envelope and spread color-photo's of the suspects. "I got these pictures from the sex offender site on the internet. In some ways they're further advanced than law enforcement."

Luther looked closely at the pictures, then handed them to Dee. "Do you recognize either one?"

She shook her head. "No."

"I'll take these with me and check them out with our witnesses and the homeboys."

Ray looked pleased as he turned to Dee. "We're gonna get this bastard, Dee, bet on it." Then he looked at Jill who had been strangely quiet. "How you doing, hun?"

"I'm alright, I guess."

"We all hurt, Jill. Maybe it'll get better someday."

Jill stood up and started for the door. "I know everyone here hurts, but at least it's not your fault. I killed my baby and her friend. I live with that."

Ray stopped and embraced her while she cried softly. His voice was soothing, "What happened is not your fault. Stop blaming yourself." He gently pushed her away and holding her arms looked into her eyes. "I'll make you a promise. When we resolve Luther and Dee's baby girl, we'll find the guy that hurt you, or I'll die trying."

She looked up into his unsmiling face. "I believe you, Raymond. Thank you." She accepted a hanky from May and dabbed her eyes. She looked at her concerned friends. "I'm sorry for falling to pieces. I know all of you have pain, too." The meeting ended as each person hugged Jill and whispered words of encouragement to her.

Ray walked Jill to the parking lot. "Buy you a cup of coffee, lady." Jill stopped walking and turned to Ray. She didn't speak, but he could see large tears well up in her eyes. "Please?" he asked again.

"I guess." They drove in Ray's car to a nearby Denny's and after ordering apple pie and coffee Ray started it. "Stop feeling sorry for yourself and get some backbone, girl. What's done is done and there's not a damn thing any of us can do about it. We're fighting back, don't you understand that? Do you want out? Because if you haven't got the stomach for this, just say so. But understand, with or without you, we're gonna put some hurt on the pervert community. And that, girl, may just make a few of those creeps think a bit before they hurt anyone else."

"Okay, Ray, I'm still with you," she whispered.

He smiled. "Good. Now, I know you don't have a job. Get one... Tell you what; I'll talk to some people at the University. There's always an opening. They have over a thousand employees so I'm sure you'll fit in somewhere." He reached over and took her hand and for the first time really looked at her. She wore no makeup and didn't do much with her long brunette hair as it hung straight down to her shoulders. He realized that this petite woman was beautiful and unconsciously he visualized her dressed up wearing makeup. When he realized what he was doing, he immediately pushed the thought from his mind. Later, as he relived the moment, he realized that that was the first time since he lost Elizabeth that he thought of a woman like that.

A week later Jill was working for the University in the History Department as a research analyst. Months later, as her demur and wardrobe gradually changed, the transformation prompted the Group to refer to her as the new Jill.

***

SUMMER TURNED TO FALL and eventually winter. By that time Ray and Jill began seeing each other between the weekly meetings, usually dinner at a family-style restaurant or a University function, such as a play, concert, or an athletic event. Ray didn't consider these dates, but rather friends enjoying each other's company. What he didn't realize was that Jill was falling in love with him. On a Friday night, after a Tiger basketball game, the couple sat across from each other at a small table in Subway. As Ray sucked the last few drops of root beer through the ice chips, Jill reached across the table and lightly held his arm. "I want to share something with you, Raymond."

He looked up expectantly.

"For the first time since, well, you know. I heard the birds singing and I watched the sun set. That might seem like a small thing, but to me it was wonderful." She hesitated a moment before continuing, "I don't mean that I'll ever forget what happened, but I am able to enjoy some of the simple things again. Our dates for example, I look forward to these like a schoolgirl. I think I'm getting on with my life and it feels good. Thank you."

He leaned across the table and kissed her lightly on the lips. "I'm glad."

***

THE CHRISTMAS SEASON brought parties and Jill invited Ray to the History Department's politically correct "Holiday Party." It was held in mid-December at "Howie's Steaks and Fine Food" a swank restaurant in downtown Columbia. When Ray picked Jill up, he whistled as his eyes drank in her beauty. She wore a tight fitting red dress with a glossy, thick, black belt. The dress allowed enough exposed skin under her chin to wear a Precious Topaz pendant that matched her earrings. Her hair was done in a wave, held in place with several gold barrettes. Her lipstick was a pale red, her cheeks lightly highlighted with pale pink rouge, and the purple eye shadow complimented her deep blue eyes. Two-inch red stilettos completed the look. "One lone word escaped Ray's lips. "WOW!"

As he looked up and down he commented, "Girl, you are smokin' hot."

Jill blushed and in a small voice said, "Something new, something borrowed."

At the party Ray met anybody who was anybody in the History Department and all the rest too, at least all of the men as they kept Jill busy most of the night dancing.

***

THE PHOTO'S LUTHER showed around the neighborhood didn't jar anyone's memory, but the Group was far from square one. Brooke worked every spare moment she had for the next two months and at a weekly meeting, in early March, had four fresh photo's that she handed to Luther. "This is a lot of hours, Luther, but these guys are registered; all owned Ford Club Wagons, and lived within 150 miles of Columbia. Only two of them served time for offenses against children, but just because a guy hasn't been caught doesn't mean he hasn't offended against a child. Three of these are from the St. Louis area and the other from Kansas City."

Ray missed that meeting. He was in Chicago tracking the attorney that defended Robert Morgan, the man who destroyed his life. He walked into the office of Anthony Drazza late on a Friday morning, unannounced and was told by an extremely young receptionist that Mr. Drazza was unavailable, and furthermore he wasn't accepting any new clients. Ray's logic for the Friday visit was that he knew most professional men liked to take Friday afternoon off to get an early start on the weekend and otherwise kept Friday a light day. "I'm not here to retain him."

"Okay, what is your business?"

"Private and personal, miss."

The secretary was perturbed. "Sir, Mr. Drazza hasn't got time to waste on..."

"It's about my daughter, he got her pregnant...Tell him it's Raymond Blackburn. He'll see me."

"OH!" the girl squealed as she bolted from her chair and rushed into the inner office. In a matter of seconds Anthony Drazza stepped into the room with the secretary following close behind. The attorney, a tall thin man in his 70's, had a huge grin on his face as he looked back at the girl while extending his hand. "Mr. Blackburn, come into my office." After they were seated the lawyer looked at the closed door and laughed.

"That's my granddaughter, Mr. Blackburn. I can only imagine what she's going to say when she gets home tonight." He chuckled. "I don't think she'll ever look at me the same way again. Anyway, what can I do for you?"

"Two things, counselor, first, you do know who I am?" Drazza nodded. "Okay. How do you sleep at night after you got that monster off? I guess some people will do anything for money."

Anthony Drazza leaned forward, only inches separated their faces. "I took an oath before the bar to defend, to the best of my ability, any client that entrusts me with their defense, regardless of guilt or innocence. That was a pro bono case. I didn't make a dime and I really didn't want the publicity of being his lawyer either. You do know what pro bono means?"

"Yeah, I know. So, why did you defend that rat? You could have said no."

"No, I couldn't. Pro bono cases are assigned on a rotating basis. It was simply my turn." He leaned back in his chair and continued, "I've had a lot of sleepless nights over what that guy did. The whole affair made me sick. It still does."

"I guess you weren't so sick that you couldn't help him clean me out. You know, the judgment he got against me that took all of my material possessions? What was your cut, a third?"

"Look, Mr. Blackburn, you got a raw deal all the way around and I really feel for you, but you need to understand, I didn't have anything to do with his civil legation. After the State's Attorney refused to prosecute, I didn't want any more to do with him and when he asked about a civil lawyer I told him to forget it, he already did enough to your family. You know the rest. He found a sewer rat to sue you, there's plenty of them around."

Ray lowered his head in contrition. "I'm sorry, Mr. Drazza. It's just that the greedy ninety–eight per cent of the lawyers make the rest of you look bad." Drazza gave Ray a long disapproving look before he reached into his shirt pocket and produced a cigarette. After he lit it he held it up slightly. "This is a nasty habit, Mr. Blackburn, but it helps me control my emotions."

Ray leaned toward the attorney. "You seem like a decent guy, will you help me?"

Drazza shrugged his shoulders. "That depends. I won't do anything illegal."

"I understand. I need to find this Robert Morgan and I don't know where to start. The prick took my money and disappeared. I think he changed his name because I can't find a Robert Morgan with a stub for a right index finger anyplace, and I've exhausted everything I can think of."

Anthony Drazza stood and walked to the window, and for a moment watched the miniature cars crawling twenty-two stories below. "Well, he's not my client anymore and I didn't represent him on the other matter, so there is no client privilege involved." He turned to face Ray. "I know some people over at the courthouse, maybe I can find out about this guy. I'm not gonna ask you what you plan on doing if you find him. I don't need to be an accessory before the fact and if I help, it stays strictly between us. Understood?"

Ray scribbled his cell phone number on the back of the lawyer's business card, dropped it on the desk, and pocketed another. Then he stood and walked to the door. He turned and accepted Anthony Drazza's hand.

"This may take a while, Mr. Blackburn. Be patient. I'll be in touch."

***

A WEEK LATER RAY and Jill visited the Stadium Mall where Amy, Jill's daughter, was abducted two years earlier. As they sat in the outer office of the Mall Manager, Ray leaned over and whispered to Jill, "Remember, don't show any emotion. As dolled up as you are, he'll never recognize you."

After a brief wait Warren Roteg, the manager, walked into the office. As he looked at his watch he murmured his apology, "Sorry, folks. I'm running a bit late today." As he opened the door to the inner office Ray and Jill followed him. He flipped on the lights and went behind the desk and sat in a large, black office chair. "Have a seat."

Ray sat next to the desk and Jill sat in a chair against the near wall. "I'm Warren Roteg, the manager here. What can I do for you?"

Ray leaned over and offered his hand. "Raymond Stiller, and this pretty lady is Jill Roberts." After shaking Ray's hand Warren Roteg smiled and nodded to Jill.

Ray looked at the man for a brief time before speaking, as if deciding whether to entrust him with the purpose of this visit.

"Mr. Roteg, Ms. Roberts and I are from NBC's Dateline; specifically, from Chris Hansen's office. Chris is doing a story on children and what attracts them to the malls of America and what hidden dangers they face. We pretty much know what draws the kids, but now we want to find out about problems they cause and the security necessary to protect them."

Warren Roteg leaned back in his chair and lit a cigarette. He took a long drag and exhaled the smoke away from his guests. "Some people drop their kids off when the mall opens at ten in the morning and pick them up around nine, just before we close. I can't imagine what they're thinking. Malls have become hunting grounds for the most perverted members of our society. We try to watch out for that, but sometimes it's hard to tell the difference between a parent spending time with a kid and a pervert trying to pick one up. The bad guys don't have big X's on their backs and believe me, many are master of disguises, so it's hard for us to tell if one is hanging around."

Jill spoke for the first time, "Mr. Roteg, we know most of the regulars are fairly street smart. It's the kids that come to see a movie, or maybe to play a few video games while mom shops that are in the most danger."

"You're right, Ms. Roberts. The kids that hang out here aren't the ones in the most jeopardy. The pedophiles watch out for kids that know everybody and leave them alone. They look for the first timers and the ones mom dumped at the arcade for an hour while she gets her hair done."

Ray watched Jill for any signs of stress and was impressed with her professional demur. "It sounds like the video arcade is the trouble spot. Why not just eliminate that business, or have an age requirement?"

"You're right again, miss, but that's what pays the light bill and a lot more around here. As far as an age requirement, don't you think we already have enough rules? I mean, don't the parents have responsibility anymore?"

This conversation wasn't going anyplace and Ray changed it. "What about security and surveillance?"

"As far as security goes we hire retired guys who patrol the stores and streets. They're not armed, but they do wear uniforms and carry a can of mace."

"So, they patrol the parking lot. Too?"

"No. By streets I mean the walkways between the stores and shops. If a crime occurs outside, we call the city police."

Jill was taking notes and barely looked up until Ray asked about the two young girls who were abducted from the mall and murdered two years earlier.

"That was tragic. But there is no clear evidence that those children were even in the mall. The mother claims she dropped them off and a teenaged sister says they were here, but kids often lie about what they were really doing, so we're not sure."

Ray knew Jill was ready to explode so he went right into his next question. "What about surveillance cameras?"

We got 'em everywhere now, but before those kids disappeared we only had a few and none were outside. We had the exits and a few of the streets covered and that was it."

"Do you have the tapes from the day the kids went missing? It'd be a big help to compare those with what you have in place now."

"I think so. The police gave them back to us, but of course I'll need permission from the mall owners to turn them over to you."

Jill stood up, walked over to the desk and looked down on the mall manager.

"Mr. Roteg, the way we slant this story will either make you look very good or very bad, cooperating fully would certainly put you in a favorable light with Mr. Hansen."

Warren Roteg thought for a moment and gave in. "Okay. But if you use any of the footage you'll need a release from the owners. I can't do anything about that."

"Fair enough," said Jill.

They got what they came for and now Ray wanted a bonus.

"Mr. Roteg, one last thing. Who are these sick people that prey on our children? I know you run them off when you can, but what's the deal?"

Roteg leaned back in his chair. "The guy next door, your brother in law, a guy you work with, or even the choir director. Mr. Stiller, these people can be anybody. They don't have horns protruding out of their head; they look like any one of us." He looked at Jill as she stood back from his desk. "And they're not all men either. If you want to find out who they are, check the internet, virtually all of them are into pictures. That's what a big percentage of them are after, pictures of naked kids, or better yet, children doing something sexual. The authorities don't always find them because they're willing to pay the kids to take pictures, and the more graphic the more they pay. For a couple of hundred dollars some of the kids would do about anything and even if caught they never cooperate with the authorities."

Ray stood and offered his hand. "Thank you, Mr. Roteg. If you could find those tapes we'll be on our way."

On the way home Ray explained why the tapes were so important. "The cops may have missed something that we can find." He looked over at Jill. "It's going to be hard to view them. Are you sure you want to do this?"

In a strong voice she replied, "I'm sure."

Chapter 14

Coach Johnson looked expectantly at Johnny Ray as he they watched the two men in Navy Blues walk out of the gymnasium. "How'd it go?"

Johnny Ray faced the coach. "I'm not officer material, Coach. I told them I wasn't interested."

"You what? Nobody turns down an appointment to the Naval Academy. What are you thinking?"

"I didn't exactly turn them down, Mr. Johnson. I just never gave them a chance to ask. Maybe they didn't want me anyway."

"Son, I'm trying to help you, but unless I know what you're thinking, I can't. What do you want to do with your life? That should determine where you go to school."

"Coach, I want to find the no-good bastard that destroyed my family. That's what I want to do with my life."

"John, let it go. Your folks wouldn't want you to live with all this anger. Make something of yourself. You're a smart kid, use your head."

"Okay, if you really want to know, I wanna be a cop. If I make detective, I'll have the tools to search for that guy."

Coach Johnson shook his head. "You'll never pass the physiological tests. They've got a slew of lawsuits because of cops beating suspects. With your temper, forget it.

"Then I'll be a private investigator."

The coach frowned. "You'll never get a license."

"The hell I won't. And if I don't, I'll just get a gun," Johnny Ray shouted.

Coach Johnson put his hand on Johnny's shoulder. "See what I mean? That's stupid talk and if you get this worked up just talking to me..."

Johnny Ray put his head down and began to sob. "Mr. Johnson, my mother, my brother, and my father are all dead because of me." His voice trailed off to a whisper, "If I don't do something, nobody will."

"Come back tomorrow and we'll talk about your future. Okay?"

Johnny whispered, "Okay."

***

THE NEXT DAY, Johnny Ray sat across the desk from Coach Johnson in the small office he shared with the basketball coach. "Have you thought about what you want to do?" Coach Johnson said as he thumbed through the letters of interest he received from eight different colleges and universities.

"I think I'd like to be a photo journalist."

"How'd you come up with that?"

"Well, I'm like writing. I'm good with computers, and I like taking pictures."

The coach leaned forward. "You think you'll be privy to a lot of information if you work for a newspaper or a magazine, don't you."

"Yeah, I hope so."

Coach Johnson took a deep breath and exhaled hard through his nostrils. "Okay, journalism it is." The coach set the letters down and picked up the telephone and quickly punched in a local number. "Joe, Ezra Johnson here. I need to ask your opinion about a good school of journalism." After a brief response the coach laughed. "No, not for me. One of my guys is being recruited and he's interested in a literary career, and since I consider you the best newspaperman in the Midwest, I thought I'd ask." The coach turned and winked at Johnny as he listened. Then he read the name of each school as it appeared on the letterheads until he was interrupted. "Mizzou? The University Of Missouri in Columbia?... Okay, Joe, thanks." He set the phone down and looked at Johnny Ray. "You heard. If you want, I can make arrangements for a visit to the school and you can have a look around the campus, and they'll pay all your expenses. I know Coach Winston personally and he runs a very aggressive program. It's a good football school, but more importantly, a good fit for your journalistic ambitions."

"Sounds good, Coach, set it up."

The trip to Missouri was set for spring break, the first week in April.

***

IT WAS THE LAST Saturday in March when Johnny Ray and two of his teammates tossed a football on the beach at Castle Rock State Park on Lake Michigan's North Shore. It was an unusually warm day for March and although the water was cold, the beach and park were filled with people. When they stopped to rest at a park bench, Johnny Ray noticed a small crowd of children surrounding a man as he sat on the break wall. The man had a monkey on a leash and Johnny could hear the children as they begged for permission to pet the animal. Visions of that day so long ago filled his mind as he walked over and stood on the outside of the group. The man was so engrossed with the children that he didn't notice Johnny.

"I need to brush Oscar. Who wants to help?" the man asked.

The children all jumped up and down screaming in unison, "Me, me, I want to."

The man, in his thirties, of average size and weight, wore a straw hat and covered his face with large, dark sunglasses. "Okay. I only need one helper and the brushes are in my car." Johnny Ray pushed past the small children. "I'll help."

"What?... Uh, okay." When the man started to walk towards the parking lot the children followed. Johnny Ray, who was on his heels, turned and shouted, "Get the hell out of here you little bastards." He didn't know how else to get rid of them and when he turned for a second time the kids scattered and ran.

The man in the straw hat and the dark glasses decided he didn't need help after all and when he got to a tan windowless van he slid the cargo door open and called over his shoulder, "That's all right, fellow, I can handle it."

Johnny Ray leaped on the man. "Like 'em a little younger, huh?" His fists were blurs as he beat the man unconscious. His friends found Johnny banging the man's head on the pavement while the monkey screeched and cried. If they hadn't stopped the assault when they did, Johnny Ray would have killed him, and that's what he intended to do. After they pushed Johnny back, his friends simply threw the man into the van and closed the sliding door. As the three walked briskly away, the monkey cried out in vain for his master to do something.

Minutes later, safely in the back seat of his friends Jeep, Johnny rubbed the knuckles on both of his hands while one friend turned to face him from the passenger seat. "Man, what the hell got into you. That guy might be dead. What happened?"

"You guys don't know, do you?"

"Know what?"

"I got my reasons. Keep your mouths shut and I hope the bastard doesn't die right away. I hope he lingers for a long time."

His friends looked at each other and neither wanted to be on Johnny Ray's bad side. "Okay, man, you got it." Both agreed.

The man didn't die, but a newspaper account gave a far different story of what happened. He claimed to have been robbed by a group of Latino youths and since he was attacked from behind he was unable to identify his attackers. When investigating detectives ran the man's name through police files, he was tagged as a convicted child molester and that, of course, didn't endear him any sympathy. The police simply buried the report suspecting that the victim may have hit on the wrong kid.

***

THE FOLLOWING WEEK Johnny Ray was picked up at the Columbia, Missouri airport by the team's defensive coach. During the short ride to the campus of the University Of Missouri it was made plain that he would be a welcome addition to the team. "We've watched your films and our scouts like your aggressive nature, son. We think you'll be a good fit for our program and of course this school has an excellent School Of Journalism. You'll get a fine education here and your ride is guaranteed as long as your grade point is at least 2.0, even if you get hurt and can't play. We'll even get you a little job where you can earn spending money and it won't interfere with either your studies or football."

Johnny Ray knew exactly what he was talking about. They'd give him a job that nobody would even check on, such as watering a small lawn, sweep the gymnasium, or wash the athletic department vehicles, all paid for by the alumni association.

The plan for Johnny Ray's visit was to spend the first half of the day with the football people and the other half with a school advisor. His overnight stay at The Holiday Inn and breakfast with Coach Winston would finish the visit after which he would be driven back to the airport for a mid-morning flight back to Chicago.

***

EARLY THAT MORNING, RUSK called Ray. "How are things at that big hospital of yours?"

"What?" Ray replied. "Who is this?"

"It's Rusk, damnit. You do remember me, right? I hired you?"

"Sorry, boss, I didn't recognize your voice. Things are good here. What can I do for you?"

"The school bought a new x-ray machine for the locker room over at the football stadium. It's just like the ones at the hospital and I know you've put a few of those in service. Could you give me a hand?"

"Sure. I can get loose around ten. Is that good for you?"

"Yeah, and leave those pretty nurses do their job, hotshot."

Ray grinned. "Don't I wish."

***

AFTER TOURING the practice field and Tigers Stadium, Johnny Ray was led into the bowels of the stadium to the locker room where large, gray lockers adorned each wall. The room was huge and nearly empty, except for a student athlete doing his "job" mopping the floor and the equipment manager going through, and sorting various pieces of equipment and jerseys. When entering the trainer's room, four whirlpool tubs, two gurneys, and various pieces of exercise equipment greeted them. Over in the corner two workmen were busy installing a new piece of equipment. The coach glanced over at the machine. "We're updating our x-ray system. With this one we'll have results within minutes." When Johnny Ray looked at the x-ray machine his heart nearly stopped. Two men wearing dark blue coveralls worked to install the new system. One was short with thinning gray hair, but the other closely resembled his dead father, although the man wore his hair short and was a bit heavier. When Ray felt Johnny Ray's eyes on his back he turned and gave the stranger a smile before returning to work. He gave no sign of recognition because he had none. Many years had passed and Johnny Ray was only eleven years old then.

Johnny Ray was sure his mind was playing tricks on him and that his memory of his father must have faded after all the years. He reasoned that he missed him so much that anyone bearing a close resemblance would play tricks on his mind. He'd had other sightings before, but never like this.

The next morning when he had breakfast with Coach Winston he decided to accept the school's offer. He agreed to live on campus and report for football practice at the end of July. He would also be employed by the Athletic Department as a grounds keeper assistant. His job would be to check that the automatic sprinkler system turned on and off at the proper times and during the winter he was responsible for shoveling snow away from the side entrance of Tiger Stadium. A great job since the annual snowfall for Columbia Missouri only averages ten inches. For this he would be paid $100 a week and furnished a car.

***

DURING HIS FLIGHT home Johnny Ray thought more about the encounter with his father's look-alike than the scholarship he just accepted. He tried to reason that the workman's likeness to his father was just a coincidence. Still, he wished he had engaged the man in conversation, just to hear his voice. After a while he scolded himself and tried to think about college life and the changes it would bring. He thought about the curriculum his advisor suggested and decided the sixteen credit hours would be manageable, even with football, and still leave time for college life.

Martha picked him up from Chicago's Midway Airport and as they drove home asked if he made any commitments. "Yeah, I signed a letter of intent... I have to be there July 23rd."

"That's great, Johnny. I'm really happy for you."

He turned in his seat and faced Martha. "Aunt Martha, I need to ask you some things. I'm not a little boy anymore, so you don't have to protect me like you always have."

Martha glanced at him. "Okay. What do you need to ask?"

"I didn't get to go when my mom and Cory died. I've never even visited their graves. Where are they?"

Martha's mind retraced the years before speaking. "I didn't go either. I took you away. Under the circumstances I thought that was the best thing to do. Your mother's church paid for the funeral and buried them in their cemetery close to the church in St. Charles, Missouri." She paused a moment before continuing, "Your father was in jail and they wouldn't even let him attend the services. That was heartbreaking to say the least. The public outcry was loud, but the judge wouldn't budge." That seemed to satisfy Johnny and he didn't speak again until they pulled into the driveway at home.

"I saw a guy that looked like my father. When I try to remember him it's not clear anymore, but when I saw that man, I remembered. He was a little older, but if you didn't tell me he was dead, I'd swear he was my father. He is dead, right?"

Martha shut the engine off and turned to Johnny. "I'm going to tell you all I know about your parents. Please keep in mind that I wanted you to have as normal a childhood as possible, so there were things I didn't talk about." She paused briefly. "I loved your mother. Elizabeth was not only my best friend she was like my sister, if you can understand that." John nodded. "Okay, your grandmother had your mother when she was sixteen. Her marriage fell apart and she was divorced a year later. When she remarried, her husband adopted Elizabeth, but he never had the love a parent should have for his child. When Raymond entered the picture your grandmother viewed him as a street-wise kid who wasn't good enough for her daughter, a kid like her first husband. She did all she could to keep them apart, but couldn't. When Elizabeth went to college, your father went to the Army. After boot camp he spent his first leave with her at a house she and I rented at school. When her mother found out Elizabeth was pregnant, she disowned her and never made contact again. Meanwhile, Elizabeth decided that she wouldn't tell your father and would give the baby up for adoption." She looked deep into Johnny Ray's eyes. "She never considered abortion, although that would have been the easy way out. Anyway, when she was full term and started to labor, she was having a terrible time and I contacted your father's army post. He got an emergency leave and was there when you were born."

"Is this the part where they got married and were supposed to live happily ever after?"

"It should have been, Johnny, but there was a problem. Your mother signed papers and they weren't allowing for a change of heart. What they didn't know was that Elizabeth was carrying twins, so they took your brother, but you went home with your parents. I thought your father was going to be arrested when he argued that he wanted his other baby too, but it didn't happen."

"My god, I've got a brother somewhere?"

"That's not all, John. As you know your father went to prison, but he didn't die."

"What? Why did you lie to me?"

"He asked me to." Martha pulled a Kleenex from her purse and dabbed her eyes. "I only did what he asked. I know it was wrong and I hated to do that. I still have the letter he wrote me. You can read it for yourself."

"So, the man I saw could be my father?"

"Yes. He served his time only a short distance from Columbia. It probably was him."

"Aunt Martha, I don't know whether to be angry or elated. Ten minutes ago I had no blood family and now I have a brother someplace and my father back."

He leaned over and hugged Martha. "I could never be mad at you, Aunt Martha, you've been a great mother to me."

"Even though I could never have children, I consider you my son. I love you as much as any mother who birthed a child, don't ever forget that."

"I won't." Johnny promised.

Chapter 15

The weekly Group meetings eventually turned monthly and were more business-like in nature. The mid-April gathering brought a huge change. May smiled at everyone and bubbled with excitement. "My son came home. He finally came to his senses and called from Costa Rica where he was living in a commune. I'm so happy I could burst. I don't know if you still need me, but if you don't, I'm not coming anymore." One by one each member hugged and wished May well, and then she was gone.

Brooke was next. "This is bittersweet for me," she began. They finally made an arrest in my brother's case. Even though they never found Jimmy, they found his DNA in the trunk of the suspect's car. There was a trace of blood and at least we know what happened to him. The State's Attorney assures me he'll get a murder conviction, even without a body." She tried to state the facts in a controlled voice, but finally broke into deep sobs. Dee stood and walked behind Brooke's chair, leaned down and hugged her. "It's okay, baby girl, let it all out."

Ray, Jill, and Luther got up and walked to the far side of the room while Dee continued to console Brooke. After several minutes they were again seated and Jill addressed Brooke, "Honey, if this is too much for you we understand. Nobody has to be here if they don't want to."

Brooke dabbed her eyes and blew her nose. "After what that man did to Jimmy, I wanna be here." She set her jaw in a determined manner and looked at each person individually. "If I can do anything to help you guys catch these slugs, I'm gonna do it."

Ray looked at Luther. "Anything on those photos Brooke gave you?"

"There's been a lot of gang activity lately and the cops are all over the place. This isn't the right time to be asking questions. When things cool down a bit, I'll check with the homeboys and see if they know anything."

"I don't want you to be alone. Let me know when and we'll go together."

***

THREE WEEKS LATER, on a Saturday afternoon, Ray and Luther walked into "Birdie's Lounge" on Broadway Boulevard. Luther took the lead as a group of neighborhood men surrounded them. There was an icy silence before they were recognized. A man in a dress hat, wearing a loud suit jacket, walked up to Ray. "Hey, brother, remember me? I still got your hand print on my throat." He laughed. "What's up, man?"

Both Ray and Luther breathed a sigh of relief as Luther pulled the photos from a large, business envelope and spread them on the pool table.

"One of these guys might be the dirt-bag that ran my little girl down," Luther said. And as he and Ray stepped back the homeboys picked up the pictures and passed them around. After a brief discussion the leader handed Luther one. "This guy used to come around here, but we ain't seen him for a long time."

Ray asked, "What can you guys tell us about him? Does he have people around here or does he come through on business or something?"

One of the men laughed. "Business, yeah, you mean monkey business. That's what that cat was up to."

"What'd you mean?" Luther asked.

"That dude was trying to sell sex stuff. You know, toys, pictures, pills, that kind of thing." Immediately memories of the meeting with the mall manager played in Ray's head. "What's his name?" he asked.

Nobody knew, but one guy remembered seeing him at a store in the neighborhood. "I saw that fool going into the bookstore on Pleasant Street. That place has a lot of nasty stuff."

Hardball, the cat in the hat jumped on that. "A lot of high school kids hang out in that place. That dude sells a lot of shit, and a lot of shit he ain't supposed too."

"Like what?" Ray asked.

"You're not going to the law with any of this, right? 'Cause we ain't about to give up a brother to the stinken' cops."

Luther stepped in front of Ray. "No, brother, we ain't gonna to the cops and we don't care what the guy does. We just wanna see if he knows anything about the shit-head we're looking for."

"Look, the dude's making a living, that's all you need to know. Cuzzy Watson owns the store, and he's mean and carries a piece. If you wanna talk to him, I better go with you, or he might sig some of those kids on your ass-es."

Fifteen minutes later they entered Watson's Books and Gifts, a storefront that had heavy mesh over all of the windows. Hardball took the lead as a heavy-set older man with a puffy, gray Afro stepped from the rear. He wore charcoal pants and a white shirt open at the collar; he also wore a dirt-stained tan holster around his waist that housed a large framed revolver.

"Hello, Mr. Watson," said Hardball.

The old man looked over his visitors while addressing Hardball in his deep baritone voice. "Yeah, hello. What you want, boy, and who dis with you?"

"Mr. Watson, this man," he turned to Luther, "lives in the neighborhood. It was his baby that got run down a couple of years ago walking home from school."

The old man offered his hand and mumbled his sympathy, but when Ray offered his hand it was ignored. "Who dis white boy, a cop?"

Ray walked up and stood inches from the man's face. "No, I'm not a cop. I'm just a guy who had his family murdered by a perverted son of a bitch and I'm trying to get a little payback."

Cuzzy grinned. "Next time you meet a stranger you better keep that rod hid a little better, son. That's why I thought you were the heat. I knew you were packin' the second I laid eyes on you." Now Cuzzy extended his hand. "Pleased to meet you. Now, what can I do for you gentleman?"

Luther showed Cuzzy Watson the picture.

"Yeah, I know that guy. I had to run him off a couple of times. Selling porn and shit to the kids. He tried to sell me too, but I got my principals. I sell magazines. Some of them pretty rough, but I won't sell anything with humans and animals, and worse yet, with children involved. I haven't seen him for a long time and if I never see him again, that's alright with me." Ray ignored the sermon. They weren't there to discuss morality. They were there to find a killer.

"Mr. Watson, do you know his name and where he's from?"

"Sorry, man, I don't. But I think he said he's from St. Louis."

Luther persisted. "Do you think any of the kids would know anything about him?"

"Sorry, boys, but I told that jerk to stay away from here or else."

When they started for the door Hardball looked back. "Thanks, Mr. Watson"

"Wait a minute. He gave me a card once. I think I still have it."

Cuzzy Watson walked to a cooler and brought back three bottles of Bud Lite. "Have a beer while I look boys."

Several minutes later Ray read aloud from the business card, "Candyman Photo Service, photo's bought, sold, and traded." He turned the card over and silently read the name, address and web address.

Cuzzy turned and sat on a tall bar stool. "I know he handles a lot of child pornography. You know, film, photos, and that pervert even told me that if I had anything good, he'd reproduce it and split the profits with me."

Ray and Luther both shook Cuzzy's hand and turned to leave.

"Ain't you boys forgetting somethin'?

Luther stopped. "Thanks, Mr. Watson, you've been a big help."

"Thanks don't buy no beer. You boys owe me for those Bud Lites"

Ray reached into his pocket and peeled off a fifty. "Keep the change and thanks again, Mr. Watson." Cuzzy

Watson looked at the greenback and grunted before disappearing into the back room.

Later, after thanking Hardball, they dropped him at Birdie's and left a hundred dollars with the bartender. On the way back, Ray and Luther discussed the day's events. Luther was ecstatic. "We got it all, Ray. Eric Sounder, 3452 West Park Street, St. Louis, Missouri and we even got the prick's web site. I'd say we did real good today."

Ray agreed. "Yeah, this is one of the good days. You know, Luther, maybe the cops keep track of where these perverts live and warn the neighbors, but then he just does his shit someplace else. I guess the bottom line is that society still gives the bastards enough leash to do their dirty work. Let's go to your house and see if Dee can bring up this creep's web site. I'll just bet its real creative."

Later as they sipped hot coffee, Dee entered the web address of Candyman Photo's. They took the virtual tour and nearly became sick when young children appeared partially dressed while modeling in provocative posses. With a major credit card the site operators promised more, a lot more with the privilege of exchanging instant messages with others sharing the same tastes.

Luther wanted to go deeper into the site, but Dee warned of using their credit card. "That's an electronic footprint. When that guy goes missing they might start looking into his personal life and wham, we're there too."

"Okay," Ray said, "we've seen enough anyway. This is our guy. Now we have to figure out when we can get to St. Louis and cancel his ticket." He thought for a moment. "Luther, with your consulting business you can just take off, but I still work fulltime and I'm always on call. This might take a bit of planning."

Dee smiled. "This may not be as hard to as you think. I'll talk to May and use the library computers to contact him. I'll sign his private guest book and say that we have a large collection of original photo's and VHS tapes never shown anywhere. We can buy a Trac Fone at Wall-Mart and see if we can lure him into calling us. If we pay cash and use a fictitious name, there won't be any traceable record of the calls. Then we bait the trap and get him to come to Columbia. If he's greedy, he'll see the business opportunity and jump at the chance."

At the next meeting all the facts were discussed and agreed upon. Dee would use the internet to lure Mr.Eric Sounder into the ambush. Luther would carry the Trac Fone and promise pictures of children engaging in various sexual acts with each other and with adults taken in Thailand. He would also promise same-sex acts committed on children by adults, featuring American children. Ray felt the bile rise in his throat as the plan was discussed and realized that he would be unable to be the phone connection. In his mind he thought of a child being hit by a car, compared to being tortured, abused, and then murdered. The result was the same, but it was a different road.

Unlike with mrTed, where instant messenger was used, Dee gave no contact information other than the Trac Fone number. It was decided that this was the best way, since she couldn't give a workable email address. Besides, people dealing with smut usually cover their identity the best they can, always fearful of the authorities. The Group hoped that Eric Sounder wouldn't be leery, since sting operations usually targeted those making contact with minors, not those trading in pictures and film. But the Group also realized that their target knew that if arrested again, they'd throw the key away since he had already been convicted twice before.

The message Dee left on Candyman's private guest book, was brief and to the point.

I need cash ASAP. I am willing to sacrifice my lifetime collection of youthful candy shots, consisting of thousands of never before viewed photos and hundred of hours of unedited VHS tapes. I'm a professional photographer and I shot this material at various locations throughout the world. This is the opportunity of a lifetime. For more information I can be reached at 573 544 8700.

photobug

Ray and Luther worked out a plan, if and when the target called. It was agreed that Ray should be the front man since the Group felt Luther would have trouble controlling himself in the presence of his daughter's killer, but Luther insisted. "I need to do this."

Two days later when the Trac Fone rang Luther was in his home office and stared at the ringing telephone for a long moment before answering. He knew that he'd probably be talking to the man that took his daughter's life and his heart beat hard in his chest as he tried to overcome his nervousness. "Hello."

"Is this photobug?"

"Yeah."

"This is the candyman. You sent me a message?"

"Yeah. I got some stuff for sale."

"Tell me about it."

"Here on the phone?"

"No, goddamnit.. Send me smoke signals."

Things were going according to plan. Candyman already felt that he was in charge and that he was dealing with a rookie.

"Alright, I just never did nothing like this before. I got pictures and video's, lots of them with anything you can think happening and all the kids are young."

"Look, I've been through this shit before. I don't want any twenty year olds that look fourteen. I'm interested, but only if they're young and if they're doing the things my customers want. Do you understand me?"

"Yeah, I got you."

"Okay, how much?"

"I need ten grand."

"Ten grand? What the fuck do you think I am, The Federal Reserve?"

"Look, man, you don't have to buy them all. Look at the goods and make me an offer."

"Fair enough. How far are you from St. Louis and how long will it take you to get here?"

"You come here or there is no deal. I'm not traveling around the countryside with all that in my car. Besides, I don't need to get robbed."

"Where are you?"

"Just west of St. Louis. Columbia."

"Okay. Is tomorrow afternoon alright?"

"Yeah, that's good."

"Meet me at three in the Sears parking lot at Stadium Mall. I'll be driving a white Dodge van and I'll be wearing a Cardinal baseball hat."

"I can't make it by three. Is five okay?"

"No. Be there at three or forget it."

"I guess I can go home sick. Three it is."

With that Luther hung up the phone before candyman could ask about what vehicle he would be driving and what he looked like. Later, as he told Ray about the call, he grinned. "We're gonna get that bastard, Raymond. I never thought it would happen, but now I know it will."

"Call Able Brown at the funeral home so he's expecting another customer."

Luther nodded his reply.

***

THE NEXT AFTERNOON, Ray ducked out of work early. That was the beauty of the job he had, nobody ever knew where he was and if he was in a noisy area he couldn't hear the two-way radio he carried.

Ray sat in his car near the only entrance to the parking lot and watched for the white Dodge van. He had Luther on speed dial and as agreed, when the Dodge van pulled slowly into the lot, he rang his cell phone as a warning. Ray watched as the van drove slowly up and down the six isles and finally parked off by himself at the edge of the lot. As planned, Luther drove his Ford Explorer close to the Dodge van. When candyman opened the door and walked the few feet to Luther, Ray whispered to himself, "Make the bastard get in, Luther." After a moment the man walked around to the passenger side and climbed in alongside of Luther. Luther had his Ultra Z Force Stun Gun ready and gave candyman a dose that rendered him helpless. Ray quickly drove up and parked a short distance away. When he opened the door, he turned the candyman around and bound his hands with Flex Cuffs before searching him.

He handed Luther candyman's small semi-automatic and billfold, which was thick with cash. Next, Ray opened the back door of the Explorer, and after checking for by-standers, dragged the semi-conscious man from the front and pushed him onto the floor of the rear seat. Then he pulled the man's belt off and tied his feet with it. "If he comes around and starts hollering, Luther, zap him again. I'll see you over at Brown's."

***

WHEN THEY GOT THERE Ray wanted to get it over with quickly, but Luther had other plans. As Ray and Able Brown stood back and watched, Luther went to work on the candyman. When he realized what Luther was referring to, candyman tried to reason with him. "It was an accident, man. She walked right out in front of me. I couldn't help it. Take me to the police, I'll confess."

Luther grabbed him by the hair. "That ship sailed a long time ago, mister."

Able Brown wanted the beating to stop, but Ray held him back. "He killed that man's child. You know how angry you were when your daughter got raped. Do you think you'd react any different than Luther if she was murdered too?"

Able Brown stood back and never said another word until Luther told him. "Okay, Mr. Brown, it's time to cook some candy."

The whole exercise was redundant, since candyman was long dead when pushed into the furnace. The only thing they kept from him was his money, twenty five one hundred dollar bills. Ray peeled off ten and handed them to Able Brown.

"This should help out with some of the expenses, Mr. Brown" He pocketed the semi-automatic and said, "We'll dump this thing out of town."

Later, when Luther told Dee the mission was a success, she cried softly as he held her. "I know it wasn't enough, Dee, but it was all he had to give. It's finally over." They embraced for a long time and both wept as thoughts of their vibrant six year old filled their minds. Finally Dee looked to the ceiling and whispered, "Now you can rest in peace, baby girl."

Chapter 16

At the next meeting, Ray addressed the Group with a smile. "As everyone knows, we closed the matter concerning Luther and Dee's daughter... Jill, tell us what you and Brooke are doing."

As the group watched, she exhaled a deep breath.

"Okay, I've made copies of the surveillance tapes from the mall on the day Amy disappeared. I've studied them a thousand times and found some shots of the girls. They're in black and white so that made it harder to identify Amy, but that day she wore her Rams jersey, number sixteen. They never went into the theater; instead they spent over an hour in the video arcade playing the games. Since there were no cameras in the arcade I couldn't see what they were doing, but we have a clear view of them in front of the arcade. Next, I found a shot of them standing by the exit doors with two guys, and then they all left the mall together. I couldn't see their faces, but from the clothes they were wearing, I found other shots of those guys from different parts of the mall. I got several facial shots, but they were too far away to recognize, even with a magnifying glass." She tried hard not to show emotion, but the strain was too much and she put her head down on the table and cried.

Brooke picked up the story. "Jill put the still shots on a CD and a friend at the Crime Lab, using advanced computer technology, got us these prints." She spread several photos on the table. The pictures showed a clear view of the suspect's faces. "I can't just show these around the station house, there'd be too many questions. What we can do is try to compare these with the photos that go with every registered sex offender. If these guys are registered in Columbia they should be easy to find, but if they're from out of town, this could take a while."

Ray had a question. "What if these guys are students at the university? Where would they be registered as sex offenders?"

Brooke answered, "Their legal residence."

"That's just great," Luther said. "The bastards could be from the moon for all we know."

Dee looked at Luther. "Don't be so negative. With us three girls checking the registry, we'll find something. We can start with the closest zip codes and work our way out from there. Right, girls?" Both Jill and Brooke agreed.

Brooke chuckled. "This is what criminal investigations are, mostly just grunt work. Cases on television are solved in an hour. In real life it takes a lot longer." She paused briefly. "We could turn this over to the detectives. They've got more resources than we do and would probably find these guys a lot sooner than we could."

Ray slammed his fist on the table. "No, damnit. Once we show our hand we're done. If the bastards are arrested, get off, and later go missing, guess where the first place the cops are going to look? I've had a taste of what the judicial system calls justice; it cost me eight years of my life and everything I've ever had. No, Brooke, we'll find and deal with them ourselves, and remember, we don't plea bargain. They'll get exactly what they deserve." He looked at the Group and smiled. "Of course any help we can get from law enforcement will be appreciated."

"I'm walking a tightrope, Ray; I can only use my friends in the department so much without raising suspicion. My friend that did the pictures wanted to know what that was all about. I told him that my cousin worked at the mall and met one of the suspects, but didn't know who he was. I told him that she thought he was cute and wanted to try to find out his name and if he was married. He just shook his head and said, 'Woman.' Remember guys, the people I work with aren't stupid. It's their business to be nosey and believe me they're always asking questions about everything."

Jill entered the conversation. "Everyone here appreciates what you do, Brooke, and we realize the consequences if we're ever caught. But as Ray said, the wheels of justice don't always turn the way they should."

Ray wanted to take the pictures to the mall manager to see if he recognized either suspect, but was voted down. Dee had the final word on that idea. "Look, Ray, if he does know them and they go missing, it'll wind up in your lap. Let us do our search. And stay away from that arcade, they got plenty of cameras now and we don't need them watching you. Meanwhile, all of us can watch for these guys in our everyday travels, we could get lucky."

As the months melted into summer, the search proved fruitless. The girls eliminated over a thousand suspects, but were undeterred and continued the pursuit. Ray made monthly calls to the lawyer in Chicago concerning Robert Morgan, and was told to be patient; he had people looking into the matter. Luther decided to take another avenue. With the blessing of the Group he entered the slimy world of smut. With Dee's computer skills, he was able to open an untraceable account with AOL using fictitious information and paying a year ahead. In the ensuing months 'lethalpower' became a regular on several of the popular underground pedophile sites, exchanging conversation via instant messenger. His aim was to make 'friends' with people within a several hundred-mile radius of Columbia, Missouri. The conversation turned his stomach, but in order to interact, he had to get down and dirty along with the dirt-bags. He soon discovered that several overseas countries were most favored vacation destinations, mainly third-world nations where officials looked the other way, as long as they got a share of the wealth. Thailand and the Philippines, where sex is sold in legal brothels, and is advertised in many shop windows in a manner similar to how the western world would dress manikins, were the most popular. But the big attraction for lethalpower's new friends to travel that far was hardly hetro- or homo-sexual activity. They wanted kids of both sexes and the younger the better. Luther found that desperate parents in those countries would often sell their children for a week at a time to a broker for $100 USD. Sadly, many of these children contact STD's and are disowned by their families and left to wander the streets. Several of lethalpower's contacts urged him to make a vacation trip where '$1000 would buy you the time of your life'.

Luther wanted to take out as many of these slime balls as he could, but Ray told him to remember Jill, and why they were working her case. Luther set up several meetings in public places, mostly St. Louis and Kansas City with sellers. He always disguised himself with heavy beards and dark glasses, hoping that he could never be identified in the event that things went bad. The only reason he bought the porn was to establish a reputation in that world. Both he and Ray agreed that if he stood up the sellers, word would quickly spread and he would lose all credibility. Ray was always close by and always made mental pictures of the people Luther dealt with as he traded fifty dollars, the going price, for ten of the most sickening photos imaginable.

In late June, Luther met with Ray at Burger King. "I might have good news, Ray. Turns out a guy I've been talking to wants to meet in Columbia. I told him I have some stuff he might be interested in. He said all he was interested in was bagging a young girl. Now get this. He's got a buddy that wants in, too. I casually asked him about how old he was because the chick I know is afraid of old guys; something about how she hated her grandpa. Anyway, this guy tells me both he and his buddy are both under thirty. So I try to get him to send me a picture, but he won't. He's afraid of a police decoy and said he's going to check me out with a few people he knows before they'll meet with me."

Ray frowned. "Could be our guys, but if you can lure them here, we'll need bait for this to work. The only one we can use is Jill and I hate to do that again."

"Why? It's her daughter's killers we're after. You don't think she'll want to help?"

"Yeah, I'm sure she will… Okay, make this tough on them so they don't get suspicious. Tell them a thousand each for an afternoon with a pretty thirteen-year-old. Let 'em talk you down to $1000 for both, but don't give in to soon. We'll leave Jill out in your Explorer where they can get a look at her from a distance. Insist you meet them in a place like McDonalds. Tell them you're afraid of being robbed and of having the girl abducted. Sit by a window, so they can get a peek at Jill without going outside. Then tell them you've got a motel room nearby. That ought to wet their appetites."

"Right. Now, what if these aren't our guys, then what? You want to take them out anyway?"

"Yeah, we'll take 'em out, since they'll only go back and rat us out to their friends."

***

AS MUCH AS HE HATED to do it, Luther sent a picture of a naked young girl that he purchased from another player when the mark insisted on seeing the merchandise. After the negations were completed, the meeting was set for late on a Friday afternoon. When Luther walked into McDonalds, a half hour early, the two men were waiting for him at a corner table in the rear of the restaurant. The store was crowded, but as agreed, both men and Luther wore black baseball caps. Luther recognized both men immediately from the mall photos that Brooke had made from the security tape. He slid into the booth next to one of the men. "You lethalpower?"

"Yeah," Luther answered. "You got something for me?"

One of the men reached into his jacket pocket and pulled out a roll of bills wrapped with a one hundred dollar bill and flashed it toward Luther before putting it back. "Where's the stuff?"

"She's outside in my car."

"Where? I wanna see her."

"You will." Luther pointed to the far window. "She's in the Ford Explorer, wearing a red hooded sweatshirt. But I want my money first." The man opposite Ray got to his feet and walked to the window. When he saw Jill he headed straight for the door. When he reached the Explorer, Jill pretended to lock the doors and as expected the guy ran around the opposite side and swung open the back door. Two things happened in a split second. Ray, sitting on the floor, greeted him with a two-second zap from his stun-gun, immediately immobilizing the man. "Evening, asshole," Ray mumbled.

In seconds Ray bound his hands behind his back with Flex cuffs, and using a short piece of rope tied his feet. He wasn't unconscious, but instead stared blankly ahead as Ray pushed him on the floor. Ray knew it would only be a minute or two before his confederate appeared. A moment later his accomplice walked briskly into the parking lot and up to the SUV. When he saw Jill's face he knew he had been had, but it was too late. When he turned, Luther zapped him and Ray came from behind the vehicle and both men stuffed him into the back seat. Jill jumped from the passenger seat and disappeared into the parking lot. Ray ran around the other side and got in the back while Luther hurriedly jumped into the driver's seat and sped away down Broadway Boulevard. Ray flipped the other guy around, cuffed his hands and pointed the stun-gun at both men. "Make a move boys and you'll get another shot."

Luther made the call Able Brown was waiting for. "We're on our way."

Fifteen minutes later, the two men were shoved into the small crematorium room where they were pushed on the floor and met Jill.

"YOU BASTARDS! Why did you kill my baby?"

One of the men spoke, "We don't know what you're talking about, lady."

Jill shoved the pictures of them leaving the mall with Amy and her friend under their noses. Does this jar your memory?"

"That's not us."

She pulled out the other pictures, the ones with their faces wearing the same clothes. They remained silent. Jill had to ask the question. "Why? And how did you get them to go with you?" Neither man looked up until Ray spoke, "Mr. Brown is going to cremate you two. Now, if you answer the ladies questions, it'll be fast. If you don't, you go in there alive." He nodded toward the furnace.

One of the men sneered. "You better call the police, because, mister, we're gonna sue the balls off of you."

Ray looked at Able Brown. "Open the door, Mr. Brown. This guy just ran out of life." Luther and Ray lifted and shoved the screaming man into the narrow chamber. The mortician closed the door and fired the furnace. Ray looked at the other man. "You gonna sue, too?" When there was no reply, he continued, "Your pal ought to be done in about an hour, friend. Now, you get the same treatment, or like I said, it'll be fast; your choice."

Luther sniffed at the air. "Damn, you shit your pants didn't you? Scared huh? So were those kids when you raped and murdered them. And we're not the ACLU, so we don't care how sorry you are. Now, are you going to answer the ladies questions?"

In a small tearful voice he responded, "We treated them to a few games in the arcade and when they said they were going to the show we talked them into taking a ride in Cliff's Mustang GT. Well, it's his car and he tells the girls we'll get some beer if they want. So, we get a twelve pack and drive to..."

"We know where you drove to," said Jill. "Why did you rape and kill them?"

"They wanted to go back. By then I knew these weren't that kind of girls. They couldn't even finish a beer between them. Cliff and I got out to take a whiz and he says let's tap 'em anyway. I told him that I didn't want any part of that, but he just laughed. A little later, when I was in the back seat, he started choking the chick with the football jersey when she told him no. When she went limp he pulled her pants off and did it."

Jill, standing back listening to the last minutes of her daughter's life finally couldn't take any more as she rushed to the hot crematorium. She banged her hands on the door screaming, "You rotten bastard, burn in hell."

Ray gently led her from the room to an empty upstairs chapel. "It's over, Jill. Now, I want you to calm down and go home. Okay? I'll have Luther drop me at your place when we finish here." She bobbed her head up and down and slowly walked to the door. Ray went back downstairs to finish the job.

When the doomed man saw Ray he tried to bargain for his life. "Look, man, I got money in my pocket. $1200. It's all yours if you let me go. Please, I never touched either one of those girls. Cliff did it all. Please, man, you gotta believe me." Luther rolled him over and took the $1200 from his pocket and looked down.

"Twelve hundred! I'm not even going to count it. We believe you."

"Okay," Ray said. We're gonna put a plastic bag over your head and then drop you off outside of the city. Don't worry, we'll put some air holes in it so you don't suffocate. As Luther slipped the double garbage bags over his head Able Brown stepped out of the room. Ray pulled out his Glock .40 and put two rounds through the man's head. Instead of waiting for the first man's body to be completely cremated Able turned off the gas and Ray, with Luther's help, stuffed his companion in alongside of him. It was done. Jill finally got the closure she needed. This made Ray more determined than ever to have his day.

Chapter 17

As they sat around the table, Brooke opened the meeting. "The heat is on. folks. One of the guys we took out was Clifford Lewsinski, Jr., the son of Deputy Mayor Clifford Lewsinski and he's on the Police Commissioner to find his son."

Ray finished the thought. "And since manure rolls downhill, the case is on everybody's priority list, right?"

"You got it, but that's not all. When they found the Mustang at McDonalds, they pulled the security tapes and got a nice shot of Luther's back leaving with the guy. We did get lucky though, the camera out in the parking lot malfunctioned, so they don't know about Luther's Explorer, and they can't find anyone that saw you guys grab those perverts."

Luther looked at Ray. "Now what do we do?"

"I'm not finished, guys," Brooke said. "The guy that made the pictures from Jill's CD asked me if those were the guys that went missing. Of course I said no, but you know cops. He'll have that in the back of his mind for a long time. Now, for the rest of the bad news, they're looking at all the recent missing person cases and found a trend. Three registered sex offenders are missing and their cars recovered within the city limits in public parking lots. Those last two guys, including the Deputy Mayor's kid, aren't registered and that's why we never found them. But Clifford junior was arrested twice for solicitation of a minor and his pal for exposing himself to a group of high school girls. With his father's political clout, Junior's charges were dropped both times. The other guy was with Junior on one solicitation charge, so his was dropped too. And the high school girls never looked at his face; they were busy looking at something else. So nobody could identify him in a photo lineup."

It was Ray's turn. "Guys, we've accomplished just about everything we set out to do, at least we resolved most of our personal issues."

The Group looked at each other, as Ray continued, "If we keep going, some good detective work will put all of us behind bars. I've been there before and I don't want to go back again. It's time to call it a day."

Brooke spoke, "Ray's right. We've got some very good detectives in this city and when they investigate a case they're like fighting bulldogs and they won't let go until it's solved. And, with the mayor's office involved it's going to be real intense for a long time. I don't know if any of them suspect I know anything, but guys, it's been quiet around the water cooler lately and I don't dare use police resources for any of our purposes until this blows over."

Everyone stood and Dee hugged Ray as she cried softly. "Thank you, Raymond. I'll pray for you." Luther gave him a man hug and shook his hand at the same time. "You are my brother, Ray. Just call me and I'll come, anytime anyplace."

Brooke hugged him next. "We couldn't have done any of this without you, Brooke," Ray mumbled.

She pulled back slightly. "Whenever you need help, just call and I'll see what I can do. I have a lot of contacts with other law enforcement agencies and I'll always do what I can."

"Thanks, I will."

After the others left, only Jill was left. She embraced Ray and held him for a long time as she whispered in his ear, "I'll always be grateful for what you did for me. You gave me my life back, and now Amy can sleep in peace."

Ray wasn't thinking about any of the things he'd done for the others. He was thinking about Elizabeth and Cory. Tears sprang to his eyes as he thought about why he entered into this world of violence and death. Yes, he helped other people, but he was still at square one in his search and he vowed he would never stop until he found Robert Morgan and got justice for what he had done to his family.

When Jill stepped back and looked into Ray's face she realized he hadn't heard her, he was alone with his own thoughts. "Ray?... Raymond?"

His head jerked as if coming out of a hypnotic trance. "What was that, hun?"

"What about us? Does it end here?" Ray looked away in an unconscious effort to stall for time, but Jill wanted answers. "Raymond, I'm in love with you. Under all that anger is the man I want to spend the rest of my life with. Do you love me?"

He looked deep into her eyes. " I'm not sure. I think I do, a little."

"A little! Do you somehow think you'd betray your dead wife if you loved again, because if she was the kind of woman I think she was, you're wrong? Did you know that I've had a lot of offers to date, but I always turn them down because I'm waiting for you. Am I wasting my time, Raymond?"

"I guess you can go out with a guy if you want to."

"If I want to! I've waited a long time for you. I know you still go to that "Hallo Cub" to find woman. I understand that, but now it's time for you to get on with your life. If you continue hating so much you'll wind up in prison again."

He took her in his arms. "Jill, give me a little more time. I really do care about you and no, I don't want you going out with other guys. But until I resolve this thing, I can't commit to anything."

She leaned back in his arms. "Okay. But I'm in this with you, all the way. Agreed?"

He looked down on her. "Okay, agreed." The deal was sealed with a warm kiss.

***

SEVERAL WEEKS LATER as the University Of Missouri Tigers football team filed into the locker room, one of the players, wearing a sweat and grass-stained #72 white, practice uniform, spotted the man he'd been looking for installing a new electric motor on one of the whirlpool tubs. "Excuse me, Mr. Rusk. My name is John Blackburn and I'd like to talk to you for a minute."

Rusk looked up into the sweaty face that hovered over him. "Well, maybe if you'd give a guy a little room to stand up...."

"Excuse me, sir," John said as he stepped back.

"Now, what'd you want?"

"Mr. Rusk." Rusk winced whenever addressed as Mr., but didn't interrupt. "I was here a couple of months ago and saw you working with another man. Can you tell me who he is?"

"Son, I'm in here a lot and I've got eight men working for me. That could have been any one of them, or it may have been a contractor." Rusk recognized the name right away, but didn't want to give up any information without talking with Ray first. "You say your name is Blackbird?"

"John Blackburn, Mr. Rusk. Johnny Ray Blackburn."

"What'd they call you, boy?"

"JR or Blackie, but most call me John."

"Tell you what. I'll mention you to my crew and see if anybody knows you. Who do you think you saw?"

As he walked away Johnny Ray called over his shoulder, "My father."

After the team showered and left, Rusk went into the coaches' office and called Ray. "I think you better come over here. We need to talk."

"You got a problem, Rusk?"

"No, you do."

On the short drive over to the football stadium Ray tried to think about what could be wrong. The first and only thing he could think of was something to do with the Group, but he dismissed that thought, it wouldn't be Rusk calling on the phone, it would be detectives flashing gold plated badges.

When Ray pulled up to the gate, Rusk was waiting for him.

"You caught up over at the hospital?"

"Pretty much," Ray answered.

"Good. Let's go downtown and get a beer."

"In the University truck?"

"Would you rather walk?"

"You're serious. Okay, get in."

Twenty minutes later as they started on their second large draught, Ray looked at Rusk. "You didn't bring me down here to talk about how hot it is and how good a cold beer tastes. What's going on?"

"A kid that came by today while I was working in the locker room thought he recognized you."

"What kid?"

"A football player. One of the new ones. He's a scholarship freshman out of Chicago. Saw that on the coach's desk."

"So how does the kid think he knows me?" Ray laughed. "I haven't been to Chicago in a lot of years."

"Says his name is Johnny Ray Blackburn and he thinks you're his father."

Ray's mouth fell open as he mumbled, "Huh?"

"If you don't want to see the kid I can tell him he must have seen a contractor and that I have no idea who he saw. Or, if you want to see him, just come down after practice. Think it over and let me know, but don't take to long, that boy seems like a nice kid and I don't want to string him along."

"Thanks, I won't."

There was no doubt in Ray's mind that the John Raymond Blackburn that asked about him was his son. The next two days he struggled with the decision he need-ed to make and unable to decide, asked Jill.

Jill beamed. "I didn't know you had another son. Of course you should meet with him. Why wouldn't you?"

"He probably hates me for abandoning him. What could I possibility say?"

"Tell him that you love him and that you want him back in your life. That's what you tell him." He thought for a moment and then looked at Jill.

"God I'm nervous. Would you go with me?"

The Justice Club

She smiled and embraced him, finally feeling a part of his life. "Of course I will."

Rusk set the meeting up for the following evening at the "Blue Cat Supper Club." Ray and Jill got there early for the eight o'clock dinner and left word with the maître'd that they were expecting John Blackburn. Ray wore a sport jacket with an open collar and Jill wore a modest blue dress that did little to hide her natural beauty. When the waiter greeted them they both ordered drinks, Ray, a glass of tap beer and Jill, a Bloody Mary. Even as they exchanged small talk, both glanced over at the reception area watching for Johnny Ray. After a brief wait they saw a tall, athletic-looking young man, dressed in a sports coat and tie, walk up to the matre'd.

Ray never hesitated as he bolted from his chair, rushing past the tables to embrace his son. Not sure what to do, Jill simply stood by the table until father and son walked smiling, back towards her. Both men wiped tears from their eyes as the past flashed through their minds. "Jill, this is my son John." Jill reached out and gripped John's hand momentarily. "John, this is my very dear friend. Jill."

Jill felt uncomfortable, intruding on such a private moment and decided to excuse herself. "You two have a lot of catching up to do. I'll just grab a cab. Enjoy your dinner."

As Jill turned to walk away, Ray gently, but firmly, held her arm. "No way, girl. You're part of this now. I want you to stay. We'll have plenty of time later to talk. I'd really like to keep it upbeat, at least for tonight."

Johnny agreed. "Sounds good, Dad."

- 163 -

Ray grinned. "It's been a long time since I heard those words. They sound strange, but good. So tell me son, how'd you ever get here?" Johnny Ray shrugged.

"I guess I'm a pretty good football player. Anyway, I got a lot of offers from big schools. I chose Columbia because I knew it wasn't far from where we lived and I thought it would make me feel closer to...you know, you and Mom and Cory. And, I think I want to be a journalist and everyone says that Mizzou is the best, so here I am."

"I wanna hear all about you growing up. You stayed with Martha and Jim, right?"

"Yes. Aunt Martha is great, Dad. I love her as much as I love you. But Jim is an asshole." He looked at Jill. "Excuse me, ma'am, that just slipped out."

She patted his hand. "That's okay, John."

When the waiter returned, he asked if they would like another drink or if they were they ready to order. Ray looked at Johnny. Would you like a drink, son?"

John grinned. "Dad, I'm not old enough, and besides I'm in training."

Ray looked at Jill. "A refill, hun?"

Jill felt on top of the world when Ray referred to her in such a personal manner in front of his son. "No, thank you."

Ray looked at the waiter and read from his nametag. "Carlo, unless my son wants something, I guess we're ready to order. The waiter repeated the nightly specials from memory and then looked at Jill with his order pad and pencil ready. "Are you ready, ma'am?"

"The breaded tenderloin with a double-baked potato, with the salad bar, please."

"Thank you, ma'am."

He then looked to Ray. "The 12oz. Kansas City sirloin, medium, baked potato, and the salad bar."

"Thank you, sir."

While he was still writing Johnny added, "Same thing for me."

When he finished writing he mumbled, "Thank you." and turned away.

John looked at his father. "I had a long talk with Aunt Martha a couple of months ago, after I saw you. She said she'd tell me everything she knew about you and mother, and I think she did."

"Like what?" Ray asked.

"About how much trouble you had with mom's family..." He paused and lowered his voice. "About my birth and all."

"What all?"

"Dad, she told me about my brother."

"Then you know we tried to get him back?"

"Yeah, I know. Do you think we could ever find him?"

"I don't know how. We tried hard for a long time and got nowhere. When they say the records are sealed, they mean it. Even after a couple of years, when we knew we'd never get him back, we still tried to find him just to see that he was alright. To her dying day mom always blamed herself, even though I told her not to."

John hesitated briefly. "Mom and Cory are buried in St. Charles, in mom's church cemetery. At least what they found of them is buried there. I'd like to go. Will you go with me?"

"Of course."

The rest of the meal's conversation consisted of lighter subject matter, about Ray's job and Mizzou football.

Jill added little to the conversation, but felt privileged to be included in Ray's most personal moment.

Chapter 18

Two weeks later, on a Sunday afternoon, Ray and Johnny Ray drove the 125 miles to St. Charles. The ride down was mostly in silence, as each man had his own thoughts for company. It was a hot August day and the cemetery was empty. After walking the rows of neatly kept graves, John stopped when he found a white, marble stone, bearing the name of his mother and little brother. When Ray, looking down a different row saw John fall to his knees, he rushed to his son's side. John stood and embraced his father for several minutes as both wept openly and unashamed.

Finally Ray spoke, "They buried them together. I'm glad."

John ignored his father. "Mother, Cory, I'm so sorry for what I did. I promise you that that monster's blood will flow before I die. I will find and punish him. I promise."

Ray looked at his son. "Johnny, neither your mother, Cory, or I blame you for anything that happened and I know mom would never want you to spoil your life with this. That bastard did enough to our family; let me handle it. Please, son, I know what I'm doing."

Ray looked at the grave and then at Johnny Ray. "I promise all of you that he will be held accountable." His voice lowered to a whisper, "I promise."

On the ride back Ray told his son about prison and his life after, including the sanctions he did with the Justice Club. "I have no regrets. I only wish our guy was one of them, but his day will come. I won't quit until I find him. Meanwhile, I want you to study hard and do the football thing. Jill's in this too, and she'll help all she can."

"Dad, when you find him I need to be there. Please, that's important to me."

"We'll see," Ray whispered.

***

THE NEXT DAY RAY called Attorney-At-Law Anthony Drazza.

"I planned to call you later today, Mr. Blackburn. Morgan's lawyer convinced a liberal judge in San Francisco to allow a name change when he argued that Morgan couldn't live a normal life because of the publicity in your case. His new name is William Gorman and he got a passport in that name eleven years ago and left the country. We know he landed in Vancouver, British Columbia, but we don't know if he stayed there or connected to another flight. What we do know is he never came back into the country, at least not legally. We know that because he never reregistered as a convicted sex offender and if he's caught in the country without doing that, he'll go to jail. But, getting back wouldn't be much of a problem. All he has to do is show some sort of ID that he lives in the United States and he's back. Sorry, I can't tell you more, but even this wasn't easy to come by. This guy's as lost as an Easter egg."

"Thanks, Mr. Drazza, I really appreciate your efforts. I'll give you my address so you can send me a bill for your trouble and expenses."

"Mr. Blackburn, Ray, I didn't help you for a fee, and if I did, you'd go broke trying to pay me. I used up a lot of favors and I'm indebted to a lot of folks over this, but you need to know that not all of the legal community is heartless. This certainly falls short of what society owes you, but please accept my help as a small down payment."

"What can I say, Mr. Drazza? Thanks."

"You're welcome, Ray; good hunting."

When the line went dead Ray looked at the telephone and gently hung it up. He was beginning to realize that the whole world wasn't out for itself and that was a good feeling.

Ray assumed "lethalpower" as his internet name, a name that Luther made well known in the world of porn. His hope was to enter general conversation in an open chat room and to lure a prospect into a private room where hopefully he could get a lead on the elusive Robert Morgan. He had two target areas, St. Louis and Vancouver, British Columbia.

While setting this up, Johnny was kept abreast of the effort and asked questions frequently. "Dad, why aren't we looking into taxidermists? Or have you?"

"What in the world would a taxidermist have to do with anything?"

"Nobody ever told you did they? That's what Morgan does. It was in the news accounts?"

"I never read any newspapers about him. I was in jail and they kept me in isolation. I never saw a paper... Tell me more."

"There isn't a whole lot to tell. Aunt Martha kept me away from all of this until a couple of months ago when I told her about seeing you. Then I got to read all the news clippings she saved and according to the paper they found several animals in various stages of processing, and a drugstore full of chemicals that taxidermists use in that guy's basement."

"Is that what he did for a living?"

"I don't know, but before he got caught molesting kids, he was an elementary school, physical education teacher and at the time he lived by us, the only income he claimed was from unemployment benefits and food stamps."

"Did it say where he taught?"

"Yeah, it was Haywood Elementary School in Columbia. I remember because we played them in football

Ray thought for a moment while he digested the information. "He had to have some kind of earned income after his conviction to be eligible for unemployment benefits and we know it wasn't from teaching school. Did the papers say anything about that?"

"No. They didn't say."

Ray smiled and patted his son on the back. "This is very good information, John. Well done."

Neither said the obvious about why that demented sick man saved the heads of his victims, but his intention was clear and if possible, that only added to their resolve.

Ray rationalized that if they could get Robert Morgan's Social Security number, then maybe Brooke could find out what kind of work he did after being fired from the school. Since it would take a court order for Social Security to provide that information, it was decided that Jill would visit Haywood Elementary School and ask to see his employee file. It was also decided that Jill would impersonate a Columbia police detective instead of Ray. The logic was, that if Ray was caught and arrested, he would be sent back to prison for a long time, while Jill, in all probability, would receive a slap on the wrist.

"This could be dangerous, Jill. Are you sure you want to do this?"

"I'm sure. Look, Ray, we've been over this a hundred times. I show the badge and the picture ID without being asked."

"Don't hold the ID out too long, but let 'em see the detective badge all they want. That computer-generated ID is a long way from perfect, but at a long glance it'll do. The main thing you need to do is take charge. Don't bully anybody, but make it plain that this matter is official police business and that their cooperation is both expected and appreciated."

She smiled. "I bluffed that guy at the mall. I can do the same thing at the school."

"There's a big difference." He worried. "This time you're impersonating a police officer."

***

THE NEXT DAY JILL took off early in the afternoon on the pretense of having a dentist appointment. It was Friday and she knew that most, if not all of the higher school officials had already left to get an early start on the weekend and that since all of the urgent school business would have been dealt with by this late on a Friday, only low level clerks would be left.

Jill wore a dark-blue pants suit with a light-blue blouse. Her hair was pulled back tight into a ponytail and the only jewelry she wore was plain silver earrings. The bulge under her jacket on her right hip completed the look.

When she walked into the principal's outer office a smiling older woman looked up from her desk. "May I help you?"

Jill flipped open a black, leather billfold with the ID on one half and the Detective badge on the other and held it up. As she spoke she slid her thumb over the ID but displayed the badge for several seconds. "I'm Detective Razzlo, ma'am, and I need to see the file on one of your past employees, Robert Morgan."

"I'm not sure if... could you come back Monday?"

Pretending impatience Jill explained, "No, I can't come back Monday. I'm here now and this is official police business."

"Well, I'm not authorized to..."

"Look, lady, I'm doing a criminal investigation and unless you don't want me to arrest you for obstruction of justice, you need to cooperate. I'm not asking you to do anything illegal; this type of information is routinely provided to us. Furthermore, I'm not taking the records with me. I just need to look at them."

"Uh, I guess if you're just looking it'd be alright."

That evening Jill called Brooke. "I'm sorry to bother you with this, but could you check out this guy Robert Morgan with the Department Of Unemployment. We need to see what he did after he got fired from Haywood Elementary School and who he worked for. We've got his Social Security number which should make it a lot easier."

"It will. I'll check it out."

"That won't be a problem, will it?"

"It shouldn't be. We work with those folks a lot."

A week later Jill read from the report that Brooke faxed to her at the University.

"Seems as though he wasn't allowed to get work anywhere around kids after he did his stint in Fulton."

Ray's head snapped up. "He did time in Fulton?" Memories of his prison time at the same institution played in his mind.

"Yes, eighteen months," Jill quietly replied. "When he worked, he did construction. There are a lot of holes in his employment record. Apparently, this guy didn't work very steady."

"Does it say what kind of construction work he did?"

"No, but on his claim forms it has the kind of jobs he applied for, all construction laborer." She looked at Ray. "With his education you'd think he could do better than that."

Ray chuckled. "Do you have any idea what a construction laborer makes an hour?" She shook her head no.

"Around the big cities it's about $33 an hour. If a laborer works steady he makes a nice living. Over 65 grand a year without overtime, skilled craftsman make even more."

Jill ignored the lecture on construction pay scales. "Now what? All we know is that he went to Canada twelve years ago. With your money, maybe he never went back to work."

"Maybe he didn't for a while, but eventually he'd have to find a job. The question is what and where."

"Do you think he found a job teaching in Canada?"

"I don't know, but if I can get the time off, I'm going up there to see if I can find out."

***

EARLY THE NEXT MORNING, RAY met Rusk in the hospital cafeteria. Before he had a chance to ask about a two-week leave, his boss dropped a bombshell. "We got a problem. One of the doctors saw that swastika on your neck and turned it in to the hospital board. They contacted the University Offices and they went through your employment application and found out about the time you served. Now, they're going to hold a hearing on whether to dismiss you on the grounds that you're an undesirable. I wrote a letter explaining why you're inked, but so far I haven't heard anything back."

Ray rubbed his neck. "I should have had this removed a long time ago. I always tried to wear collared shirts, but I guess somebody saw me in a tee."

He paused for a moment and realized that even if the board decided to keep him, it would never approve his leave. He stood and offered his hand. "Thanks for all you did for me, Rusk. But if that's how it is, I'm out of here."

Rusk, ignoring his hand, stood and embraced Ray. "It doesn't have to end like this. We can fight it."

Ray patted him on the back. "No. I've got other things to do and I don't need this in my face."

***

THAT EVENING Ray sat across from John Mullio, owner of The Hallo Club and his former boss. "I'm ready to put in some work, Mr. Mullio, if you still want me."

John Mullio took out a thick cigar, moistened it in his mouth and lit it. He looked around the nearly deserted club and finally spoke, "You know, Ray, things have been really good. We're expanding and of course that means we can always use good help. And to answer your question, yeah, I got work for you. I got a crew working in Jefferson City and right now they're a bit short handed. Interested?"

"Yes, sir."

"Good. Here's the deal. Some of our business ac-quaintances are showing appreciation for... let's say, some past favors. A couple of months ago I was invited to a sit down and they offered me a little piece of a new territory. I guess you know how the system works. When you're allowed to do business, you kick upstairs to the next level. We're somewhere in the middle of the ladder." He leaned towards Ray in an unconscious effort to emphasize the importance of this information. "This isn't entry level. Your work will be much more substantial and so will the pay. The only reason I am offering you this opportunity is because I trust you and believe you'll be loyal to me. I hope I'm not wrong."

"No, Mr. Mullio, you're not wrong. One thing though, I'm still working on finding the guy that killed my family and from time to time I'll need a little time off. Will that be a problem?"

Mullio smiled and leaned back. "No, that's not a problem. You'll work with the crew, but only answer to me. I've got an issue with some locals and I'm putting you in charge of that."

"What's the deal?"

"My new place, "Club 54" is a play on the highway that runs through the city. It's pretty much the same oper-ation as this place, strippers, a little live entertainment, and our main thing, gambling and short term loans."

"Mr.Mullio, I don't know anything about running a nightclub."

"You won't be. I'll be working between both clubs; they're only a half hour apart. Don't worry, I'm sure you can handle what I'm giving you, or I wouldn't be making this offer."

Ray offered his hand across the table.

That sounds great, Mr. Mullio. I won't disappoint you."

"Good. Now here's the deal. We got a gang of Latino's that want to push drugs through the club and won't take no for an answer. Drugs bring heat and we got a few public officials sitting on the fence about working with us. There's a lot of money in dealing, but a lot of grief too. That's why I gave it a pass. The average guy doesn't care about a little prostitution or gambling in his town, but he doesn't want his fifteen-year-old daughter strung out on drugs. And that, Ray, is what's called negative public opinion. These guys are vicious. They wrecked the club a couple of weeks ago, beat up the bartenders, and took two of our girls to their clubhouse and raped them."

Ray set his jaw in a determined manner. "I can take care of that."

"I don't think you understand. I don't want a war. I just need this problem to go away."

"I understand, Mr. Mullio. Give me a couple of weeks and I'll have it taken care of."

***

RAY DEALT WITH gangs before, when he was in prison. And he knew that the only thing that they respected was power, and violence was power. He understood that he would probably have to kill to accomplish this mission, but that didn't bother him. He killed before, for the Whites, and he killed for himself. And if he clipped a couple of sewer rats, so what?

A week later he had the background he needed on the "Tulley Street Gang." They were independent and didn't kick upstairs to anybody. That would make it easier, Ray reasoned. He wouldn't have to deal with any of the strong street gangs infecting the United States. He thought about making an example out of one of the bangers selling outside of the club, but instead, decided to talk first.

Ten o'clock that evening, a guy sat in a red Lexus SUV in the parking lot of Club 54. Ray walked up just behind the driver's window with his Glock semi-automatic in his left hand behind his back. As he leaned forward the man rolled down the window. "What's your pleasure, amigo?"

Ray put the Glock to the man's head. "Put both hands on the steering wheel, and do it very slowly."

With the cold steel of the semi-automatic pressing into his temple, the man offered no resistance. In a heavily Mexican-accented voice he warned, "You don't know what you're doing, bro. This money and merchandise belongs to Tulley Street. That's major grief for you. Just walk away and I'll forget all about this."

As he yanked open the door Ray ordered, "Shut up and get out, hands first... Now put your hands on the roof and take a step back...spread you feet." After patting him down Ray pulled a semi-automatic from the man's shoulder holster. As he looked at the Glock model 22 he remarked, "My brand. Okay, lock the car; we're going for a walk."

Several minutes later, after entering a back door to the club, they were sitting opposite each other in the back office. Ray stared hard at his prisoner as he popped the clip from the Glock 22 and ejected the round from the chamber. He slid the gun across the desk.

"What's your name?"

"Jose, man, and you're in some deep shit, amigo."

"First off, I'm not you amigo. Second, you're stepping on my toes and I'm giving you a chance to get out of my world."

"You got some stones, mister. I don't think you realize what you're doing."

Ray ignored the obvious threat. "I wanna meet with your leader. I believe that's Big Six, Mr. Juan Swarze. He's your main homeboy, right?"

"He'll step on you like an ant."

"You know, you're starting to piss me off. Keep it up and I'll get another errand boy to deliver my message...You do wanna go home tonight?"

Jose didn't reply. His bluff wasn't working and he didn't need to die over this. Big Six would take care of this wise guy, he was sure of that.

"You can tell Mr. Swarze that this time he's not dealing with college bartenders or women. I know how to play rough too. I'd rather work this out, but if he won't work with me, I'll give him more grief than he's ever had to deal with."

"He'll tell you to fuck off, mister."

"Look, asshole, I didn't ask for your opinion. Just tell him."

Ray scribbled the phone number of his new Trac Fone on the back of a Club 54 business card. "Tell him he can call me at this number and we'll set something up."

As the man rose he picked up his Glock and put it in his shoulder holster, then looked at the card. "I'll tell him."

When he turned to go, Ray issued a warning. "If I find anybody selling around here again, they won't go home. Do we understand each other?"

"I'll tell him."

After updating John Mullio, Ray offered his opinion. "Either they'll arrange a meeting with the idea of taking me out, or maybe they'll come back in force and wreck the club again."

"Maybe, Ray, but they may just try to do business as usual. Only this time nobody will walk up and get the drop on them. I still prefer to handle this without a major incident."

"We got enough people staying at the club around closing time to stop anything and the police have assigned a car to sit there at night. I think we're covered. If they can't do business, I expect a call. And if they come back, we'll scratch the salesman."

"Okay, keep me posted."

For a week nothing happened. No phone call and no pushers, but on a busy Friday night, with the parking lot full, a man started doing business out of a white Monte Carlo. After no word from Big Six, Ray knew it was just a matter of time before a showdown occurred. He knew the pusher wouldn't be alone and when word reached him, he had people walking through the lot pretending to look for their cars. Two men were spotted parked in the row behind and several cars down in a GMC Tahoe. Ray sent four men, dressed in yellow parking vests and packing plenty of heat to run them off. After a brief confrontation the GMC slowly exited the lot. Ray approached the Monte Carlo from behind, before any phone messages could warn the seller. When the man saw him approach in the side mirror he half turned in his seat and rolled down the window. It was the last thing he ever did as two 9mm slugs ripped his head open. Ray wiped the semi-automatic clean and threw it in the car. Two minutes later a tow truck lifted the Monte Carlo onto its winch and drove away. Ray had no idea where the truck went, but he knew that car and gun would never be seen again. He also knew he'd be meeting Big Six.

An hour later the Trac Fone bought especially for the purpose of dealing with the Tulley Street gang rang. Ray let it ring several times before answering. "Yeah."

"Listen you motherfucker, if anything happens to Pablo you're dead. Do you hear me?"

"I assume this is Big Six."

"You damn right it is."

"Now you listen. Pablo's telling God how sorry he is for all his sins right about now. I warned you. Now you have a choice, either work this out with me or lose some more homeboys. Your choice."

Big Six paused for a moment. He decided to meet and rid himself of this enemy once and for all. "Okay, when and where?"

"I'll let you know. Call me Monday morning at ten sharp and don't send anybody else around Club 54 until we talk. If you do I'll consider it an act of war. By the way, I'm going by your rules, so don't fuck with me." With that he hung up.

Ray called in the crew he was working with. "Don't let up. That maggot is capable of anything....We've gone over this enough, any questions?... Okay. Get everything ready Sunday night and I'll meet with him Monday. Make sure everything is done right, guys, or I'm a dead man."

***

MONDAY MORNING at exactly ten, Ray answered the cell phone. "Six?"

"Yeah, it's me."

"You know where Saint Jude Catholic Church is?"

"I guess I do. My wife and kids go there."

Ray smiled to himself. "I'm sitting in the middle of the church right now and I've got some people watching my back. Meet me here; you got ten minutes."

"What the hell are you doing in a church? That ain't no place to meet."

"Just be here and use the side door up front, I don't wanna get strangled from behind."

"Are you serious, man? That's a church."

Ray was pretty sure that even a violent gang like Tully Street wouldn't desecrate a church, especially a Catholic one.

Eleven minutes later a huge figure walked in from the side door of the church. Ray chuckled as the man dipped his forefinger into the holy water font and made the sign of the cross. When Six spotted Ray he walked to the pew and genuflected before entering and sitting. He looked at Ray. "I don't like this. Let's go somewhere else."

"Where? Your clubhouse?"

"Look, man, I don't like doing business in the house of the Lord."

"Then just listen, because I'm going to tell you how it is. First off, your family guarantees my safety. My people picked up your two kids on the way to school. Don't worry, they're fine and they'll stay that way, as long as I do. If you don't believe me, look at this." He pulled out his cell phone and played back a video showing the children watching cartoons in front of a large screen television."

"If you hurt those kids I swear…"

"Chill! The kids are fine and unless you get stupid, they'll stay that way."

"What kind of people are you, messing with my kids?"

"The same kind you are. Your rules, remember? I know what you're capable of."

"Okay, what?"

"Let's go outside, unless you got some homeys waitin' for me."

Six pulled out his cell phone and punched in a number. "It's me, back off... Yeah, I'm sure. Go home... everybody. I got it covered."

As he exited the pew, Six again genuflected, and when he left the church he re-blessed himself. Ray chuckled and thought about how screwed up the world was.

"There's a little coffee shop across the street. Wanna grab a cup?" Six said.

"Sure."

Over coffee Ray laid it out. "Look , Juan, all the big hitters are on my team and I have organization behind me. You might win a battle or two, but I promise you'll lose the war. And if you think we can't get to you, think about this, underneath your car is a fake bomb. Four red road flares, wrapped with duct tape. We even put a detonator on it and if you don't believe me I'll show you when we leave. All I need to do is place a call and it's activated. Instead of flares it could be dynamite. Then puff, no more you."

"Alright" Big Six said. "What's the bottom line?"

"Stay away from our club with drugs. If you got other business there, come see me first. We don't do pills or powder, it brings too much heat. At least we're not into it at this time. I don't know about the future. That's not up to me."

"I can live with that."

"Good. The other thing, you owe us street tax."

"Street tax," screamed Six.

"Look, Six, if you wanna play ball with the big guys, step up to the plate. You kick up five percent of your gross and in return you get your territory protected, our goodwill, and access to our contacts. That could keep you and a lot of your boys out of jail. Just don't abuse the privilege; it's not a get out of jail card free card. I'm not even sure about five, but I'll push hard for you." Ray picked up his coffee and took a long swallow. "Well?"

"I'll have to think about it."

"While you're thinking, let's go look at your car and I'll show you that I mean business."

They walked the long block in silence, each with his own thoughts. Six looking for a way out and Ray thinking about his life and what brought him to this point. When they reached the classic 1970 Chrysler Imperial, Six reached underneath and pulled the fake bomb off the frame and laid it in the street. Ray took out his cell phone and punched in a number, pushed send and watched as the detonator ignited the fuse with a loud bang. Ray then looked at Six. "Satisfied?"

Six stuck out his hand. "Deal!"

"Good. My people will drop your kids off at school in about half an hour."

Later that day John Mullio grinned as Ray recounted the story. "Ray, that's great. Just getting him off our back would have been enough, but taxing him is unbelievable. Great work."

"Mr. Mullio, after we get the small print taken care of with Tully Street, would it be possible to have some time off? I've got a lead and need to go to Vancouver, Canada."

"I don't see why not. Take a vacation and take that girlfriend with you."

Chapter 19

Johnny Ray found school challenging. With football and his 'job' there were not enough hours in each day. But with his father back in his life he was as happy as he could ever hope to be. The Missouri Tigers were under-rated in national surveys; at least that's what football insiders thought. And although some freshman practiced with the varsity, most were not included on the playing roster. Johnny Ray Blackburn was the exception. After two games, the crowd liked his aggressive play at middle linebacker so much that when he made a tackle they'd shout "BLACKIE." They shouted that a lot in his first season. The team did so well that they were invited to participate in the "Coors Bowl" in Denver, Colorado on New Year's Eve. Their opponent, Texas State, ranked #7 in the country.

The Mizzou Tigers practiced hard for several weeks before the bowl game, with only two light workouts scheduled at Denver's Mile High Stadium on the two days preceding the game. Texas State had the morning practice the first day and as a few stragglers left the home team locker room Johnny Ray walked past them with a group of Missouri Tigers. One of the opposing players stopped in front of him. "Forget something, Chas?"

"What?"

"Where are you going? That's the enemy you're walking with, man."

Johnny Ray thought that this was an attempt to get inside of his head before the big game and grinned as he walked by. "I forgot the keys to my Benz."

***

WHILE RAY WAS keeping busy with Club 54 Jill assumed the identity of "lethalpower" but since several internet posters suddenly disappeared from their world, porn site members were extremely cautious about accepting anyone they didn't know personally. Jill realized that this would be a slow process before it bore any fruit, but she was patient and decided on a ruse. At times she counterfeited names of-well known posters, hoping to lure information that would be useful at a later date. It was easy. She joined the various sites using a familiar screen name and when filling out the profile information, simply used a capital I instead of the lower case l, a change seldom noticed. An example of this type of change would be "bIuesman" instead of "bluesman."

***

THE ONLY place where Ray's true identity was known was the University Human Resources Department and that information was buried in a maze of computer files. He used the name Raymond Black and that's how all of his identification read. Besides Jill, only Rusk and John Mullio knew his true name. The name change proved to be a good thing, since many Americans are stopped at the Canadian border where authorities check criminal and driving records. Even a convicted drunken driver is denied entry into the country.

When Ray left St. Louis's Lambert Field the late January temperature was 14F. Five hours later when he landed at Vancouver International Airport is was –17F at noon. After renting a four-wheel drive Toyota Rav-4, and with the help of a city map, he drove to the Government operated Labour Employment Bureau, reasoning that that would be the logical choice for a foreigner to find work. This whole trip was a long shot since twelve years had passed since Robert Morgan, alias William Gorman fled to Canada, but if he did look for work, this would proba-bly be his first stop. Before leaving home he decided not to use the fake detective badge, instead choosing to im-personate an attorney looking for the beneficiary of a wealthy estate. He reasoned that all government offices work only through official channels and he knew that what he was attempting was not only unethical, but illegal as well. When he walked into the building it was late af-ternoon and only a few applicants were sitting at the long tables, filling out paper work. He walked up to the recep-tion desk wearing a big smile. "Good afternoon, ma'am."

A chubby girl in her mid-twenties looked up. Her expression was hard and unfriendly. "What can I do for you?"

Ray reached into his shirt pocket and produced a business card that Jill made on her computer. He handed it to her. "Edward Egnever, Miss, and I need to see the person in charge, please." He watched her face as she read from the card. It didn't change.

Edward Egnever

Attorney at Law

12 South Dearborn St. Chicago Ill.

312-264-5545

"So you're a lawyer, what'd you want?" Immediately Ray stereotyped her as a smart-mouthed bitch and real-ized he needed to get tough. As she tried to hand his card back he replied, "I guess I stuttered. Get your boss....now. This is an important matter."

His tone frightened her and she immediately rose and walked to an inner office where a moment later an elderly man wearing a dark-blue suit and holding the business card followed her to where Ray stood. The man glanced at the card. "Mr. Egnever, would you follow me, please?"

When they were seated the man spoke across a generic gray desk. "My name is Ronald Savor, I'm the Office Constable. What can I do for you today?"

"Please, call me Edward, Mr. Savor. Now, I'm an estate attorney and I'm looking for William Gorman and I have reason to believe that he registered with this service, but it has been a number of years. Mr. Gorman is a very wealthy man, only at this time he doesn't even know it. You see, sir, he was estranged from his mother and she recently passed away leaving a sizable estate and a will naming him, her only child, as sole beneficiary. She was a retired school administrator and made many successful investments. She lived alone and very modestly, and nobody knew how wealthy she was. I'm not sure she even knew, but her accountant did and he hired me to find William before the State of Illinois confiscates her assets."

Ray reached into his pocket and produced an obituary from The Chicago Tribune dated several months earlier. That was Jill's idea, and from the look on Ronald Savor's face, a convincing one. After he read about Mary Louise Gorman and her only living relative, he looked up. "Edward, we're not allowed to give out that information. I'm sorry."

"Mr. Savoy, I'll find Mr. Gorman with or without your help, but if you could just tell me if he was here and what type of work he applied for I'd be extremely grateful and willing to show my appreciation."

"Look, Mr. Egnever, the government runs a point man through this office every now and then looking for cracks in the system. I'm close to retiring and don't need to get fired for taking a bribe."

"Sir, I'm not trying to bribe you. Call my office if you don't believe me." Thoughts of the message he put on his Trac Fone flashed through his mind. The same Trac Fone he used with The Tully Street gang. Ronald Savoy picked up the telephone and dialed the number from the fake business card. He put the phone on speaker and hung up the receiver. They both listened as it rang six times before voice mail activated.

"Thank you for calling the office of Edward Egnever. I'm unable to take your call at this time but if you'll leave..."

After he pushed the phone button ending the call Savoy looked at Ray. "I'll help you, but not because I'm looking for anything. I'd hate to see the government get some working stiffs inheritance. Is that clear?"

"Yes, sir."

He turned to his computer. "What's the guy's last name."

"Gorman."

In a matter of seconds a long list of Gorman's popped up. "First name."

"William."

After entering the information he looked at Ray. "We got a lot of William Gormans. I need more information. Where was he born and is he a Canadian citizen?"

"He was born in the States. Missouri I think, but I'm not sure, and he's not a citizen of this country. If it would help, I have his American Social Security number."

"We don't use that." After several minutes Savoy looked up. "Did he do construction work?"

"Yes. I'm pretty sure that's the type of work he was looking for."

"Okay. I've got him applying for a school custodian, but he didn't wait for a background check." He looked up. "We don't allow just anybody to work in our schools."

Ray bobbed his head in agreement. "Good idea."

After scrolling for a moment Savoy looked up. "Here we go. Mr. Gorman went to work for The Pacific Construction Company in April of 1996. I realize it's been a while, but that's the last we have on him. I'll write down the address for you."

Ray wanted to show his gratitude, but was careful not to insult the man. "Are you a married man, Mr. Savoy?"

Ronald Savoy grinned. "Forty-three years this Saturday and to the same woman."

Ray leaned forward. "Would you do me just one more favor?" He reached into his shirt pocket and produced two crisp 100 dollar bills. "Would you take your wife out to dinner? Please? You saved me a lot of footwork and this is just a small business expense."

The man thought for a moment and took the bills from Ray's hand.

Well, if it's an anniversary present, I guess I can accept it."

Ray stood and, after thanking Savoy, drove to a downtown hotel where he stayed until morning. He did call Jill and told her of the success he had. The next morning he drove to the offices of The Pacific Construction

Company, located a short distance from the Port Of Vancouver. When he asked to see the manager, a short stout man with thinning, gray hair in his early fifties appeared. By his demeanor Ray could tell he was a "no-shit" boss and with that in mind decided to level with the guy. Ray offered his hand. "Ray Black, mister..."

"Red. My name is Red. What'd you need, Ray."

"I'm trying to find a William Gorman. He worked for you in the late 90's."

Red never asked what Ray's interest was, but instead volunteered his opinion.

"Three Finger Bill. Yeah, he worked for us, off and on. He's a perverted piece of shit, that bastard." When he heard him called three fingers, Ray knew he was on the right track.

"Does he still work here?"

"No. We run him down the road a long time ago. We had a Holiday party at a nice hotel and that asshole got caught taking pictures of some of the kids. You know, not such nice ones. The prick got a room in the hotel and gave the kids booze and money to pose. The Mounties got him out of there before we killed him."

"Didn't he get charged or something?"

"No. The parents didn't want to put their kids through a trial, so he got away with it... Are you a cop?"

"No, I'm not a cop. He murdered my wife and son and I'm going to find him or die trying."

Ray was invited into Red's office where he told the whole story about what Robert Morgan did to his family.

Red looked at Ray. "Sorry about your loss, mate. I thought you Yanks had a double-jeopardy clause. You know, he can't be tried for the same crime twice."

"He never went to trial. But I plan on settling out of court."

"Hmm. I hope you find him and if I can help in any way, I will."

"Great. Do you know if he's still in Canada, or where he might be?"

"I'm sure he's not here. As an undesirable alien he probably got the boot a long time ago."

"By law he has to register back in the States as a sex offender. If he doesn't and they catch him, he goes to jail. And he's not currently registered. But if he's not in Canada, where the hell could he be?"

Red stroked his chin several times. "He liked the boats. He was always talking about getting a job on a cruise ship. Whenever we had work around the docks he wanted it. I heard that he even went there on Sundays when the passengers got off and on. Several cruise lines port in Vancouver; I wouldn't be surprised if he found work on one."

"Doing what?" Ray wondered.

"Unless the ship is dry-docked, it sails fifty two weeks a year and does running maintenance all the time. They have all kinds of people on board, but since the pay is so low and the hours long, usually only third world people apply."

"If that's where he went, I'd just bet that he's found a spot working with kids."

Ray stood and shook hands with Red. "Thanks, man, you've been a big help."

"You're welcome. I hope you find him and get even."

Ray reached into his shirt pocket and handed Red a lawyer card. "If you ever get anything more on the dirt bag give me a call. And no, I could never get even."

After Ray left Red examined the business card and realized that Egnever was just revenge spelled backwards.

Chapter 20

When he returned home, Ray had a quiet dinner at Jill's house where they discussed how to continue the search for William Gorman.

"I don't think he changed his name again," Jill said. "It's been over twelve years and he probably thinks everybody forgot about him."

"Well, I haven't," Ray, growled.

"I know, honey. There's something else we need to talk about."

He smiled. "Sorry, baby, I just get so worked up over that bastard. What is it?"

She got up from her chair and walked around the table and sat in his lap with her arms around his neck. "What about us, Raymond. I'm still young enough to have children and I'm madly in love with you. I need to know about our future."

He looked up into her face. "I love you, too, but until this is resolved...."

She didn't let him finish the thought as she put her index finger over his lips. "Shhh."

Later, over coffee, they decided to contact the cruise lines that sailed out of Vancouver. Using her computer Jill located the addresses of Royal Caribbean, Princess, and Carnival Cruise lines. RCL is in Miami and Carnival has several branch offices in the Miami area. Princess Cruise Line's home office was located in Santa Clarita, California.

"Let's go to Miami and pretend to be cops," Ray suggested. If he's on a ship we got a fair chance of finding him there."

"Let me talk to Brooke first and see if those cruise lines cooperate with law enforcement. I know they fly foreign flags, so I'm not sure how cooperative they'd be."

"Good idea. Call her now while she's at home."

Ray wandered to the refrigerator and pulled out a beer and sipped on it while Jill and Brooke engaged in a lengthy conversation. When she finally hung up, Jill turned to Ray. "She doesn't know."

Ray just laughed. "Pack your bags, we're going to Miami."

"I can't just pick up and go. What about my job?"

"Can't you take two personal or vacation days?"

"Let me make a call. I'll check."

**

EARLY THE NEXT MORNING the couple boarded Southwest Airlines flight #721 non-stop to Ft. Lauderdale. They rented a car and made the twenty-six mile trip to Miami, arriving shortly before noon. When they questioned the people at Royal Caribbean they got complete cooperation, since they represented themselves as Law Enforcement. But William Gorman or Robert Morgan, currently, or formerly, never worked for the cruise line. After a light lunch, they rented a motel room across from South Beach and spent the rest of the day enjoying the ocean.

The next morning they drove to Sunrise, Florida, a Miami suburb and home to Carnival Cruise Lines. Again the folks were only too willing to cooperate and this time they struck gold. They were told that William Gorman was currently in the second month of a nine-month contract sailing to the Western Caribbean aboard the Carnival Valor, sailing out of Miami. He was part of the entertainment committee, with his job title listed as assistant to the cruise director.

After assuring the Carnival people that this was merely a follow up to an investigation concerning a property dispute and that Mr. Gorman was in no trouble, they drove back to Ft. Lauderdale and caught an early evening flight back to St. Louis.

When they returned home Jill started her search of the Valor. Through various vacation sites she was able to get the deck plans and after sifting through passenger reviews got a handle on what to expect on Valor. For the next month both she and Ray learned where everything was and how to get to it. When they felt proficient Jill started looking for a cruise.

"We need passports or we can't board the ship," Jill said. "And in order to get one you need to produce your birth certificate, certified by the governing body where you were born."

Ray chuckled. 'That's a problem? I'll pick one up on the internet."

"It won't be that easy. They do a background check. You'll have to get one in your own name or you won't get one."

Ray sighed. "Then I'll get one in my own name."

"You know that means you'll have to use your right name with the cruise line."

"Whatever it takes, Jill, but I need to get aboard that ship."

Ray looked over Jill's shoulder as she surfed through the Cruises Only web site checking to see what cabins would be available. "Look for a cabin as close to Camp Carnival as possible, one with a balcony." Ray knew that Camp Carnival, a children's room where parents left their kids under the supervision of staff, would be William Morgan's favorite hunting ground. "I'll bet the bastard spends a lot of time there," Ray said as they studied the Panorama Deck plan. Ray pointed his finger at the middle of the screen. "There, that one, 7063. It's close to the elevators, one floor below Camp Carnival, and it has a balcony."

They booked two months ahead, with Raymond J. Blackburn and Jill Collins sharing cabin #7063. That would give Jill time to set up her vacation and also provide time to get the necessary passports.

In the weeks after the March 22nd cruise to the Western Caribbean was booked, Ray had continuing nightmares about how Cory and Elizabeth died and what was done to their bodies. In the dream he tried desperately to save them, but he was always too late. When he finally got there, Robert Morgan's hands were dripping with blood and all he could do was wrap his hands around his neck. The dreams always ended the same; he'd wake up sobbing and choking his pillow. He didn't share this with Jill; she had her own nemeses to deal with.

Meanwhile Jill, using several counterfeit names, managed to download numerous "stills" of nude children and of adults engaging in various sex acts with them. As disgusting as they were, Ray and Jill viewed the pictures looking for clues. Using Jill's computer and a magnifying glass they determined most of the hardcore material came from overseas, but a lot of the soft shots were taken of American children in cheap motel rooms or in outdoor settings, such as campsites. The thought of Cub Scouts and Brownies being abused was sickening, but the pictures that created the most interest were taken in a game room with pictures of cuddly animals decorating the walls. Upon closer inspection, Jill spotted something barely noticeable. At the very top of one picture was a border of the unmistakable Carnival Cruise Line emblem. A red, white, and blue, rectangular symbol featuring Carnival's logo.

"Look at this, Ray," she said as she pointed. "This could be our guy."

Ray looked closely at the photo of a naked boy and girl posing in a provocative manner. "Maybe, but we won't be able to tell until we get inside Camp Carnival when we're on the Valor. Make a couple of copies, they could come in handy." As she thumbed through the other pictures taken inside of the Carnival playroom Jill noticed something else. "Whoever took this picture got a piece of their finger over the lens."

"Yeah, and it's not Morgan. That finger is dark skinned." He looked at Jill. "It looks like our guy has a partner, unless this is a different ship. I guess we won't know until we sail."

"Maybe we won't have to wait that long. The people that post on the vacation sites are always trading information. Maybe someone has a picture of little Suzie up in the playroom on Valor."

"Check it out."

***

TWO DAYS LATER Jill matched the picture taken by a past passenger with the ones she had. She couldn't wait to tell Ray so she called him on his cell.

"Good news, darling. I got a picture of Valor's Camp Carnival playroom and it's a match. I'm sure, because our pictures and the pictures the past guest took have the same lion missing most of its tail. All of the other pictures show the other lions with full tails. Somewhere along the line, some kid must have torn it off."

"That's great news, Jill. That means we're definitely on the right track and that he's not alone."

***

ALTHOUGH WILLIAM GORMAN and what he did was never far from his thoughts, Ray still needed to concentrate on business, namely affairs that concerned John Mullio and his strip clubs.

It was long after closing time when Ray sat in the office of Club 54 with his boss. A boss who long ago gave up trying to have Ray call him John.

"We had a good month, Mr. Mullio. I think we're through the teething process."

Mullio nodded his agreement. " There's another matter I want to run by you. I got some outside work, if you're interested."

"Try me."

"You know that hustle I do every now and then? The one where we tell a guy he's marked?"

Ray chuckled. "Yeah, and we can make it all go away... for a price."

"You got it. I've never done it around here, but there's a local guy that needs a good taking down. You wanna work on this? You get five grand when we collect."

Ray whistled through his teeth. "Who, when, and where?"

Mullio laughed. "The mark is a big television personality in North Central Missouri, Russell Hamilton, and he's loaded. He's also one of the biggest assholes that ever breathed on this planet. His television personality is nothing like who he really is. He's one ignorant dude, but he enjoys a lot of popularity and some of his best friends are high-office politicians. Still wanna do this?"

"Yeah. If he's the prick you say he is, it'll be a pleasure."

John Mullio frowned. "He is."

***

FOR THE NEXT three weeks Ray stalked Hamilton. He was there when he left his upscale townhouse and he was there when he went to bed. The only time he had to himself, was when Hamilton was at the studio doing his television show, a late night entertainment spot that was taped in the afternoon. By the third week Ray knew the routine. Do the show, stop by one of his favorite watering holes, and then have dinner at Wally's Steak House. He always returned home before ten, probably to watch the news and then his own program.

On a Wednesday night, after quickly checking for an alarm, Ray used a key pick to let himself into Russell Hamilton's townhouse. It was only 8:30, but Ray was patient. He was also careful not to leave any evidence of himself. The police style gloves would prevent fingerprints and he was careful not to leave any trace of anything that DNA could be extracted from. Ray used his small flashlight to make a quick survey of the premises. What he found in the spare room turned his stomach, hundreds of photo's, all pornographic and many involving children. He also shuffled through stacks of videocassettes and compact discs, silently reading some of the tittles. "Naughty Children, Bad Girls of Thailand, Boys with Men, and Violent Children Misbehaving." He also found several instant messages printed from porn sites that identified his screen name as "dIamondCutter" "So you have a secret life," Ray whispered. "I'll remember that when the time comes."

As Ray sat in the dark he wondered what his life would be if none of the bad stuff happened. But it did and he killed, and not just for revenge, he'd killed for money. What did that make him? Was he simply a murderer or was he a vigilantly ridding society of its worst. His thoughts were interrupted by the sound of a key in the door lock. He sprang to a spot behind the front door and drew his Glock, raising it to a position even with his right ear. When the lights went on and Russell Hamilton closed the door Ray greeted him, "Welcome home."

The man turned and faced his intruder. "What? What's this all about, and who are you."

"Well, I'm not Joe the Plummer."

Ray pointed to the couch with the semi-automatic. "Have a seat, Russ."

"I will not. I'm calling the police, mister."

Ray raised his voice to just under a shout. "Sit down, and shut up."

When the man sat, Ray quickly sized him up. Fifty something with thick salt and pepper hair, big, slightly overweight, and well dressed.

"You, my friend," Ray warned, "have made some enemies and somebody wants you dead. The organization I represent has been contracted to punch your ticket."

Russell Hamilton, for the first time in his life, was speechless and all he could do was mumble, "Huh?"

"Now listen and listen carefully. The people I represent respect you. Me, I don't care one-way or the other. You could be lying on that couch with a hole in your head. The only reason you're not, is because somebody likes you, but as I said, business is business."

Russell Hamilton, the guy with the reputation for not taking any sass from anybody leaned forward. "What can I do?"

That's what Ray wanted to hear. "Okay, Mr. Hamilton, here's the deal. We were offered fifty k to whack you. Normally the fee is ten grand for an unknown, but since you're a big shot, clipping you will bring a lot of heat. So, I guess you could say you're a victim of your own success. Besides, we know you can afford a lot more. Here's the deal, pay us the same and your problem goes away. Believe me, Mr. Hamilton, you'll buy the best friends you ever had. Either way we get paid, and personally I don't care which way it is. So, the next time we meet, you're either going to give me 50 large, or I'm going to blow your shit into the next life. Your choice and if you call your cop friends and I get arrested, you still go down. What's it gonna be?"

Russ Hamilton's voice quivered, "Fifty thousand is out of the question. I could probably go twenty..."

Ray stood up and holstered the Glock. Okay, I'll tell 'em you said no."

As he started for the door Hamilton's voice stopped him, "Don't tell them that."

Ray turned and looked at him. "What do I tell them?"

"Tell 'em yes. How do we do it?"

Ray walked to the front door and opened it. "Someone will be in touch."

***

JOHN MULLIO LOVED IT. "I told you twenty grand and you get us fifty. Great work."

"The bastard is a pedophile, Mr. Mullio. I just added a little tax."

"Okay, Ray, we'll handle it from here and there'll be a nice bonus for you when we collect."

Chapter 21

On Sunday, March 22nd Ray and Jill waited in line to go through security before entering the restricted area where they would register with Carnival personal before boarding Valor. Jill whispered in Ray's ear, "Are we carrying anything we're not supposed to have?"

"No, we're fine. If we weren't, the airport people would have stopped us."

After checking in they walked up the gangplank, where security officers photographed each passenger. As they entered into the twelve-story atrium, several attractive women in island costume gently ushered each group to one of the several photographers taking pictures. Ray muttered, "No thanks." and took Jill's arm leading her to the mid-ship elevators. A few minutes later they entered cabin 7063 on Panorama Deck. To them the room seemed small, but by cruise ship standards the 185 sq. foot room was considerably more than many ships offered. They dropped their carryon bags on the bed and took the elevator to Lido Deck where they had lunch at the open style buffet.

As they dined Ray reminded her, "Don't let anyone take your picture if you can help it. And don't make friends, that's not what we're here for."

Jill looked around. "I like the theme, America, 1776 style. It's neat."

Ray looked around at the paintings of frontiersmen, muskets, and cannons gracing the walls. "Looks a bit overdone to me, but the ship is nice."

Ray ended the conversation about the ship's decor. "I'm not positive, but I think I saw Morgan when we boarded. He stood off to the side and behind the ship's officers. He looks a bit older, but don't we all?"

Jill looked at her watch. "Dinner is at 6:15, are we eating at our assigned table tonight?"

He smiled. "If you want to."

"Yes. I'd like that."

The rest of the afternoon they explored the ship and with their previous study, knew it well. When they visited Camp Carnival the room was unoccupied, but they found what they were looking for, the half-tailed lion. After the Muster Drill, which all cruise ships are required to hold; they returned to their cabin and found their luggage already inside the room. As Jill unpacked, Ray scanned The Carnival Capers, a daily entertainment guide that highlighted the activities taking place on the ship. What he was looking for wasn't there. He set it aside and found a hard-cover manual that he thumbed through. "Bingo," he said. "Here's a section about children and the services available, including babysitting." He looked at Jill as she hung her clothes in the closet. "Tonight, while Mommy and Daddy get blitzed and lose next month's house payment at the Casino, I'll bet our boy is busy making friends with their kids. After dinner let's just poke around a little and see what the deal is."

Ray and Jill dined at one of the few two-person tables available in the formal dining room. Although most people enjoy the fellowship of their shipmates, they avoided it. After several futile attempts to engage them in conversation, the waiter and her assistant stopped trying. After dinner, the couple found deck chairs a short distance from Camp Carnival's outside entrance and watched as numerous children were left with the babysitting service.

Ray, sporting the short beard he grew to mask his identity, wore a floppy, blue hat that hid most of his face as he and Jill wandered into the room. There were four babysitters, two men, two women, and an energetic group of happy kids ranging in age from infant through pre-teen, but no Robert Morgan. When they left Ray turned to Jill. "I'll bet he's in the video arcade. Some of these parents are so stupid that instead of paying eight dollars an hour for a babysitter, they give the kids ten dollars and send them to the arcade for the night"

Ray's theory proved correct. The arcade, located on the same deck as the casino and only a short walk away, was packed with kids of all ages, and right in the middle of them was a three fingered man passing out complimentary tokens and making all the friends he could. Both Ray and Jill knew that Morgan was hunting, looking for weak prey; children whose parents were more interested in their own good time than the safety of their kids. What those parents failed to realize was that the ship was like a city and held the same dangers.

They found a small table in the hallway just outside of the arcade where a three-piece band entertained a small group of passengers. The volume of the band made conversation difficult, so as they their sipped drinks, they mostly just watched as Robert Morgan endeared himself to as many children as possible. Morgan worked the room like a professional and spent a bit of time with each child explaining the games and dropping in complimentary tokens. After an hour Ray leaned over to Jill. "Let's go play a little blackjack while the crowd thins in there. I'll bet this guy is just waiting to see who's left around midnight, you know, the kids on a loose leash."

Two hours later, just after midnight, Ray and Jill again sat outside of the Video Arcade, only this time the band was gone and only a few children were still playing the games. Later, Morgan walked past them to the bar, returning minutes later with a tray of drinks. They could see three cans of Coke, along with several bar drinks featuring wedges of fruit. Morgan seemed oblivious to them as he sipped on a Coke, while laughing and joking with the kids. By this time, the video games were forgotten as the group retreated to the back of the game room.

Ray stood. "Let's go. Our boy put in a good foundation, but he doesn't have time to do anything tonight."

Early the next morning as Ray and Jill ate breakfast at the buffet, Ray again scanned the Carnival Capers. "Today is a fun day at sea. Let's just see what the staff has planned." As he went down the list, Jill agreed with him that Robert Morgan would most likely be involved with children activities and that's what he looked for. "Here we go," Ray said as he read from the newsletter. "Camp Carnival orientation and registration from nine until twelve, lunch at noon, pool games in the main pool from one-thirty to three, and story time from three-thirty until five." He looked up. "Then it's the eight dollar per hour babysitting service, if you don't want to be bothered with your kids. That's available until 1 AM."

When he looked at Jill, tears were running down her checks. "It's not fair. Some people shouldn't have children. I took care of my baby and she's gone. Some of these people ignore their children and get to be grandparents. I hate them."

Ray reached for her hand and stroked it softly. "Nobody ever said life was fair, but we're not here to feel sorry for ourselves. If we stop this monster, some folks, maybe even some good parents, will be spared what we live with."

"I know," Jill whispered as she dabbed her eyes with a tissue. After breakfast they casually walked by and looked into Camp Carnival, searching for Robert Morgan. He wasn't there. Later that morning they spotted him as the MC of a game on the pool deck. This game didn't involve children, but instead, many bikini-clad young women who took time out from sun bathing to participate in the hula-hoop contest. The crowd roared with delight as several older men, with enormous beer bellies, tried in vain to compete and cheered as the girls gyrated to the beat of loud island music.

Jill looked at the nearly empty pool and shouted into Ray's ear. "Let's get our suits and take a dip." He grinned his reply.

LATER, AS THEY ATE lunch, Jill asked, "Now what?"

"Let's just check out all of the activities and see what he does." He pulled the Capers from his pocket and read down the list. "Trivia contest at two, a tour of the wheel house, also at two, and Bingo from three to six. He's gotta be doing some of this."

"What about tonight?"

"Let's see," Ray said as he looked down the list. "Captain's reception at 5:15 and 7:15, followed by the Formal Night dinner and pictures." He looked up from the list. "All kinds of lounges featuring entertainment all night; everything from Disco to karaoke."

"Anything with the kids besides babysitting?"

He studied the lineup. "No, nothing."

"So, what should we do, Ray?"

"If I'm right, Morgan will be off duty by nine and will probably be doing something involving the kids. I don't think he does babysitting, but we can check that out tonight."

***

THAT NIGHT AS JILL PRIMPED, Ray quickly dressed in his rented tuxedo. When she came out of the bathroom, wearing a long black evening gown accented with pearl accessories, he was sipping on a Coke from the mini-bar as he sat watching television. He stood and whistled through his teeth. "Wow, you're absolutely gorgeous." When he took her in his arms she leaned back and smiled.

"Looking for a date, handsome?"

Ray grinned. "Yes, ma'am, I am."

They kissed very passionately and held a long embrace. When Ray tried to gently back away, she held tight for a long moment. The embrace hid her face and he knew she was feeling deep emotion and he didn't want to intrude into her thoughts.

Finally she ended the moment. "We better go or we'll be late for dinner."

After dinner they again peered into Camp Carnival. This time Morgan was wearing a clown suit and doing a puppet show. They stood in the doorway for a few minutes before a woman, also dressed as a clown, told them that adults distract the children and she would appreciate it if they would leave. They knew Robert Morgan observed them, although he barely glanced their way. They hoped that the staff wrote them off as concerned parents just checking out the playroom.

Later that evening, around ten, they sat at a table outside of the Arcade and again Robert Morgan was hosting a group of children, only this time he had another adult with him. The slightly built man, in his thirties, was obviously not American or Canadian, but probably Philippine or Indonesian, since many crew members hailed from those countries. Mostly he remained silent and acted like Morgan's assistant. Ray nudged Jill. "His partner in crime." They both realized that this impromptu gathering was not part of the ships scheduled curriculum, but also understood that staff officials would look favorably upon employees who donated time to passengers on their own. From information Jill gained on the vacation sites, they knew ship employees were forbidden to appear in public without wearing their ship nametag and although Morgan and his companion didn't wear company uniforms, they still wore the nametags.

Ray and Jill left after an hour and played blackjack until nearly 1 AM, when they strolled past the semi-darkened arcade. Again a small group was huddled in the back, surrounding Robert Morgan, as sounds of laughter floated into the hallway.

At breakfast the following morning, Ray again scanned the Capers. "Treasure Hunt for the kids at three, that's the big gig. The rest of the stuff looks about the same as yesterday."

"I'll bet that pervert made himself a lot of friends by now. Do you think he's ready to do anything?"

"Tomorrow will be his day," Ray said. "When we port in Cozumel, most of the passengers will go ashore and that will give him the opportunity he's waiting for."

"Shouldn't we do something? You know, when the ship is nearly deserted?"

"I don't know, Jill. I don't think we should do anything yet. Let's get him the night before we get off the boat. That way when he goes missing they won't have much time to investigate before we debark."

"What about that man with him?"

"Let's just see what his part is. He could be just a tag along. Maybe that's not his finger on that photo."

That day they covered every activity the ship offered and found Robert Morgan hosting the Newly Wed Game at ten and the children's pool games at one. By this time it was obvious he was extremely popular with many of the children, as they referred to him as "Uncle Bill." And also to the parents, who were delighted to have such a loveable grandfather figure onboard overseeing their children's activities. Ray and Jill also gave special emphasis to all other children's activities, searching for clues as to whether the man with Morgan at the Arcade was also a child abuser.

Later, while sitting at a table near the rear of the ship and watching the pre school children frolic in the wading pool, they were approached by a husky man wearing a security uniform. As he introduced himself they silently read from his nametag. "Arlo Hoez, Philippines."

"Good afternoon, folks. My name is Arlo Hoez. I'm the Valor Security Chief." Ray looked up and offered his hand. "Ray, and this is Jill." Jill just smiled.

"May I sit down?"

As Ray gestured toward an empty chair he thought. "So much for imminently."

"I need to be blunt, guys. You've been seen on numerous occasions observing the children, although you don't have any with you."

Jill got defensive. "Is that against the law, Mr. Hoez?"

"No, ma'am, it's not against the law, but it's my job to see that everyone, including children, are safe on this ship and since your behavior has been a bit odd, I need to talk with you."

Jill raised her voice slightly, "We haven't done anything wrong and I resent the fact that you're insinuating that we have."

"Ma'am, I'm not insinuating anything."

Ray held up his hand in a stopping motion. "You're a good detective, Arlo. If you'll bear with us for a bit, I think we can clear this thing up. We've got something in our cabin you need to see. If you'll wait here, I'll get it."

Arlo Hoez stood. "Let's all go."

The Security Chief led the way as they walked in silence to the elevator and down the hall to their cabin on Panorama Deck. When inside the cabin he stood by the door as Ray searched through his carryon bag. "Here, look at this." He flashed the Columbia Detective badge Brooke gave him and then handed Hoez a picture of Camp Carnival. The one featuring the naked teenagers. The Security Chief grimaced as he studied the photo. "You think this was taken on this ship?"

"We know it was," Ray said. "Let's go up to the playroom and I'll show you."

Jill stayed in the room as the two men went up to Camp Carnival. The room was still filled with jubilant children and would be for the next twenty minutes. They found deck chairs in the shade while they waited for the room to empty. Arlo Hoez started to question Ray. "Are you working a case, Mr. Blackburn?"

"Yes, I am."

They sat in silence for a few moments before Hoez spoke. He talked softly and it was almost like he was alone, "I was abused by my uncle when I was four, until I turned nine. I hate that memory. That bastard robbed me of my innocence. He got away with it because nobody wanted to believe me." He turned to Ray. "If you can prove to me that we got someone like my uncle on board, I'm on your side. Do you have a suspect, and if so, what do you think he did?"

"Yeah, I got a suspect. He abused and murdered my son, and then murdered my wife."

"OOH!" Arlo Hoez listened, as Ray told of the crime and how Morgan got off, omitting any part he played in the drama.

They again sat in silence until the noisy children, waving the pictures they drew, poured from the playroom to their waiting parents. A few moments later Arlo Hoez looked at the photo Ray handed him and then compared it to the decal of the lion missing half of its tail. He patted Ray's shoulder. "You do realize that you have no jurisdiction here, Mr. Blackburn, and we only have one small jail cell on board."

"I understand, but I'm not planning to arrest him. Let's just say that I plan on settling out of court."

Hoez ignored Ray's passion. "Who's the guy?"

"His real name is Robert Morgan, but he had it legally changed to William Gorman."

The Security Chief was stunned. "Uncle Bill? That's the guy? Are you sure?"

"I've been trailing him and his three fingers for a long time. Yeah, I'm sure."

"Do you have a plan?"

"Not yet, but I know how he gets the kids." Ray then explained about the arcade and the underage children who hung in there without parental supervision. He looked at Hoez. "He's got to have some place he can take these kids. He can't take the chance of being caught in the playroom. Is there some other place he can hold his little parties where he won't get caught?"

Hoez thought for a moment. "Yes. This ship does running maintenance and we always have at least ten cabins that are being renovated on every cruise. We know that some of the crew have romantic liaisons in them, but we look the other way. They're not hard to get into. Some of the cabin stewards have pass keys that allows access to any passenger cabin on the ship. I'll bet he either has a key, or someone else involved does."

"One more thing, Mr. Hoez, who fingered us?"

He shook his head no. "I'm not sure. We got the complaint through the Purser's desk. It could have been anyone."

"Yeah, even Uncle Bill."

Ray offered his opinion about the following day, when the ship docked. "I'll bet it's party time in one of those cabins."

Hoez smiled. "Guess we'll just crash the party." He reached into his shirt pocket. "Here's my card. Dial my number from any ship telephone and it'll page me."

Before Ray went back to his room he decided to bring back Jill an iced tea. Instead of walking across the crowded pool deck to the mid-ship elevator he decided to use the forward one and walk the hallway on Panorama deck to his cabin. As he walked from the bow to mid-ship, he passed several room stewards, including the man with Uncle Bill from several nights earlier. When he got to his cabin Jill was gone. While looking for a note the telephone rang. "Yeah?"

"Mr. Blackburn! I don't know how you found me, but I guess I always knew you would. You probably wonder how I knew you were aboard. I always check the passenger manifest before we sail looking for friends, and watching for you."

"Where's Jill, you son of a bitch."

Robert Morgan chuckled. "In a safe place."

"If you hurt her..."

"You're gonna do what? Now, listen to me. What's done is done. I can't change any of that, but if you keep up this vendetta, you'll have her blood on your hands. I promise you that. Now there are a few things you need to know."

"I know all I need to know, you prick."

Morgan shouted into the phone forcing Ray to hold it away from his ear. "Keep it up, asshole, and I'll hang up and you'll never see Ms. Collins again."

"Alright, calm down. Let me talk to her. I need to make sure she's okay."

"She's fine and she'll stay that way as long as you do what you're told."

"I'm supposed to take your word for it?"

Ray could hear Morgan's voice as he talked to someone.

"Ray, I'm okay."

Immediately Morgan returned to the phone. "Satisfied?"

"Okay, what do I need to know?"

"That's better," Morgan said. "Look, I'm sorry about what happened to you wife and kid, but I didn't do it. All I wanted was a few pictures of the boy."

Ray was fighting himself. He wanted to scream into the phone, but knew if he did it was over. "So you didn't do anything?"

"I didn't say that. Yeah, I got the boy to go home with me, but while he was there this guy I knew came by and got weird."

"Weird, how?"

"Look, I wanted to let the kid go home, but Mac didn't."

Ray didn't say anything, but instantly remembered every Mac he ever knew or heard of. The list was practically endless.

"What's his first name?"

"Look, man, I'm not here to give anybody up. I just want you off my back. You half killed me once. I don't need any more of that."

"I guess suing me for all I had made it all better, right?"

"Do you want to know what happened or not?"

Ray remained silent. "So the kid starts fighting and crying, saying he wants to go home and won't shut up, then Mac shuts him up. I wasn't even in the room."

Ray's knuckles were white from squeezing his fist so hard, but he still remained silent. Robert Morgan paused a moment as he sobbed. "It wasn't me, Mr. Blackburn. I love kids."

Ray used all the restraint he could. "What about Elizabeth?"

Morgan sniffed a few times and then continued, "Mac came by every day while they searched for your son doing drugs and spending time with the body. When the mother came I wasn't home. He said when he got her in the house he just killed her too."

Ray knew he had to ask about the taxidermy equipment, even though he didn't want to. "What about the taxidermy stuff?"

"I got another friend who was working out of my basement at the time. That's why Mac.... did what he did to the bodies. He wanted to preserve them. He said if they could stuff a horse they could surely do the same to a person."

"What happened to their bodies?"

"I don't know, man. Mac took them out at night. I never saw them again and he didn't say what he did with them."

Ray was getting sick. He felt like he was going to vomit as he changed the subject. Look, Morgan, let Ms. Collins go and I'll believe your story.... We got a deal?"

Morgan just laughed. "I'll call you back later, be in your room." When Ray heard the phone go dead he wanted to collapse on the bed in a fetal ball and cry, but instead he dug for Arlo Hoez's card and called the number. He left a short voice mail, "Come to my cabin, now."

Fifteen minutes later, after he was filled in, Arlo stared at Ray. "We need to be very careful. If Jill goes overboard, he's in the clear. The only way he won't hurt her is if he still thinks you can get at him."

"What can we do?

"Wait until he calls. Until we know what he has in mind, we can't do anything."

"I saw that little worm that he had with him the other night doing cabins about an hour ago. Maybe he knows something,"

Arlo Hoez started for the door. "Wait, and when he calls try not to piss him off. I'll nose around a bit and see if I can come up with anything. And whatever you do, don't get anybody else involved. You never know who his friends are."

It was after eight before Arlo returned. "I found Uncle Bill on the stern by the rock climbing wall with a bunch of kids. They loosened several bulbs and were barely noticeable, but a guest reported it and when I got there I could smell the grass they were smoking. Gorman told me that he had a group of kids out listening to the night sounds. All I could do was run 'em off and call maintence to fix the lights. That guy has brass balls."

When the phone rang it was nearly midnight. Ray sat with the Security Chief in his cramped office as he answered the forwarded call. With the call on speaker, Arlo listened intently as Robert Morgan outlined his instructions. "Tomorrow morning, Mr. Blackburn, when we port in Cozumel, you leave the ship and don't re-board. If you don't try any funny business, I'll let Ms. Collins off in Grand Cayman. I'll have to give her a little something so she stays quiet, but if you do like I tell you, she'll be unharmed. If on the other hand, you try anything funny, she goes for a swim. Do you understand my instructions?"

Ray looked at Arlo who nodded his approval. "Yeah. I understand. Now you listen to me," Ray said as Arlo shook his head no, "If you so much as..." When the phone went dead Ray cursed and set it back in its cradle. He looked at Arlo. "If that asshole thinks I'm going to leave Jill on this boat while I stay in Cozumel, he's full of shit."

"He's gonna watch for you to get off. So you get off, but when you get back on an hour later he won't know, because I'll be at the entrance and take you off to the side and you won't have your ship and sail card punched. I suspect he has access to a ship computer and can watch in real time as passengers and crew debark and embark the ship. Before the ship sails at five, he'll hear the announcement looking for passenger Raymond Blackburn, cabin 7063 Panorama Deck. Then he'll know you're on shore."

"What's that gonna do?"

"I think he plans to go ashore and pay some of the locals to get rid of you. All he has to do is describe you and what you're wearing, and then puff, you disappear. He's been on this itinerary for a long time and knows a lot of people in these ports. These islands are so corrupt that he could even have the police do it. If I'm right, you'll go awol, and Jill will go missing before we get back to Miami."

"And Mr. Morgan's life goes on as usual," Ray said.

"You got it, but while he's on shore setting things up we'll search the ship." He patted Ray's shoulder. "Don't worry, we'll find her."

***

RAY DIDN'T SLEEP that night, and as agreed, stayed away from Arlo Hoez and any other security personal. When he got off the ship with the first passengers, he carried his overnight bag making it appear that he really planned to stay ashore. He was sure he was being watched as he got into a Taxi and ordered the driver to take him to "Shell Beach." When he got there he waited for the cab to disappear from sight and quickly got into another taxi and returned to the ship. After walking up the gangplank Arlo took him firmly by the arm. "This way, sir." As he was ushered past the screening machine and the metal detector the security officers on duty hardly took notice. They went directly to Arlo's office where Ray left his duffel bag. "Okay, Ray, I got a list of the empty cabins.

An hour after their search began, Arlo Hoez, using his passkey, entered R306, an inside cabin on the lowest passenger deck on the ship. Jill lay on the bed with hands and feet bound and a gag covering her mouth. Ray rushed to her side and carefully removed the duct tape holding the gag. "Are you alright?"

She looked up into his eyes as they filled with tears. "No, I'm not alright, but I guess I'll live."

Arlo was already on the phone making arrangements for a different cabin. After a brief conversation he turned to the couple as they held the long embrace. "Don't go back to 7063. I got you a cabin on Emerald Deck, that's deck six. You guys stay there until I can get this guy into custody."

Ray gently pushed Jill to his side. "I don't think so. We can put Jill in that safe cabin, but I'm going to be there when you catch that pervert."

"Look, Ray, I got enough on him to put in him in jail, but since we fly under the Panamanian flag, that's where he'll have his day in court. Remember, we're both police officers. Let's just let the law do its thing."

"I'm gonna be there, Arlo."

"Okay. Just remember, we're professionals and no matter what our personal feelings are, we need to do this the right way."

As they waited in cabin R306 Ray and Arlo heard the expected announcement concerning passenger Raymond Blackburn. The message was repeated four times and finally the Valor set sail for Grand Cayman, twenty minutes late. The two men sat in silence, each with his own thoughts for nearly an hour. Arlo Hoez with thoughts of incarcerating Robert Morgan and Ray with visions of ending the man's life.

A slight click from the door lock brought both men from a sitting position. Ray ducked into the bathroom while Arlos stood facing the door with his semi-automatic in his right hand. When the door swung open, the room steward Ray observed with Morgan appeared, carrying a food tray. After determining that he was alone, Arlo ordered the man into the cabin. "Pablo, I'm surprised at you." The man remained mute as he stepped further into the room. Ray swung open the bathroom door as their prisoner turned to face him. Ray took the tray and threw it into the shower. "Where's your buddy?" Ray asked. Silence was his reply. Ray grabbed the man by the throat. "When's he coming here?"

"That's enough, Ray," Arlo said as he pulled Ray away. "Turn around, Pablo."

When he obeyed, Arlo cuffed him and pushed him into the bathroom with a warning. "Make any noise and I'm gonna let this guy come in there and quiet you down. You understand?"

"Si, senor."

Arlo instructed Ray, "I don't think Morgan has a key. He'll knock on the door thinking Pablo is in here. Arlo opened the bathroom door. "When's Uncle Bill coming?" Pablo shrugged. "I don't know."

"Ray, you ask him."

"No, senor, Hoez. I remember. He comes late tonight after everything close. He tells me that. I just bring food for the lady."

Arlo looked at Ray. "Stay here, just in case. I'm gonna keep an eye on Uncle Bill tonight. Stay with Pablo. I can't take the chance that somebody will see me hauling his ass to the brig, and don't hurt him. I'll be back later. If I need to call, I'll ring once and call right back. Got it?"

"Yeah. Let me call Jill before you leave. I wanna be sure she's alright."

Arlo nodded his approval. "What room, Arlo?"

"614, an inside cabin."

Ray dialed the telephone; Jill answered on the first ring, "Ray?"

"Yeah, it's me. Stay there and don't leave. I'll ask Arlo to bring you something to eat." Arlo nodded. "I don't want anybody knowing where you are."

"Are you okay?" Jill worried.

"I'm fine. I'll probably be out until late, so don't worry."

"Be careful. I love you."

"I know. Bye."

***

TWO HOURS LATER, when Arlo Hoez couldn't find Uncle Bill, he decided to search the empty cabins. After an otherwise futile search he pushed open the door to cabin 9745 on Lido Deck. As his eyes took in the scene he drew his sidearm. Uncle Bill, dressed only in boxer's shorts, stood behind a tri-pod that supported a video camera while two naked teenaged boys hunched over an equally naked pre-teen girl of about twelve. The room was vacant, except for several chairs and the blankets lining the floor against the far wall where the girl lay. The boys jumped to their feet and grabbed their clothes, but the girl barely moved. Arlo realized that she was so intoxicated that she was unable to resist any unwanted advances. Memories of his uncle played in his mind as he faced Uncle Bill. "Turn around and put your hands behind your back."

While being cuffed Morgan pleaded, "This isn't what you think Mr. Hoez. We were..."

" Sit down and shut up."

"Alright, boys, give me your ship and sail cards."

Arlo took out a small notebook and wrote down the information. He handed each boy his card back as he surveyed the room and the empty beer cans lying on the floor. "How old are you kids?"

The youth closest to him answered, "We're both fifeteen, sir."

"Do you have any idea what the penalty for rape is in Panama?

They looked at each other and mumbled in unison, "No, sir."

"Hanging, and nobody gives a shit if you're fifteen or fifty. If I arrest you, you'll be tried in Panama, because that's the flag this ship flies, and mommy and daddy can't do a damn thing to help you."

Both boys started to whimper as Arlo continued to tell the horrors of the Central American judicial system. "They won't hang you right away, they'll leave you in prison for a couple of months where the inmates will sell your asses to each other."

After they begged, Arlo warned them. "Now, listen to me. I think you boys just made a very bad mistake and are truly sorry for being involved in this. I'm going to give you a break. I'm not reporting this or arresting you, unless you get into more trouble. You keep this to yourself and stay with your parents the rest of the cruise. If I see either of you out alone after dinner, I'm going to arrest and charge you with statuary rape. Do we understand each other?"

"Yes, sir," both answered.

"One more thing. Do you know this girl?"

"Uncle Bill brought her. We don't know her."

"Alright, hit the trail."

When the boys left, Arlo turned to Robert Morgan. "Lie down on the floor."

His prisoner shook like a wet dog as Arlo ripped the cord off the video camera and tied his feet. Next, he tore several long strips from the blankets and gagged him. He opened the bathroom door and dragged his captive inside and closed the door. He walked over to the girl and helped her to her feet. "C'mon, miss, let's get you dressed." Arlo debated what to do with her and decided to take her to medical. They would contact her parents and tell them that she was disorientated and possibly bumped her head or suffered heat stroke. Either way, she would remain in the nurse's station long enough to sober up. Sadly, this scenario plays often on every cruise ship.

"How's Pablo?" Arlo asked when he returned to cabin R306.

"He hardly made a sound since you left."

Arlo opened the bathroom door and stared at Pablo's lifeless body for a long moment. "I TOLD YOU NOT TO DO THAT."

"Well, while I was choking the life out of that useless bastard, all I could think about was my wife and son, and this is as close to the killer as I've ever been. If you're feeling sorry for Pablo, think about your uncle and all the other kids he probably abused besides you."

When Arlo said, "Now we got to get rid of his body." Ray realized that he had a partner, another victim who not only hated the sin, but also the sinner."

With all pretence of arresting Robert Morgan gone, a scheme was hatched. Arlo Hoez would pretend to arrest Uncle Bill and bring him to deck three aft, the lowest deck that offered a rail overlooking the ocean. Ray would wait in the shadows and help push Uncle Bill to the same fate he planned for Jill.

The plan worked well as Ray met Uncle Bill, face to face, for the first time since Cory and Elizabeth died. While Robert Morgan pleaded for mercy, Arlo removed the handcuffs. "Please, don't do this I have money."

"Yeah, my money," Ray said.

"I beg you, please. I didn't hurt your boy or wife. It wasn't me."

Ray spoke just loud enough to hear over the breaking surf, "This is your come to Jesus moment, Uncle Bill, don't waste it."

The doomed man looked at Arlo. "You can't let him do this. You're the law; you're supposed stop crime, not commit it."

"I am stopping crime, by stopping you. And now I'm gonna change hats. I'm judge, jury, and executioner." With that said, they grabbed Robert Morgan and threw him overboard. Arlo glanced at Ray as they watched the tiny figure disappear into the ship's frothy wake. "Let's get Pablo."

Fifteen minutes later it was done.

The next morning Ray and Jill debarked the ship in Grand Cayman, explaining to ship authorities that they had an emergency at home. The helpful Security Chief, Arlo Hoez, arranged transportation to the local airport and assisted in booking a flight back to Miami.

Chapter 22

Nearly two years had passed since Robert Morgan met the Lord. By this time Jill and Ray were married and Johnny Ray was named on the AP All-American football team as one of the three best linebackers in the nation.

Far from Columbia and the University Of Missouri, a mother clutched her son's hand in their cardiologist's office as she cried softly. "Are you sure, Doctor?"

"Yes, Mrs. Stellon, I'm sure. The virus weakened the heart muscles to a point that medicine can do very little. The damage is similar to what Rheumatic Fever causes."

Charles Stellon spoke. "Are you telling me that I won't ever play football again?"

"Charles, it's much more serious than that. You have the heart of an eighty year old man." The doctor paused for a moment. "You probably won't live to see your thirtieth birthday. I'm sorry."

The virus that Charles Stellon contacted was from an unknown origin. The initial symptoms were similar to the flu, but when it persisted after several weeks and grew worse, he sought medical attention where he was diagnosed with a rare, but particularly aggressive virus.

That evening Charles and his mother had a heart to heart talk. "Mother, is there anything more you know about my natural parents?"

"Just what I told you, your mother was a girl in trouble and your father was a soldier. They gave you up. What else is there?"

"What about other family. Did they ever marry and do I have any brothers or sisters? She shook her head. "I don't know. We never had any contact with them."

Paul Stellon stood in the doorway before entering the room. "Catherine, the boy has a right to know everything pertaining to his adoption." He looked at his son. "Chas, you know how much we love you, but mom just feels a little threatened by the past."

Charles softly took his mother's hand and rubbed it against his cheek before kissing it. "You're my mom. I don't have, nor ever had any other mother. I just want to know about myself."

As Catherine stared into space she began, "You were born at St. Bernard Hospital in Montgomery City, Alabama. Your birth mother was indigent. She was a student at a small Christian College when she found out she was pregnant. When she refused to denounce your biological father, her mother and stepfather disowned her. From what Elizabeth told us, her family wasn't super rich, but they weren't poor either."

"That's her name, Elizabeth?"

Paul Stellon smiled. "Yes, and she was very pretty."

Catherine went on. "Before we adopted you, I miscarried and when the doctors told me I couldn't have any children, I started having mental issues. Your father and I decided to adopt, but the wait would have been years, so we talked to Aunt Birdi. She volunteered in an outpatient clinic in those days and when Elizabeth came in she was near term without a doctor or any other prenatal care. Birdie talked to her and set it up through a lawyer, where we paid her expenses in exchange for signing the papers giving you up."

"What about my father. You said he was a soldier. If he loved her, why didn't he take care of things?"

Paul and Catherine looked at each other as Paul resumed the story.

"He didn't know. Elizabeth didn't want to burden him. She told us that it was her problem."

Charles got angry. "What the hell kind of guy is he, leaving her high and dry like that."

"It wasn't like that, son," Paul continued. "She was in Alabama and he was in Seattle. They talked on the phone every few days, but she never told him."

Catherine picked up the story. "Elizabeth's friend called and told him that she was about to deliver his child. When he got there, things changed quite a bit. He wanted to marry Elizabeth and take you home, but Children Services wouldn't hear of it. We told them that we understood the situation and were willing to give you up, but they told us that if we did, you would go to an orphanage. So we took you home, but there was a twist. Elizabeth was carrying twins and your twin brother was born three minutes after you."

"I've got a brother?" Charles grinned. "I always wanted a brother. Wow. Do you think it's possible to find him?"

Paul frowned. "I wouldn't know where to start, Chas, but I'll help all I can if you wanna try."

***

THOSE FIRST DAYS after getting the news about his health and that he had a brother, Charles Stellon did a lot of thinking. He didn't want to die, not at twenty-one, but he didn't have a choice. His main concern was for his parents, but close behind was his determination to somehow find his brother. After reviewing all of the legal papers that his parents had, he tried contacting the attorney who arranged the adoption. The barrister was deceased and no one in his family knew about any records he may have had concerning adoptions. Next, he tried the hospital and also drew a blank. They claimed to have no information and even if they did, it would take a court order to release it. Child Services was also a stonewall and informed him that the case was sealed and, like all similar cases, would remain sealed to protect the parties involved.

Chas wondered what his brother was like and if he was still alive. He also wondered if he was an identical or a fraternal twin, the former with an exact DNA makeup and the later only half. Since this matter came to his attention, he researched twins and discovered that identical twins formed from the same egg, where fraternal twins came from separate fertilized eggs. Thoughts of dying were pushed to the back of his mind as he daydreamed about his brother. Late one night, while again trying to visualize what his twin would look like, he bolted up in bed as he remembered the words from a teammate during Bowl week in Denver, "The guy's your twin, Chas. You gotta see him." With the excitement of the game he forgot about it, until now.

Chas knew it was a long shot, but the next morning he was on the phone to the University of Missouri and ordered the current "Tiger's Football" a publication that recapped the last two seasons and projected the next. It also contained a photo lineup of the team with a brief autobiography of key players.

The following week, when the book arrived, Chas tore open the wrappings and hurriedly thumbed through the pages. He saw nothing at first, but after looking very carefully he spotted a possible look alike. Johnny Ray Blackburn, who faced the camera crouching with both arms outstretched and wearing full equipment. Only a small portion of his face was visible, but his size appeared similar to his. As Chas read the short biography his heart sank. "Blackie" was described as a ferocious linebacker, defensive captain, and leader of "The Holy Hell" defense, along with being named to several All American teams since his freshman year at Mizzou. His hometown was listed as Chicago, a long way from St. Bernard Hospital in Alabama. Charles spent hours studying the photo with a magnifying glass and although he thought he saw similarities, he realized that maybe he just wanted this guy to be his brother so bad he imagined it.

At dinner that evening, his mother questioned him. "Did you find anything in that book you ordered?"

"No, Mother.... Well, I'm not sure. I called the administration office and they promised to fax a group picture of the football team. Maybe I can get a better look at this Blackburn kid."

The following day, again using the magnifying glass, Chas Stellon studied Johnny Ray Blackburn's picture. When he brought the photo into the kitchen to show his mother, he barely held his excitement. "Mother, this guy looks just like me. I think he's my brother."

Catherine looked carefully at the picture and smiled. "I think he is, too."

***

YEARS AGO, WHEN CHARLES was a baby, Paul Stellon was transferred and moved his family from Alabama to Plano, Texas, a thriving community only a short distance from Dallas. As he boarded Continental Airlines flight #245, a non-stop Dallas, Fort Worth to St. Louis flight the following morning, Chas had butterflies in his stomach. Questions and doubts filled his mind. 'What if the guy's not my brother, he'll think I'm a nut. But what if he is and doesn't know about me?'

Four hours later, Chas Stellon parked his rented Taurus in front of Tiger Stadium. Only one entrance was open and as he walked through the gate a security guard appeared out of nowhere. "Where do you think you're going, bud? No visitors allowed while the team is practicing."

Charles stopped. "Uh, my brother's on the team and said it was okay to watch."

"What brother?"

"Blackburn, John Blackburn."

"You mean Blackie?" The security guard took a good look at Chas. "Damn, are you his twin or something? You look just like him. Go ahead."

Chas walked through the tunnel and came out close to the fifty-yard line. He stood back by the stands while he watched the team scrimmage. He watched as #65 made tackle after tackle, reminding him of the Coors Bowl nearly two years earlier. When #65 came off the field, he removed his helmet as he trotted to the sidelines. He glanced up briefly and spotted Chas Stellon standing several feet behind the players and coaches. His trot slowed to a walk as he continued past the sidelines, ignoring the coach and his teammates in the process. The coach and several players turned and watched as he stopped in front of his brother.

Chas stuck his hand out. "Chas Stellon." He paused briefly as his voice broke. "I think I'm your brother."

Johnny Ray dropped his helmet. He ignored the out-stretched hand and embraced his brother instead. "My God, man, you have no idea what this moment means to me. I've dreamed of this ever since I found out I had a brother, but I couldn't find you. How'd you do it?"

By this time the coach came up behind the boys as they held each other's arms.

"C'mon, Blackie, we got work to do." He started to turn towards the field when he glanced at Charles. "Who are you, Blackie's double?"

As tears flowed freely down his face, Johnny Ray replied. "This is my brother, Mr. Parks. We haven't seen each other in almost twenty- two years."

Coach Parks did the math. "You were separated as babies?"

"At birth, sir," said Chas.

Coach Parks' voice softened. "Hit the shower, John. See you tomorrow."

"Thanks, Coach."

While Johnny Ray showered, Chas called home. "Mom? It's him. I found my brother. He's been looking for me, too."

"I'm glad, Chas. I really am, and so will your father."

Later as they walked to the parking lot Johnny asked, "You got a room?"

"No, not yet."

"Good. I've got a "man cave" off campus. You're staying with me, brother."

Chas smiled. "You don't know how sweet that sounds, brother."

Johnny Ray turned slightly and whispered, "Yeah, I do."

Later as they sat at the kitchen table sipping on Cokes, Chas asked the inevitable.

"What about our parents? Did they ever marry? Do we have any brothers or sisters?"

Johnny Ray filled his lungs and exhaled slowly through his nose. Chas noticed his eyes moisten as he stared into space. "Our parents married when mom got out of the hospital and we had a little brother, but he died when he was six." Johnny paused briefly. "Mom died a couple of days later."

"God! What happened?"

Johnny Ray didn't want to relive that nightmare again, but told the whole ugly story and again blamed himself."

Chas was stunned. They sat in silence for a long time before Chas spoke, "Is the guy still in jail?"

"No. Dad went to prison for beating him half to death and I went to live with mom's best friend near Chicago. The bastard that did it got off because the police gathered evidence without a search warrant, and without it they had no case. He sued dad for his injuries and took everything we had. I didn't even know dad was alive until I came to school here and I saw him working for the University. He told Aunt Martha to tell me he died in prison. I guess he had his reasons."

"What ever happened to the guy that did it?"

"All I'm going to say is that dad found him and he won't be bothering any more kids."

"So, our father lives here in Columbia and works for the school?"

"He lives here, but he doesn't work for the school anymore."

"What does he do?"

Johnny Ray grinned. "He works nights."

"What's he like?" Can I meet him?"

"I think so. I'll call him later and see if he can come by tomorrow."

***

THE FOLLOWING AFTERNOON, Ray walked into the small house Johnny rented. He could hardly believe his eyes. He wasn't told about Chas, only that something important came up and that Johnny needed him. He knew immediately that he was looking at his long-lost son, as he was greeted with huge grins. Instinctively, he opened his arms and embraced both boys. As they talked Ray explained the futile search that he and Elizabeth conducted and how they finally resigned themselves to the fact that they would never be reunited with their lost son. After they exchanged stories of how they were able to find each other, Ray asked about the life Chas Stellon led.

"My parents are great people..." He looked at Ray. "I don't know what to call you."

"Ray is good. You already got a father; I know that."

"Thanks, Ray. Now, you both need to understand what my parents went through. They knew about what happened at the hospital the day we were born and offered to cancel the adoption, but Child Services told them that either way, I wasn't going home with you, Ray. My parents took me home and anguished over whether to look for my natural parents, since they knew you wanted me. But all they knew was that my mother's name was Elizabeth, a college student, and that my father was a soldier. I'm sure their search was much shorter than yours. When Children Services found that they were looking, they warned them that I could be taken away and placed in foster care, so they stopped searching. I grew up in Plano, Texas and am an only child. I attend Texas State and played football." Chas grinned and looked at Johnny Ray. "I was on the team that lost to Mizzou in the Coors Bowl, although I wasn't as good as you and didn't play."

"Are you still in school? And do you still play football?"

"I took this semester off because I got sick, but I'm still a student. I can't play football anymore. I caught a virus and it wrecked my heart, so my playing days are over."

Johnny Ray leaned forward in an unconscious effort to show concern.

"How bad is it?"

Chas shrugged his shoulders. "The doctor says I have the life expectancy of an eighty-year-old." He grinned. "Some good came out of this, mom told me about having a twin and with my time a bit short, I got on it right away and here I am."

Both Ray and Johnny Ray were stunned. They wondered how such a happy thing could turn sour so fast.

Charles stayed for three days before returning home and spent nearly every waking hour with his brother and biological father. When he returned home, he felt good about who he was and where he came from. He was saddened more by the tragedy in his brother's life than of his own prognosis. He was happy that Ray found love again and instantly liked Jill, vowing to stay in close touch with his newfound family.

CHAPTER 23

When Ray and Jill married they decided to abandon any more retaliation involving child predators. Since they caught and punished the ones who destroyed their families, they decided to move on. Ray didn't believe Robert Morgan's story of an accomplice, and in his mind justice was served. Other than explaining the circumstances to his newly-found son, the matter was buried and never mentioned again, although memories of Elizabeth and Cory were occasionally relived in dreams, as were Jill's memories of Amy.

Johnny Ray was different. He thought there was more to the story and that it involved a taxidermist in some way. He didn't share his feelings with his father, rationalizing that he'd already been through enough and that he and Jill deserved some happiness. He made personal contact with every taxidermy service listed in the St. Louis telephone directory and those in the surrounding areas, always with the same result; nobody could connect Robert Morgan with anyone in the business.

Johnny remembered the vow he made to his mother and brother at their grave, the vow his father pleaded with him to forget, but he didn't forget it. When the team played an out-of-town game he always tried to find time to contact any taxidermy businesses in the area. During his senior year the team traveled to Carbondale, Illinois, home of Southern Illinois University, for a pre-season game. The team arrived on a hot Friday night in late August. The game was scheduled for the following night and as Johnny spent the evening in his room, he searched the phone directory looking for any taxidermists in the area. He found two, both within walking distance of his hotel. Early the following morning, he walked into "Hart and Son Pawn and Taxidermy Service."

A longhaired youth about his age, wearing a Hard Rock Cafe tee shirt, greeted him, "Can I help you?"

"I'm not sure. Are you the guy that stuffs animals?"

The kid turned around and sat on a tall stool and leaned against the wall. "That's my uncle, but he doesn't do much with that anymore."

"Is he here?"

"Look, friend, Uncle Jim's a bit light in his loafers, if you know what I mean. And like I said, he doesn't do much with the business anymore."

Johnny Ray became excited, but was careful not to show it. "Sounds like you don't like Uncle Jim very much." The clerk just glared as Johnny reached into his pocket and put a twenty-dollar bill on the glass top counter. The kid stood and went for it like a puppy being offered a treat. "Does your uncle like little boys?" The guy looked at the twenty, then at Johnny.

"That's not enough for that kind of information. Are you a cop or something? What's that bastard done now?"

"No, I'm not a cop. I'm just trying to find out about someone he might know."

"Make it fifty and my memory might get a little clearer."

"Look, friend, I'm not James Bond. I don't have fifty. I barely have twenty, but I do have a dead mother and brother that I'm trying to find out about."

"Whoa... okay, man," he said as he pocketed the bill. "My uncle is a piece of crap. My father caught him abusing me when I was five and beat his ass good, and then threw him out. When I was thirteen dad was killed in a car accident and the court sent me here to live with Uncle Jim. I was older then, so he never tried anything again. Now, I run the pawn and support him while he gets drunk and does shit."

"Is he here? Can I talk to him?"

"Go around the building. He's sitting on the back porch draining a forty ounce. That's his breakfast."

Johnny Ray stuck his hand over the counter. "Thanks, man. I think your uncle might be the guy I'm looking for."

Johnny Ray found a skinny, old man with long, stringy, gray hair wearing faded, bib overalls over a dirty white tee shirt.

"Good morning," Ray called.

The man barely glanced at him.

"Your nephew said you're a taxidermist."

"Not anymore. I'm retired."

"That's alright. I'm here about something that happened a long time ago."

The old man set the beer bottle down and straightened himself in his chair. He stared at Johnny who stood on the sidewalk with one foot on the first step.

"You a cop?"

Johnny got angry. "No, goddamnit, but if you don't tell me the truth, I'm gonna kick your sorry ass into the next world. I know about you so don't try to bullshit me. I'm not asking about nothing current. I wanna know about a mother and a little boy who were murdered in Missouri about fifteen years ago."

"The Blackburn case?"

"Yeah. The Blackburn case."

"Who are you and what makes you so interested?"

"It was my mother and brother." Johnny took the two steps and stood over the man. Uncle Jim looked up at him. "'I'm an old man, if you kill me you'd be doing me a favor, son."

Johnny's voice turned gentle, "Were you involved? I need to know what happened."

"No. At least not directly." He squinted against the rising sun as Johnny sat in the chair next to him. "I always knew that someday someone would come. I thought it'd be a cold case cop, not a kid. Okay, I was friends with Bob Morgan. We had ... shall I say, the same interests. When this terrible thing happened, a friend of Bobs' called and wanted me to do the most unthinkable thing. Preserve the bodies. When he told me he severed their heads and froze them, I was absolutely sick. He wanted to bring the bodies to me and have them processed. Of course I refused."

"Seems like you were a long ways away. It must be at least a hundred miles to St. Louis from here."

"I was in St. Charles then, only a couple miles from where you lived. I even had equipment at Bob's house. I was going to teach him the business."

"Who was Bob's friend and how well did you know him?"

"His name was Russ. I never knew him by any other name. We only met once and that was enough. The guy was crazy. When he found out I was a taxidermist he started talking about some really weird shit."

"Weird, like what?"

"He saw a home improvement display where they had a family in a future home setting. He said the figures were lifelike and that his fantasy was to have something like that, with a real family, for people like us to enjoy. That scared the hell out of me and I never wanted anything to do with him."

The thoughts of what he was hearing nearly nauseated Johnny Ray, but he knew that if he got emotional, the interview was over.

"Do you know why my brother died?"

Uncle Jim picked up the bottle and took a long swig. "Bob said it was an accident. The kid wouldn't stop crying and when the doorbell rang he panicked. He told me he put his hand over the boy's face and smothered him. He didn't mean to, but that's what happened." Uncle Jim frowned. "Turned out it was only somebody delivering a new telephone book and they just rang the bell and left."

"So how did this Russ guy get involved?"

"Bob didn't know what to do, so he called Russ. Instead of devising a plan to get rid of the body, Russ decided to.... Anyway, he calls and he tells me he has a start to that family he was talking about. I hung up and didn't answer my phone for two days. Then him and Bob show up at my place and tell me they got two bodies for me to process. I told them to get away from me or I'd call the police. Then Russ tells me that I was a dead man." He looked at Johnny Ray. "I believed him. I knew what he was capable of, so I packed up and left St. Charles and here I am."

"Can you tell me anything more about this Russ guy?"

"All I know is that he worked for a newspaper or something. Bob told me that he had a lot of connections and that kept him out of trouble."

"Do you know where?"

"No, son. I didn't wanna know anymore about that crazy bastard than I already told you." Uncle Jim turned to Johnny and grabbed his arm. "God, don't tell him you even saw me. I don't want nothing to do with him."

Johnny Ray stood up. "I won't. Thanks for your help. Oh, one more thing, what's he look like?"

"Just an average-looking guy, except for his left hand. He has a big red birthmark on the back of it. Kinda looks like a big red paint splotch. He's real self-conscience about it too, according to Bob Morgan."

Johnny Ray debated whether to call his father or not. He decided not to. He played the football game that evening, but had a hard time concentrating. On the 4-hour bus ride back to Columbia he avoided conversation with his teammates, preferring to be alone with his thoughts.

***

MONTHS PASSED AND Johnny Ray still hadn't located anyone named Russ. Using the internet, he tried Russell and any other derivative from Russ that he could think of and came up empty. This effort was done after checking out every newspaper, newsletter, and magazine that was published in or around St. Louis, looking for anyone with Russ or Russell in his name. He pondered what this Russ character could be doing and realized that if he made friends with important people, he probably was, or in the past a reporter. After he thought about it and being a journalism student himself, he decided that maybe, just maybe, this guy wrote a book of some sort.

When Russell Hamilton, author of "Progressive Ideas For A Stalled Society," popped up on the screen, Johnny smiled as he read from the biography.

Mr. Hamilton received his degree in Journalism from The University of Missouri School of Journalism. He spent many years as a political reporter and Opinion Page Editor for The Columbia Times (using the byline Mac Trac) before he accepted a position at KRAU television Columbia, Missouri, hosting a talk show on current events.

Johnny Ray gritted his teeth as he whispered, "I'll just bet you're my boy."

The ironic part was that he was under his nose all the time, living in the same city. Before he ended Russell Hamilton's life, Johnny Ray wanted to know who he was and what made him tick, and most of all, he needed to be sure he had the right man. As he watched his television program, "Getting It Right" each night for three weeks, Johnny developed a deep hatred for the man and what he believed in. The agenda that "Getting It Right" pushed was for leniency and tolerance, not punishment and justice. Johnny Ray couldn't believe his ears, as night after night, Russ Hamilton preached his doctrine and caller after caller supported it. But in all that time, Russell Hamilton never exposed his left hand, until a film clip showed the birth-marked hand as he greeted the mayor of Columbia, while receiving an outstanding citizen award. As Johnny Ray watched this "on the scene report" he jumped up and punched the air. "Got ya."

Russell Hamilton was very visible and loved in the community, always making time to attend grand openings and other civic functions. He was even past president of the local Chamber Of Commerce and often entertained business people interested in coming to Columbia. But his favorite pastime was officiating at any school program he could get himself invited to. Since most school officials are die-hard liberals, he always had a full calendar and was a welcome guest speaker at many educational institutions.

For the next several months Johnny Ray followed his prey and attended many of the events where Russell Hamilton appeared. After watching him, he realized that Hamilton always sought out children, the younger the better. This guy, Johnny realized, was the man that destroyed his family and robbed him of his childhood. He could never hope to punish him enough for that, but the hatred he felt would permit him to do things he otherwise would be incapable of.

***

IT WAS A COLD RAINY night, as Johnny sat in his car across from the black Lexus Russell Hamilton drove. It was eight o'clock on a Friday night and Wally's Steak House was busy. He watched as Hamilton, with his overcoat pulled up around his collar and hat pulled down tight, bent as he walked into the wind to his car. Johnny waited a moment, then got out of his car and walked slowly towards the Lexus. He knew that in a matter of seconds Hamilton would get back out of the car and examine the flat, left front tire. Just as Hamilton got out of his car a couple passed Johnny under a security light. The woman smiled and the man mumbled an insincere, "Good evening." Then they recognized Russell Hamilton and greeted him with enthusiasm. "Good evening, Mr. Hamilton. How are you?"

As he looked away from the tire he answered, "I was good until now."

Johnny Ray pretended concern as he turned around and stopped in front of the Lexus. "Need a hand, mister?"

"No. I'll call the motor club."

Johnny smiled. "Why bother? I'll have you on your way in a jiffy. Open the trunk and I'll get the jack and the spare."

Russ Hamilton took a good look at the helpful stranger. He was young, handsome, and obviously looking to make a buck.

"Yeah, okay. I could use a hand."

Johnny Ray reached into his pocket and produced a black stocking hat and a pair of leather gloves. He pulled the hat down over his ears, nearly hiding his face. Several minutes later the tire was changed, but in those minutes several people recognized Hamilton and stopped to talk. Johnny tried not to look at any of them and after he put the jack and tire in the trunk spoke, "You're all set."

Russell Hamilton handed him ten dollars. Johnny put the bill in his pocket and waited for the next move. "You need a ride, son?"

"Uh, yeah. Could you drop me off downtown on Broadway?"

"Hop in."

After the Lexus pulled out of the parking lot, Hamilton made his move. Usually he never messed around this close to home, but this kid was obviously a college student and if he handled it right, maybe this could be a night to remember. Johnny Ray stiffened as he felt the arm casually rub against his leg. When he didn't resist, Hamilton became boulder and put his hand on his knee. Johnny turned to look at the man.

"You got money?"

Hamilton smiled. "Yeah, I got money. What'd you have for me?"

Johnny pulled a 22 caliber nine shot Taurus revolver from his pocket and pointed it at Russell Hamilton. "Keep going out of town."

"What? Are you robbing me?"

"If you don't do exactly what I say, it'll be a lot more than that."

When the car slowed and started to pull off the road, Johnny Ray fired one shot into the man's thigh. Hamilton let go of the wheel and grabbed his leg as Johnny Ray yanked the wheel with his free hand, guiding the car back on to the road.

"Next one is in your head. Now drive this car and do what I tell you."

Ten minutes later, they stopped on a desolate, gravel road.

Russell Hamilton started to reach for his wallet. "Forget that. I'm not here to rob you."

"What'd you want then? The car? Take it?"

"Turn the interior light on. I wanna see you face... Good. Now, remember a little boy and his mother you killed? That was my mother and brother. You know, the people whose heads you cut off and froze."

Russell Hamilton didn't try to talk his way out of a useless situation. He bowed his head in contrition. "Make it fast, okay?"

"Why'd you kill my mother? I know it was you." Silence was the answer.

"Get out of the car." When they stood face to face in the moonlight, Johnny Ray told the man his fate. "After I kill you, I'm going to cut your head off, just like you did to my family. I only wish I had time torture you, but I haven't." Johnny reached into the car and pushed the trunk release. "Get rid of that tire."

"Please, I beg you to reconsider."

When he turned to face him, Johnny Ray put six bullets into his chest. As the man moaned his last message to the world, he was shoved into the trunk. Johnny Ray grabbed his head by the hair and pulled out a large hunting knife. At that moment he realized that he could kill, but not dismember a body, only a cold-blooded monster could do that. For a long moment he looked at Russell Hamilton, child molester, murderer, and now victim. He uttered a curse and spit in the corpse's face. Finally, he slammed the trunk shut and drove to within several blocks of Wally's Steaks. He used the knife to cut the front seat, shredding foam and cloth, and set it on fire. He threw the revolver in a pond and thirty minutes later he was home. His clothes and skin were blood splattered and after showering, he built a small fire in the back yard and burned everything, including his shoes. With the car fire, he hoped to eliminate any possible sources of his DNA. Johnny Ray felt no remorse, only satisfaction. He kept his vow and eliminated a titan at the same time. He did the world a favor and now he could get on with his life.

Before retiring for the night, he checked his cell phone and found one missed call. As he played the lone message, a lot went through his mind. "Johnny, it's Chas, your brother. It's six o'clock and my connecting flight just got canceled. I've been here in St. Louis since noon and now I'm stuck for the night. If you get this in time, maybe you could drive down here. I'm at the Quality Inn near the airport." Johnny looked at the clock. It was nearly 11. "Sorry, Chas," he mumbled. "Catch you next time."

Chapter 24r

The fallout from Russell Hamilton's murder was felt far and wide as his popular television program reached half of the homes in Missouri. The public outcry was deafening and they wanted justice, and they wanted it now.

Since he still had his wallet and it was filled with cash, robbery was ruled out as a possible motive. The fire destroyed any usable evidence from the car's interior, but the body was a forensic bonanza. All seven .22 caliber rounds were recovered and through some very good police work, the medical examiner found what was thought to be the killer's DNA in the form of spittle, frozen on the victim's face. After searching Hamilton's townhouse as a possible crime scene, investigators discovered the secret life that Russell Hamilton led and theorized that he may have simply picked up the wrong guy. When they leaked this information to the public, interest waned and the case went on the back burner.

The only lead the detectives had was of the mysterious stranger that changed the flat tire in the parking lot of Wally's Steak House and so far that dead-ended, as eyewitnesses were unable to pick out any suspect from a photo lineup. The couple that Johnny passed under the security light that night disagreed and gave conflicting descriptions about his appearance. A police sketch artist completely ignored the man and concentrated on the woman's depiction of the suspect. Although the sketch missed the mark by a lot, both witnesses agreed, that if they could view the man in the flesh, they would recognize him immediately.

***

WHEN RAY HEARD the news about the murder, he immediately remembered Russell Hamilton and felt justice was done. His opinion of what probably happened mirrored the police; he picked up the wrong guy. He thought about canceling Hamilton's ticket himself, but because of the promise he made to Jill, he never acted on it.

A week later Brooke called Jill. "It's me, Jill. You know, your police connection?"

"Of course I know who you are, silly. How have you been?"

Brooke ignored the small talk. "Meet me for lunch tomorrow at Zambo's in the mall. It's important. Is 12:30 okay?"

"Yes." Jill knew that whatever it was, Brooke didn't trust the telephone.

"Good. See you then."

When Jill told Ray, he decided to go also. It would be good to see Brooke again, and whatever it was, it most likely concerned things he was involved in anyway.

After exchanging pleasantries Brooke came to the point. "This Russell Hamilton thing really stirred the pot. The detectives went back years and dusted off all of the unsolved cases involving sex predators and I don't mean their crimes. I mean the ones committed against them. They got a nice list of all the people that we made go away."

Ray leaned forward and kept his voice low. "So what. They can't implicate us in anything. Besides, they don't even know if a crime's been committed in those cases. They're simply missing persons."

"Ray, I know these cops. They're not stupid. All of those disappearances are now considered probable homicides."

Jill spoke for the first time, "How does that concern us?"

"Remember Mary, the monitor from The Grief Help Group? The detectives have been talking to her."

"Why?" Ray asked.

"Seems a lot of screwed-up people go to those meetings and as good cops, they cover all the bases."

"I thought she couldn't talk about those meetings," said Jill.

"They're asking about the people, not what was said. Anyway, she told them about our little group meetings."

Ray gritted his teeth. "That bitch. Her and that, 'I just want to help.' Now what? Do you know what she told 'em?"

"So far they don't think anything. They just asked me who we are and what we talked about. I told them that we just supported each other and until you lose someone close, you couldn't possibly understand what we were all about."

"That's it?" Jill wondered.

"Not quite. They already had all of our names, so they asked about us and what sort of grief we were going through. I told them that was a private matter, but I know they're searching the files and down the line they'll find out about the crimes against our families. With five people unaccounted for and now a television personality murdered, they're hungry for an arrest."

Ray had no idea who got to Russell Hamilton, only that he finally got what he deserved. He never gave a thought about Johnny Ray being involved and never knew that Russ Hamilton was involved with the death of his family.

Several weeks later, Brooke had dinner with Ray and Jill at her house. She told them that nobody suspected her of anything and that the group was not considered involved in any way with the Hamilton case. The only interesting thing was that most of the cold cases that they were investigating involved either registered or known sex offenders and the Group members all lost children, and most involved sex crimes. While checking, Ray's prison record came up and that did create some interest. "Let 'em check on me," Ray said. "There's nothing linking me to anything." His mind recalled his encounter with Russell Hamilton, but that was years ago and he was careful not to leave any evidence.

Brooke continued, "Since Luther and Dee left the state, and May would hardly fit any suspect profile, that just leaves us three. The detectives know me, so I was ruled out. But you two are considered people of interest."

"What does that mean?" Jill wondered.

"Maybe nothing. But since I know you, they keep quiet around me. Ray, they could bring you in for questioning, so make sure your place is sanitized. It probably won't happen, but they could get a search warrant for the house and cars."

"Okay, Brooke. I'll get rid of the Glock and the stun guns. Otherwise, there's nothing to find."

THE FOLLOWING AFTERNOON a high level meeting was held in Interrogation Room 2A at the Columbia Police Station. The Chief of Detectives, Police Commissioner, and three detectives sat around a large rectangular table discussing the Hamilton murder and the missing person cases. The Commissioner led the assembly. "Enough excuses. Ever since Clifford Lewsinski, Jr. went missing, his old man has been calling me every other day to see what we're doing. You do remember that his father is Deputy Mayor? Now we got this Russ Hamilton shit to deal with and I don't care if he was a pervert." He looked at the Chief Detective. "Well?"

"Uh, sir, we think all of these cases are connected. All the victims have one thing in common, they all have sexual histories."

"Great work, Chief." The Commissioner mocked. "So, it's nearly solved."

Donny Hermenson, a bald headed police officer nicknamed "Duck" was the lead detective and didn't pull any punches. "Look, Commissioner, you're a politician. We're cops. With all the laws in place protecting the bad guys it's a miracle we make any arrests. We are working on a suspect though. It's probably a long shot, but this Blackburn guy did hard time for half killing a degenerate that murdered his family. Now he's hooked up with John Mullio and that Hallo Club bunch."

"That's it? What am I supposed to tell the Deputy Mayor and all those reporters that are on my ass?"

Tell 'em we're waiting for the results of the DNA that was recovered from Hamilton's body, but that takes time."

"Then what?"

"We run the results through CODIS and see if we get a hit."

"And if you don't?"

"We'll get a sample from Blackburn and see if he's a match."

"Blackburn? Why does that name sound familiar? We got a sheet on him?"

The Chief of Detectives spoke, "No, sir. He's clean as far as we know."

The Commissioner stood and turned to the door. "Keep me informed, and damnit,, do something."

***

THE DNA RESULTS came back three weeks later and did not match anything CODIS had on file. Raymond Blackburn was then brought in for questioning and sat stone-faced in one of the interrogation rooms while three detectives questioned him. Duck Hermenson took the lead. "This is being video-taped, sir. Okay, for the record, state your name."

"Ray Black."

Duck grinned. "I guess I should have said, state you whole name, Mr. Blackburn."

"So, you know who I am."

"Yeah, we know. Do you know why you're here?"

"Yeah, you picked me up and brought me here."

"Look, smart ass, we know what you're capable of. You like to beat people up."

Ray sat in silence as Duck Hermenson read from the criminal record of Raymond Blackburn.

When he finished Ray yawned and stretched his arms. "Uh, I already know about my record and I don't need a trip down felony lane either." He looked at the other detective. "Am I under arrest or something?"

The Duck pretended anger. "You talk to me, mother-fucker."

Ray jumped to his feet and was quickly subdued by all three detectives.

When he was again seated, this time handcuffed, Duck left the room slamming the door. One of the other detectives followed, leaving Ray in the room with the remaining man. The policeman looked at the door and shook his head. "Duck's a hothead."

He walked behind Ray, took the cuffs off, and sat next to him. "I could go for a coffee, how do you take yours?" Ray ignored the peace offering and remained silent.

"Be right back."

Several minutes later he returned with two steaming cups. He set them on the table and reached into his shirt pocket and dropped several packets of sugar and non-dairy creamers on the table. Ray hesitated for a moment realizing that if he drank from the cup they'd have his DNA. He smiled. "Thanks."

The detective walked over to the video recorder and turned it off. "Look, fellow, don't take any of this personally, we interview a lot of folks during these investigations and after reading your file, I'd probably have done the same thing you did to that bastard."

As Ray sipped from the coffee he laughed to himself at the clumsy attempt of good cop, bad cop. He knew that half the police force was watching through the mirrored window; he didn't have to watch Law and Order to figure that out. The good cop thought he was making progress and outran his coverage. "Raymond, we know you were involved, and really, we understand why. Actually, you did the community a favor; we all agree on that."

Ray chuckled. "X gets the square." The detective's face turned beet red as Ray continued, "Charge me with a crime or I'm outta here. I spent eight long years in the can and I know a bit about the law, Officer." Ray stood, drained his coffee, crushed the paper cup, and then put it into his jacket pocket. Observing this, Duck Hermenson burst through the door. "Get out of here you piece of shit before I forget I'm a cop."

Ray stopped in the doorway and faced The Duck. "Listen, you bald-headed duck, if you ever see me on the street, leave your badge in the car and we'll finish what you started."

After Ray left the detectives discussed the interview. "He's not stupid." Offered one detective.

Duck chuckled. "No, he's not stupid, but he's emotional." He stroked his chin. We'll put a female officer on his ass at that Hallo Club and when he has a drink with her, she can snatch the glass and then we'll have Mr. Smart Ass's DNA. I'd bet my pension that he's involved in this shit someway."

That idea didn't work. When the decoy started hanging around the club and playing up to Ray, he informed her that if she was a working girl she better look for greener pastures and that if she was just on the make, he was married and not interested. Duck was furious. "We gotta get a perp with a conscience."

The female officer offered her opinion. "Maybe the guy's on the square."

"And maybe the pope isn't Catholic," Duck shot back. "I can smell a varmint a mile away and this guy's a rat. You spent enough time around that crap hole, don't you know somebody that could help us get a cigarette butt or something?"

She thought a moment. "He doesn't smoke. What about his car? I'll bet we can find hair or something in there."

Duck shook his head. "No, not without a search warrant and we can't get that without probable cause."

"Mimi!"

"What? Who's Mimi?"

"She's a waitress and takes care of the boys in the back room. No other waitress is allowed in there. I'll bet she'd like to make herself a fast two hundred."

"Two hundred? I don't want the guy's head. I just need a glass he drank out of."

Another detective added, "We could stake out his house and get his garbage. That might have some of his DNA in it."

"And it might not. All right, Sharon, we'll try it your way, if you're sure this Mimi won't go to the boss."

"She won't. Not for two hundred."

***

AND THAT'S HOW IT WENT down. A glass with Ray's fingerprints and DNA was whisked to the private lab that tested DNA for the state. Four weeks later Ray was again brought in for questioning. This time it wasn't a fishing expedition.

"Ray," Duck Hermenson began, "we got a sample of your DNA and ruled you out as the contributor from the Hamilton case. However, we know that the perp is related to you. Probably your brother."

Ray's mind exploded. He was absolutely blindsided. He knew immediately that Johnny Ray was involved and couldn't think of any way to keep him out of it. He looked up at the detective as he stood over him. "If I'm under arrest, arrest me. Otherwise I'm calling my lawyer before I answer any questions."

The interview was over, but the police already knew where to look, in Ray Blackburn's back yard.

It was only a matter of time before several dots were connected. Johnny Ray Blackburn may have been a major celebrity in Columbia, Missouri, and well known, but in a matter of days he was arrested and questioned in the same interrogation room his father sat in. The detectives drilled him hard, but with John Mullio's lawyer, Herman Baur present, he admitted nothing. The following day he was formally charged in the death of Russell Hamilton and over his attorney's protests, remanded and denied bail.

Although Russ Hamilton's secret life was revealed, even in death, he enjoyed a loyal following, but so did Johnny Ray Blackburn, star linebacker for the Mizzou Tigers and victim of a murderer's rampage against his mother and six year old brother. That information was unknown and the defense team never tried establishing a connection between what happened in St. Charles, Missouri, and Russell Hamilton, that would give the prosecution probable cause.

Even Ray knew nothing of his sons involvement, only a drunken ex taxidermist did and he wasn't talking. After several eyewitnesses from the steak house parking lot identified Johnny Ray from a police lineup and with his DNA a match, he was practically declared guilty in the news media. The prosecutor believed he had a dream case. One with plenty of publicity that would get him noticed by important people and one that had overwhelming evidence of the suspects guilt. The only thing he lacked was motive and it was just assumed that Hamilton's history as a pedophile was not a coincidence. And that he just picked out the wrong guy.

When father and son talked at the jail it was through a glass partition using telephones. Ray started the conversation as he pointed to a sign on the wall informing visitors and prisoners alike, that all conversations could be recorded. "Be careful what you say."

Johnny Ray nodded. "Looks pretty bad, Dad."

"Yeah, but don't give up hope. We're working on something."

After exchanging small talk, Johnny looked hard into his father's eyes. "It's over, dad. Mom and Cory can rest in peace." Ray nodded his understanding and now understood his son's involvement. His only regret was that he didn't know of Hamilton's part when he had him alone. If he had, Russell Hamilton would have faced the same fate as the other missing men and no body, no murder charges.

Chapter 25

As is customary, the prosecution presented their case first. Surprisingly, the defense didn't cross-examine any witnesses and only asked for permission to recall each one at a later date. The State's Attorney's office expected an offer to plea bargain, since the defense didn't offer a witness list into evidence, but they were wrong. On the third day of the trial, after the state rested, the defense took the floor, with attorney Herman Baur recalling each of the eyewitnesses. Only this time, with the court's permission, Chas Stellon sat at the defense table next to Johnny Ray. When again asked to pick out the man they saw on the night in question, all three of them were unable to positively identify Johnny Ray. The prosecution objected and wanted the testimony stricken and Chas put on the witness list. But since he wasn't on the pretrial list, he couldn't be called unless both sides agreed and that would never happen. The objection was denied. But the state still had its ace in the hole, the killer's DNA. The DNA that matched Johnny Ray's court ordered sample.

The prosecutor argued, "Your Honor, this man, this look alike, doesn't change anything. The defendant left his DNA at the crime scene; we don't need a witness to prove that."

Herman Baur countered, "You Honor, we have Mr. Stellon's DNA and a report from the same state sanctioned lab where Mr. Blackburn had his sample tested. At this time we would like to recall the state's expert witness from that lab."

The judge nodded to the bailiff who recalled the woman. Herman Baur gave the report to the bailiff, who showed it to the judge and then handed it to the witness.

The prosecution stalled for time. "Your Honor, can the court give the witness a few minutes to compare both DNA reports?"

"I'll allow that. We are in recess for one hour." The judge banged his gavel and went to his chambers. Johnny Ray went back to a holding cell while his defense team went into the hall. As Ray sat next to Herman Baur and Chas, he looked over at the prosecutor as he hunched over his DNA witness.

"What does this mean, Mr. Baur?" Ray asked.

"Simple. She's going to testify that the boys are twins. If they're fraternal we're sunk. If on the other hand they're identical, the prosecution has a major problem. We've discredited their eyewitnesses and now with DNA coming from another possible source, their case is blown."

They watched the prosecutor as he argued with his star witness. Herman Baur grinned. "Looks like the verdict is in."

When court resumed the expert witness confirmed that Johnny Ray and Chas Stellon were identical twins. The prosecution then argued that Chas Stellon had conspired with the defense in an unlawful manner and that he and Herman Baur should both be held in contempt of court, pending more serious charges. When that failed, they asked for a mistrial in order to gather more evidence. Both motions were denied.

The prosecutor tried one last thing. "Your Honor, I know it's highly unorthodox, but we request that you personally question Mr. Stellon. I'm sure under oath he'll testify that he was nowhere near Columbia, Missouri, on the night in question since he lives in Plano, Texas."

Herman Baur nodded to his opponent, in an acknowledgement of respect for his thoroughness. The judge looked to the defense table. "With your approval, Mr. Baur, and if I'm not satisfied with the direction this is going, I'll entertain your motion to drop all charges. With that news the court spectators gasped as the judge banged his gavel for order. Baur knew it was a risky, but if he won that point the trial was over. He conferred with Johnny Ray before answering.

"We agree, Your Honor."

Chas was called to the stand and sworn. The judge leaned down toward the witness stand. "Okay, son. Where were you and can you prove where you were on the night Mr. Hamilton died?"

"I was in St. Louis, sir. My flight home was cancelled because of bad weather and I didn't leave there until eight the following morning."

"So, in theory, you could have driven, or been driven, the hour and a half or so from St. Louis to Columbia that night and got back in plenty of time for your flight."

"I guess that was possible."

"Can anyone collaborate this?"

"If you're asking me if I have anybody to alibi me in St. Louis, no. But I have proof of what I'm telling you." He removed a business envelope from his inside jacket pocket and handed it to the bailiff. "The receipts for my flights and motel room are in there, Your Honor."

The judge carefully went through the receipts and when he looked up he scowled at the prosecutor. "Next time you prepare a case, sir, do a better job. You've wasted a lot of the court's time, not to mention the taxpayer's money, bringing charges you can't prove beyond a reasonable doubt."

He looked at Chas. "I'm not going to ask you if you came to Columbia that night, Mr. Stellon, because you're not on trial here." He looked at the defense attorney. "Make your motion, Mr. Baur."

"Motion to dismiss on grounds of insufficient evidence, Your Honor."

The judge never looked up as he banged his gavel. "Granted."

When the courtroom burst into loud talking, he banged vigorously again. "This court is still in session." He looked at the jury. "Thank you ladies and gentleman for doing your civic duty, you're dismissed." He looked at Johnny Ray. "All the charges against you concerning this matter are dismissed, Mr. Blackburn. You're free to go."

The bailiff stood in front of the court as the judge retreated to his chambers. "Ladies and gentleman, court is adjourned."

Johnny Ray hugged his lawyer, his father, and his brother in that order. He looked at Herman Baur and shook his head. "Mr. Baur, you are unbelievable... thank you."

Baur looked at Chas. "Thank your brother, John. Without him, you'd be going away for a long time."

Johnny looked at Chas as he wiped away a tear. "My brother! I feel like I've been reborn." He again embraced Chas. "Thanks, bro."

When Ray and Jill, both boys, and their attorney exited the courthouse they were met by a group of reporters and television cameras. The media group rushed from the impromptu news conference that the prosecuting attorney held and surrounded the four men. Several microphones were shoved in front of Johnny Ray's face. "Mr. Blackburn, the State's Attorney says he is going to file charges against you and Charles Stellon."

"What charges?"

"Conspiracy to commit murder, kidnapping and violation of Mr. Hamilton's civil rights."

Herman Baur stepped in front of Johnny Ray. "Those charges are absurd and no grand jury would ever hand down an indictment based on what the DA showed in court today. Ladies and gentleman, this is just a pathetic attempt on his part to save face. This matter was properly adjudicated in a court of law and the correct verdict was rendered."

When the group started to walk away, another question was shouted above the voices, "Johnny, when did you find your brother?" Johnny stopped, but his attorney pulled him on. As they got into a waiting car one final question reached their ears. "What about the American Civil Liberties Union? They're not going to like the decision."

When they were driving away from the courthouse Ray asked the lawyer. "Is this over?

"It depends how the public reacts. I'm sure the media will blitz the airways and newspaper with opinions of why justice wasn't done. But I think they missed the point; most of the interested people are parents and when they found out about Hamilton's interest in child pornography, they figured he got what he deserved." The lawyer frowned. "Going against public opinion doesn't improve ratings or sell newspapers. When the DA finds out he's rowing a leaky boat, he'll back off."

***

THAT'S EXACTLY WHAT happened After taking the public's temperature, the media backed off and the whole matter died a quiet death.

Two weeks later when Ray entered The Hallo Club the hostess greeted him. "Ray, there's a guy waiting to see you." She pointed to a booth in the far corner. It was early on a Wednesday night and the club was nearly deserted. The only entertainment was loud rock music that discouraged conversation. Ray stood over the man sitting at the table. "Well, well, if it isn't Detective Donald Duck Hemerson"

The detective looked up. "You got a place where we can talk without shouting?....Please it's important."

Ray just stared at the policeman for a long moment, then nodded and started walking towards the back of the club. The Duck followed him to the manager's office where Ray sat behind the desk as the officer settled into a chair next to him. "Well?"

Duck Hermerson chose his words carefully. "Raymond, I'm not on duty now and I'm not wearing any kind of wire. And I'm not here to make trouble for you. You need to understand that."

A soft knock at the door preceded its opening and Mimi appeared. "Can I get you and your guest something, Ray?"

Ray looked at the detective. "What'll it be?"

Duck looked at the waitress. "Plain Ginger Ale, please."

She looked at Ray. "Coffee, black."

Duck made small talk until Mimi came back. He didn't want any interruptions after he started. When the drinks were served Ray put a five on her tray. The detective pulled a ten from his pocket. "Let me get that."

Mimi kept walking and carefully closed the door. Ray chuckled. "Put your money away, Detective. I didn't pay for the drinks, that was a tip. Drinks cost seven dollars each in this place, but since you're my guest they're on the house."

Duck ignored the putdown. "Raymond, I'm not here to cross swords. I've come as a friend."

Ray laughed. "Now you're my friend? That's a good one."

"Godamnit, shut the hell up and listen." He looked around the room as he continued, "The sand is running out. This place will be a pizza parlor in five years. John Mullio is going down. Don't go down with him."

"What's that supposed to mean?"

"We know what he does and we know what you do, too. Mullio has a lot of people in his pocket, important people that look the wrong way at the right time, but now that he's getting involved with drugs, all bets are off. This is a college town and folks don't want the city to get the reputation as a drug haven."

Ray stood up. "Thanks for the warning."

"Sit down, you dumb shit. I'm not finished."

"Okay, what else?"

Duck leaned towards Ray. "I know all about that posse you hosted. You know, the folks you met at grief counseling? I've been on your asses for a long time, only I didn't know it was you I was chasing. Look, guy, I don't think you folks know the difference between vigilantism and justice."

Ray grunted. "Sometimes, Detective, there isn't any. And about the group, we met a few times, so what."

"Look, Raymond, my brain didn't fall out of my ass yesterday morning. I'm a pretty good cop and I think I figured it out. Everyone in that group lost a child, except the librarian."

"You mean May!"

"Yeah, May. Right about the time you guys were meeting we started getting some missing persons and guess what, they all had pasts that included crimes against children. Oh, and I know all about your case, too. You did a hard eight, no probation. I'm really sorry about that. The judge that sentenced you should be horse whipped."

"Water over the dam."

"Ray, I don't have proof that you pulled the plug on those people, but I'd bet my retirement you did. I never found anything on Robert Morgan, but I suspect you cashed his chips too. Now this deal with your boy, the only reasonable explanation for what he did was that Russ Hamilton had something to do with your family tragedy. I was lead detective on that investigation and it was the only time in my life I didn't follow through. After finding that porno shit in Hamilton's house nobody wanted to see your boy convicted, so when the state's attorney built his case we never mentioned the fact that his mother and brother were murdered by a child abuser."

Ray bobbed his head in agreement. "Thanks."

"Now for the rest. Either you disappear from my radar screen, or I'm going to put you away again. I don't need any more missing or dead people in my world. I got enough to do without you complicating things."

"So, either I get out of Dodge, or you'll build a case against me."

"Look, man, it won't be just you. At the end of the day, Jill goes too."

"And where are you going to get enough evidence to convict us in a court of law?"

"That's the easy part. I paid a visit to our friendly librarian and she folded like a lawn chair. She thought I was there to arrest her and started crying when I told her I was looking into the group you guys formed. She started to tell me about The Justice Club, but I didn't give her a chance to roll over. Ray, I've been doing this a long time and I know when someone is about to give up the gig."

Duck stood and leaned over Ray. "You got one month to get out of Missouri. If you don't, you'll be getting your mail at Fulton State Prison for the rest of your life."

When Duck reached the door Ray looked up and whispered, "They slaughtered my family."

Duck opened the door and turned back. "I know. That's why I'm giving you a break."

Epilogue

Five years later the world was a different place for Ray Blackburn and the people he loved. Johnny Ray cashed in on his football fame after graduating from The University of Missouri and took a job with "Sports Galore" a nationally-read magazine as a feature writer. His brush with the judicial system has retired to the faded memory of a fickle public.

Ray and Jill reside in Dorner, North Carolina and own and operate Rayjill Motor Sports, a growing company that markets rolling chassis to racecar teams all over America. Ironically, Jill gave birth to twins named Cory and Amy. The baby's names were not intended to replace the lost children, only to honor their memory.

Charles Stellon returned to his family after the trial and eventually received his degree in mechanical engineering. He is employed by Rayjill Motor Sports as a design engineer, specializing in hi-performance suspension and aerodynamic packages. His health restricts the hours he works, but Chas remains optimistic about the future since he is waiting for a suitable heart donor and is considered an ideal candidate.

Meet our Author

Patrick M. Shanahan

I grew up playing on the streets of Chicago so that makes me a city kid. I'm the second oldest of 13 children born to Irish Catholic parents and that made me a poor city kid. The big city has a lot to offer about the secrets of life and my character and who I am are reflected from that learning experience.

My literary efforts include human interest pieces, children stories, short stories and three full length novels. My favorite genre is crime fiction and each story is character driven with a believable plot and numerous twists.

Although I write mostly fiction my manuscripts are often fed with antidotes from either my life or from those I've met on life's journey. Those, along with a healthy dose of imagination often fill the pages of my manuscripts.

My articles and short stories have appeared in various newsletters, newspapers, and national magazines for the past eight years.